THE KILLING OF KATIE STEELSTOCK

Also available in Perennial Library
by Michael Gilbert:

The Crack in the Teacup
The Empty House
The Family Tomb
Flash Point

THE KILLING OF KATIE STEELSTOCK

Michael Gilbert

PERENNIAL LIBRARY

Harper & Row, Publishers, New York
Cambridge, Philadelphia, San Francisco, Washington
London, Mexico City, São Paulo, Singapore, Sydney

 For information address Harper & Row, Publishers, Inc., 10 East 53rd Street, New York, N.Y. 10022. Published simultaneously in Canada by Fitzhenry & Whiteside Limited, Toronto.

First PERENNIAL LIBRARY edition published 1988.

Library of Congress Cataloging-in-Publication Data

Gilbert, Michael Francis, 1912–
The killing of Katie Steelstock.

"Perennial Library."
I. Title.
PZ3.G37367Ki 1988 [PR6013.I3335] 823'.9'14 79-3409
ISBN 0-06-080881-0 (pbk.)

---

88 89 90 91 92 OPM 10 9 8 7 6 5 4 3 2 1

1

Jonathan Limbery sang in his thick tenor voice:

"Es zogen drei Burschen wohl über den Rhein
Bei einer Frau Wirtin da Kehrten sie ein."

[Eight varied and uncertain trebles repeated]

"Bei einer Frau Wirtin da Kehrten sie ein."
"Frau Wirtin hat sie gut Bier und Wein
Wo hat sir ihr schönes Tochterlein."

"It's very difficult, isn't it?" said Roney Havelock. "I mean, it's difficult enough learning to sing in English, but German!"

"German," said Jonathan, "is the most natural singing language in the world. Look at that last word. Tochterlein. You can really get your tongue round Tochterlein."

"What does it mean, anyway?" said Sim Havelock.

"It means 'darling little daughter.'"

The trebles thought this was funny.

"You mustn't laugh when you sing it at the concert," said Jonathan. "It's a very sad song. It's about three students who crossed the Rhine to visit this inn. They were all in love with the landlady's little daughter."

"Her tockter-line?"

"That's right. Only when they got there she was lying dead in her bed."

"Tough," said Roney. "What did they do?"

"They all go up to have a look at her. The next three verses are solos. You'll have to take one each. The first student said how lovely she looked. The second one said he'd always been in love with her. The third one said he was *still* in love with her."

"That's balmy," said Sim. "You couldn't be in love with a dead girl. What would be the point of it?"

Tim Nurse said, "It sounds a bit soppy to me. One thing, if it's in German no one's going to know what it means. It's quite a decent tune."

"It's gone seven," said Jonathan. "You'd better all be pushing off or you'll be late for your suppers."

The boys, who varied in age from Terry Gonville, nearly fourteen, to Sim Havelock, just gone nine, were disposed around Jonathan's music-cum-writing room. The windows were wide open to a late-August evening of blistering heat. They seemed disinclined to stir. Roney Havelock, who was only eleven but took the lead in most things, said, "Do us the 'Walloping Window Blind,' Jonathan. There's time for that. Just one verse. We'll sing the chorus for you."

Jonathan sighed. Then he plucked a single note from his nickel-plated guitar, a note so deep that it might have come from a bass cello. In repose his face was unattractive. ("Mean eyes, a sour mouth and an obstinate chin," Sally Nurse had said, "yet a lot of people like him." "And a lot of people don't," her father had said.) When he sang he became a different person. He became part of the song, serious or humorous, bold or sentimental. A television cameraman who knew his job would have tracked extra close, to catch every tiny detail in a dead face which came to life in such a startling way.

> "A capital ship for an ocean trip
> Was the Walloping Window Blind
> [twank-a-pank].
> No wind that blew dismayed her crew
> Or troubled the captain's mind.
> The man at the wheel was made to feel
> Contempt for the winds that blow,
> Though it often appeared, when the gale had cleared,
> That he'd been in his bunk below."

The guitar quickened to a livelier tempo. The treble voices shrilled in unison.

> "Then blow, ye winds—heigh-ho, ye winds,
> A roving we will go—oh.
> We'll stay no more on England's shore,
> So let the music play—ay.
> We'll catch the morning train,
> We'll cross the raging main,
> We'll sail to our love in a boxing glove,
> Ten thousand miles away."

Jonathan produced a final arpeggio on the guitar and Roney said, "Go on. Go on. Next verse. The one about the bosun's mate who was very sedate, yet fond of amusement too—oo."

"It's ten past seven."

"One more verse. Just one," said the boys. "Unless we have one more verse we won't go."

A head poked through the open window and Tony Windle said, "You having trouble with your choir, Johnno?"

"It's a mutiny," said Jonathan. "But I'm not going to yield to force. Come in and help me disperse the mob."

Tony climbed through the window, picked up Sim Havelock and deposited him squealing onto the front path. Jonathan was putting away his guitar. He said, "Urchins, the jam session's over. If you behave yourselves you can come again next Friday."

The boys began to disperse reluctantly. Roney was the last to go. He said, "You wouldn't get very far really. Not if you tried to sail in a boxing glove."

"Perhaps it was a boat called the *Boxing Glove*."

Roney considered the point. He said, "Well, that's one solution I hadn't thought of," and sprinted off after the other boys, who were walking arm in arm down the middle of Belsize Road chanting, "Then blow, ye winds —heigh-ho, ye winds, a roving we will go—oh."

"Roving is something I shan't be doing, not for a day or two," said Tony. "That rancid jackanapes raided *my* car last night."

"What did he do to it?"

"He took away the distributor head."

"I say! Not funny."

"Not funny at all," said Tony. "And if I catch him, I'll try to convince him of it."

"Do you think it was boys? They seemed such kids' tricks. Letting down George Mariner's tires and emptying all the water out of old Vigors' radiator."

"You can blow tires up again and refill a radiator," said Tony gloomily. "I shall have to buy a new distributor head, and the car'll be out of action for days. That's what I came about. I promised to drive Katie to this hop."

"Hasn't she got a car of her own?"

"Certainly. But she's a lazy little slut and always prefers to come in mine. Can I use your blower?"

"Help yourself."

But the telephone produced no answer.

"Hell," said Tony. "Now what am I going to do about that?"

"Borrow my car."

"Hold it. I've got a better plan." Tony climbed back out of the window and held up his hand to stop a young man who was coming up the road on a moped.

He said, "Hold your horses, Sergeant. I've got an official complaint to make. Come in."

Detective Sergeant Ian McCourt, who was young, Scottish and helpful, dismounted and followed him in.

"It's that bloody jackanapes," said Tony. "He's wrecked *my* car now by pinching the distributor head."

"I'd like to hear about that. When did it happen?"

Ian had been born in Inverness, where, as everyone knows, they speak the purest English in the British Isles. It was only an occasional broadening of the consonants and a certain formality in his speech that evidenced his origin.

"I can't tell you exactly when. I brought the car back at about midnight last night and parked it where I always do, at the back of the house."

"That's in Upper Belsize Road."

"Number thirty-four. The other side of the Brickfield Road crossing."

The Sergeant made a note. "When did you find it had been tampered with?"

"When I tried to start it this evening. I didn't need it to get to the station this morning. The chap I share the house with—Billy Gonville—he's got a car too and we take it in turns to ferry each other to the station."

"Then the assumption is that this pairson got at your car between midnight last night and first light this morning."

"I imagine so."

"It's curious, all the same."

"Why?"

"When Mr. Mariner's car and Mr. Vigors' car were interfered with we concluded that it was boys being mischievous. But that hardly fits in with something happening after midnight. Boys wouldn't likely be out at that hour."

"I suppose not. So who is it who's playing these tricks?"

"I would hardly classify them as tricks. Trespass and criminal damage. It's a serious offense."

"It seems so pointless."

"You haird nothing?"

"Nothing at all. There's no reason I should. After all, this joker had only got to hop over the back fence from the lane behind the house, lift the bonnet—there's no bonnet lock, you see—and whip out the distributor head."

"Is your bedroom at the back?"

"It is. But I'm a very sound sleeper."

"Would Mr. Gonville have been home when you got back last night?"

Tony looked surprised and said, "His car was there. I imagine so. In bed and asleep. You don't think he did it, do you? No point really. It means he's going to have to drive me to the station every morning until I can get a new part."

"If we knew why it was being done," said McCourt, "we might have some notion who it was. Well, I must be getting along."

"You wouldn't by any chance be going out through West Hannington?"

"Aye. That's where I was bound for."

"Then could you possibly leave a message for me with Miss Steelstock. I tried ringing her up just now, but either she wasn't at home or maybe she was in her bath."

"I shall be calling on the Manor House. I could leave a message with her mother, if that would do."

"That would do splendidly. Just to tell her that I'm carless and she'll have to drive herself to the Tennis Club disco."

"I'll do that," said McCourt.

"Now that's a good chap," said Tony when he'd gone. "Wasted on the police in a dump like Hannington. I must get back and change. Are you coming?"

"I can think of better ways of spending a hot summer evening than plodding around the Memorial Hall with a lot of sweaty girls."

"You have a point," said Tony.

Sergeant McCourt and Sergeant Esdaile constituted at that moment the total detective force of Hannington and District. Normally there were three of them, but Detective Inspector Ray was in Reading Infirmary with supposed peptic ulcers.

Because they were short-handed (for this, McCourt reflected, is the way of the world), their work load had greatly increased. An epidemic of country-house burglaries had broken out, starting in the area of Wallingford and spreading south through Moulsford, Compton and Streatley.

"They're cleaning up the whole area," said Detective Superintendent Farr from Reading, who had been put in charge of the counteroffensive. "And they're just about due in your manor, so keep your eyes open."

Keeping their eyes open had involved patrolling on alternate nights. Which wouldn't have been so bad, said McCourt, yawning, if they had been allowed to sleep on alternate days. However, provided nothing unexpected happened, this was his last official duty for that day. He had to visit each of the three large houses in West Hannington and urge the owners, all of whom would be going to the Tennis Club dance, to leave someone at home if possible and, if not, to leave a television set or a few lights switched on and to lock up securely. Or, better than either of these corny devices, to leave a dog loose in the house.

He tackled the street in reverse, calling first at Group Captain Gonville's house, which was the Old Rectory and lay on the far side of Upper Church Lane. The Group Captain revealed that he and his wife were both going to the dance, but he thought that his bull terrier would keep an eye on things while they were away and would the Sergeant like a drop of Scotch. He, too, liked the Sergeant, as did most of the inhabitants of West Hannington. McCourt refused regretfully. He said that if he had so much as the smallest drink he would fall asleep on his moped.

His next port of call was West Hannington Manor. This was the oldest and largest house in the neighborhood and the most likely target for burglars. It had belonged to Matthew Steelstock, the estate agent, who had broken his neck out hunting, ten years before, leaving a widow with three children: Katie, then fifteen and already beginning to turn male heads; Walter, thirteen; and Peter, six. Matthew Steelstock had been a riotous, fast-living, foul-mouthed man, and since he had left his wife well provided for, she had accepted widowhood without any undue distress. As she often remarked, she had her children.

Of these, Katie was now a first-magnitude star.

Who would have thought she had it in her? An attractive girl, agreed. One who took trouble over her appearance and was never short of boyfriends. But so were a million other girls. Then she had to go up to London and get involved with that photographer. The one who got into trouble afterward with the police. But he certainly took beautiful photographs. Artistic lighting, unexpected angles. And he *said* he had an in with the television companies. Well, people like that would say anything, but in this case there seemed to be some truth in it, because Katie started getting better parts in commercials. Well paid, too. About that time she had acquired an agent. "A very respectable man," said Mrs. Steelstock, "with an office in Covent Garden." She understood he had been to Harrow.

Then came the *Seven O'Clock Show.* The all-family quiz show that combined general knowledge, popular music and a touch of sex. The perfect condiment to season the family evening meal. And starting with one of the supporting parts, Katie had somehow managed to take it over. The producer must have had something to do with it, and the cameramen certainly lent a hand; but it was her own bubbling, self-confident, friendly extroverted personality which turned "Kate" into "our Katie," the two-dimensional friend of a million three-dimensional families; pin-up for a million adolescents; the guest, at the same time real and unreal, at a million supper tables.

"With the money she's made," said Mrs. Steelstock, "she could have gone off and lived up in London with all her smart new friends, but Katie's really a home girl. Her family and her friends are all down here in Hannington and that's where she prefers to stop. We converted the stable block into a self-contained maisonette for her." (If when she said "we" Mrs. Steelstock implied that she had paid for it, this was untrue. The cost of the conversion had come out of Kate's own pocket.) "It gives her just that bit of privacy that all real artists need."

It was Katie's brother Walter who opened the door when Sergeant McCourt rang the bell. He said, "It's quite all right, Sergeant. We're leaving Peter in charge. He's got a headache and won't be coming with Mother and me. Anyway, we'll be back by eleven. We're not night birds."

"That's all right then. And by the by. I've a message for your sister. From Mr. Windle. He won't be able to take her to the dance. Some joker's put his car out of action."

"I suppose it's the same kids who damaged the other cars."

"We're not so sure about kids. It transpires that this incident must have taken place in the early hours of the morning."

Walter considered this slowly. He liked to consider things slowly. He said, "If an adult is responsible, the whole thing seems rather pointless, doesn't it? Unless he has a particular grudge against the three people concerned. Mariner, Vigors and Windle. There doesn't seem to be much connection."

"It's a problem we're working on. I'll have to be on my way. You won't forget to tell your sister."

"That's all right. She'll take her own car, I've no doubt."

"Or maybe she'll walk."

"Not our Katie," said Walter.

One of the reasons that McCourt had taken a circular

route into West Hannington was that it was an excuse for leaving the Mariners to the last.

George Mariner had built the Croft when he came to West Hannington twenty years before. It had taken a lot of money, and the sacking of one architect, to get it exactly as he wanted it, which was odd, because it was not a house of any particular character.

McCourt raised the heavy brass dolphin door knocker and let it fall with a thud upon the heavy oak-paneled door.

When nothing happened, he said something under his breath, knocked again and pressed the bell. This did produce results. Lights came on in the wrought-iron lanterns on either side of the porch and the door was opened by a smart-looking maid.

McCourt said, "Is Mr. Mariner in?"

The maid said, in tones which would have suited a fifty-year-old butler, "I will ascertain if he is at home. May I have your name?"

"Don't be daft, Polly. You know perfectly well who I am. Buzz along like a good girl and get hold of him."

"Will you come this way please," said the maid, without abating a jot of her formality. "If you will be good enough to wait." She showed him into the room on the left of the hall, which was George Mariner's study or business room, and departed, closing the door carefully behind her. McCourt sighed and contained his soul in patience. It was a full ten minutes before the master of the house appeared.

"Sorry to keep you waiting, Sergeant," he said amiably. "I was in my bath."

The pinkness and whiteness of his face, the smartness of his lightweight linen suit, the crispness of his shirt reproved the Sergeant, who felt hot, sticky and dirty and illogically blamed this on the cool figure in front of him.

"Can I offer you a drink?"

"Not just now, sir."

"Then you won't object to me having one myself." Mariner turned his broad back on the Sergeant and mixed himself a generous Scotch and water. "Now tell me, what is it brings you out on this hot evening?"

McCourt explained. Mariner said, "Have no fear. My girl will be here until we get back. And even if the house was empty I shouldn't feel uneasy. I have Chubb locks on the front and back door, window locks on all the ground-floor windows and a burglar alarm which sounds off in your police station. I take it there will be someone on duty tonight?"

"Aye," said McCourt. "There'll be a night duty man there. I'll be getting along now."

Mariner touched a bell in the wainscoting and said, "Polly will show you out." He then sat down at his desk, inserted a sheet of paper into the typewriter and started to type, not inexpertly. The Sergeant retired to the hall, where he found the maid waiting. He said, "So you're not going to the dance, Polly?"

"I haven't been asked," said the girl, who seemed to have abandoned her impersonation of Jeeves. "As if I'd want to go anyway. A lot of toffee-nosed crumbs."

McCourt grinned, resisted the temptation to smack the bottom which, in its tight black dress, seemed to be inviting a smack, and clumped out of the door. He said, "Be good, then."

"Not much chance of being anything else in this dump," said Polly. "Tarrah."

She watched him go. She thought he was rather a dish. A bit solemn, but good-looking in a dark Scottish way. A bit like Gregory Peck, really.

At the police station McCourt found Detective Sergeant Esdaile, a Yorkshireman, his senior in years and rank, finishing an accident report. He said, "I've done the West Hannington lot, Eddie. My God, how I hate that man."

"Who?"

"The bloody Master Mariner."

"Oh, him."

"Because God made him a J.P.—"

"Not God, the Lord Chancellor."

"You're wrong, Eddie. He wouldn't accept the honor from a mere menial like the Lord Chancellor. It was a direct gift from the Almighty. It enables him to look upon policemen as supernumerary footmen."

Esdaile grunted, looked at the word he was writing, crossed it out and wrote it again.

"True, he only kept me waiting for ten minutes tonight. Last week, when I called on him about the joker who let down his tires—you'd have fancied he'd had his house burgled and his wife raped, the fuss he was making—"

"You couldn't rape her," said Eddie. "She'd freeze your balls off." He crossed out the second version of the word and scratched his head with the end of the pen.

"—he kept me waiting nearly *twenty* minutes. And when he did come down from whatever it was he was doing he spent another twenty minutes giving me a lecture on the proper performance of my duties."

"He's a bastard in any one of nine languages," said Eddie. "How *do* you spell unconscious?"

Old Mr. Beaumorris sat in the bow window of his cottage on the street. The window was wide open. Through it he observed the life of West Hannington.

There was not much happened in the village which escaped him.

He saw the Reverend "Dicky" Bird driving past in his battered Austin, the back of the car stacked with folding chairs, presumably destined for the Memorial Hall. He was glad there were going to be plenty of chairs. Mrs. Havelock came striding past. Must weigh all of twenty stone, he thought. In prime condition, though. She spotted Mr. Beaumorris, drew up, poked her head through the window and boomed, "You coming dancing tonight, Frank?"

"I'll be there. Too old and too stiff to dance, though. I imagine all your brood will be in evidence."

"I've told the three oldest they can come. Roney and Sim will have to stop at home and look after the young ones."

"You must find your children a great comfort."

"Sometimes they're a comfort. Sometimes they're a pain in the neck," said Mrs. Havelock and sailed off up the street like a barquentine with the wind behind it. Mr. Beaumorris smiled. He detested all children.

A quarter past eight. Time to be thinking of moving. He liked to be early at functions. It was too hot for his favorite velvet-collared smoking coat. Instead he would wear the white alpaca jacket, which had belonged to his father. The ends of the trousers could be tucked temporarily into his socks. This would prevent them from getting dirty when he rode, as he planned to do, on his ancient bicycle, to take part in the evening's festivities.

2

As was his habit, Mr. Beaumorris annexed the most comfortable chair in the hall, shifted it into the corner and enthroned himself upon it; and as iron filings are drawn to a magnet, the older ladies flocked up and settled around him. Among themselves they said, "Of course, old Frank's a terrible rattle. If you tell him anything it'll be round the village in half an hour." But this did not prevent them spending a great deal of time talking to him.

"We live in troublous times," he said. "Violence, dishonesty, theft and assault. I can't help feeling glad, sometimes, that I'm an old man, with not many years to go."

"I hear this gang broke into Lady Porteous' house at Compton," said Mrs. Havelock. "They ransacked the place from top to bottom."

"Poor Lucretia was in tears about it," said Mrs. Steelstock. "They took *all* the silver. She had a complete set of asparagus servers which had been in the family for more than three hundred years."

This was recognized as being a prestige point for Mrs. Steelstock, as the only person present who knew, and could use, Lady Porteous' Christian name.

"I have a number of precious objects in my own little house," said Mr. Beaumorris. "Many of them I picked up when I was working at the V. and A. Fortunately they are hardly the sort of items to attract the rapacity of a burglar."

"I imagine you have some valuable things in your house, Helen."

Helen Mariner swiveled in her chair and stared glassily at Mrs. Havelock. This unnerving mannerism was largely due to deafness. Eventually she thawed sufficiently to say, "I believe we have. I leave all that sort of thing to George."

"I saw that nice policeman going round on his motorcycle," said Mrs. Havelock. "I believe he was warning everyone to lock up very carefully."

At this moment Tony Windle and Katie swirled past to the strains of an old-fashioned waltz. The ladies abandoned burglary for a more congenial topic.

"It's time she got married," said her mother. "It can't be good for her, the rackety life she lives in London."

"I wonder she honors us with her presence," said Mavis Gonville. A life lived in and around R.A.F. messes and married quarters had attuned her to precisely the sort of remark which, without actually being offensive, could be taken in as many different ways as her hearers chose.

"She's a nice unspoilt girl at heart," said Mrs. Havelock.

"Is it true that she gets five hundred letters a week from her admirers?"

"I'm not sure of the exact number. Her agent deals with all that sort of thing."

The gyration of the waltz brought Katie and Tony within range of the battery once more.

"She's got an admirer there," said Mavis.

"Not serious, surely," said Mrs. Havelock. "He can't seriously be considering matrimony. He's got a job with some insurance company, but I don't believe they pay him very much."

"If it's as little as they pay Billy," said Mrs. Gonville, "he certainly couldn't support a wife on it. Billy can't even pay his own bills."

Mr. Beaumorris said, "In my opinion, although of course I'm completely out of touch with the affairs of the young, a much more serious prospect would be our journalistic friend Jonathan Limbery."

This produced a short silence while the four ladies digested the inferences.

"It depends what you mean by serious," said Mrs. Havelock. "If one of my daughters was entangled with that young man I should regard it as extremely serious."

"There was something in it at one time, I believe," said Mrs. Steelstock. "And he used to hang around our house a good deal. But Katie gave him no encouragement, of that I'm sure."

"It went a bit further than that," said Mavis Gonville. "It wasn't just a question of no encouragement. They had a flaming row. And since they were tactless enough to have it in the Tennis Club bar, quite a lot of people heard them having it. I believe you were there, Helen."

Mrs. Mariner rotated again and said, "Was I? I don't think so. I believe my husband was there."

"Ah," said Mr. Beaumorris, "but bear in mind, ladies, *Amantium irae amoris integratio est*."

"You'll have to translate for us," said Mavis. "We're none of us Latin scholars."

"It is a comment, dear ladies, which is attributed to the Roman poet Terence. It means, roughly, that a lovers' quarrel sometimes signifies the rebirth of love."

"There's a nasty draft from that electric fan," said Mrs. Mariner. "Perhaps you'd be kind enough to turn it away from me, Mr. Beaumorris."

*　　　*　　　*

"That's a real hanging jury in the corner," said Tony Windle as he and Katie swirled away. "One old man and four old women."

"Five old women."

"Who do you think they're tearing to pieces?"

"Us, of course. Where's Jonathan?"

"He's not coming."

"Oh. Why?"

Remembering Jonathan's stated opinion about village dances, Tony thought it more tactful to say, "He had a piece to finish for his paper."

"I should have thought it could have waited. That rotten rag of his only comes out once a week. If the piece is for next Thursday he'd have plenty of time, surely."

She sounded put out. Tony thought. "So that's the way the wind's blowing, is it?"

"The same again," said George Mariner. "Vernon?"

"Thank you. It's a gin and tonic."

"Gerry?"

"The same. It's the only possible drink on a night like this."

"Hottest for years," said Vernon Vigors. He was the senior partner in Vigors and Dibden, the only firm of solicitors in Hannington. A thin, dry man in his middle sixties, he seemed to feel the heat less than the florid George Mariner or Group Captain Gerry Gonville, tubby, bald and cheerful and recently retired from the Royal Air Force.

"Put plenty of ice in, Sam," said Mariner. "How's the new job going, Gerry?"

"Better than the last one," said Gerry.

The other two laughed. When Gonville had left the Air Force his first job had been secretary to the Hannington and District Golf Club. The story of his brushes with the lady members had become part of local folklore.

"It involves going up to London four days a week, but this one's a sensible sort of job. I help look after all the appeals for the R.A.F. Benevolent Fund. We collect the money. Our welfare department spends it."

Vigors said, "I'm glad you got the job. Cheers, George."

"Cheers," said Mariner. "And a bloody good cause, too. Though why we have to leave the care and comfort of Air Force men who've fallen on hard times to a voluntary organization is something I've never understood. Did the Air Force save this country in 1940 or didn't they? They did. All right. Then why can't this futile bloody crowd of old women who call themselves a government use a hundredth—a thousandth—of the money they put into bankrupt bloody shows like car factories that can't make cars and steelworks that can't produce steel and pay the Air Force back something of what we owe them."

"I can tell you the answer to that," said Vigors. "Fifty thousand steelworkers and fifty thousand car workers add up to a hundred thousand votes."

"I was talking to old Playfair the other day," said Gonville. "Jack Playfair. He was one of the squadron leaders in Number Six Group. He's in charge of the Recruit Training Centers at Horsham. He said the first thing these recruits ask about when they come in is money. What's the pay? Any special allowances they can wangle? What about free issues? The next thing is leave. They haven't been inside ten minutes before they're thinking of getting out again."

"The first leave *I* got," said Vigors, "was in 1941. One week in two years."

"It was a bit different during the war," said Mariner. "Though I can't help thinking a year or two of active service would do all these young gentlemen a power of good. Sometimes it makes me sick to look at them. Slouching along, with their hair down to their shoulders and their hands in their pockets. What they need is a sergeant major right behind them with a swagger stick."

"It's not their appearance I mind so much," said Vigors, "as the fact that they know it all. The other day a young fellow in our office—not even qualified, mind you—had the nerve to tell me that he thought we oughtn't to act for a man *because he was dishonest*. I explained to him, quite gently, that it was a solicitor's job to act for people who were in trouble—"

"And that half your clients were crooks anyway."

"Well, not quite half," said Vigors. "It's about time we filled those glasses up again, isn't it? The same again all round, Sam. And have one yourself."

Young Noel Vigors and his wife, Georgie, were one of the few married couples who were dancing together. They were both good performers. Noel was saying, "I saw Dad sloping off into the bar with George Mariner and Gerry Gonville. I bet they're hard at it, yackety-yack, yackety-yack, down with the young, up with the old and what they all did in the war."

"Your father was a gunner, wasn't he?"

"North Africa and Italy. Quite a respectable sort of war. Better than old George, who spent all *his* time in the R.A.S.C. dishing out spam and toilet paper to the troops. Not as good as Gerry, of course. They didn't hand out D.S.O.'s and D.F.C.'s for nothing."

It was odd, thought Georgie, how the precise way in which a man happened to have behaved forty years before still seemed to make such a lot of difference forty years later.

She said, "It's difficult not to agree with some of the

things they say. I only wish they wouldn't say them quite so often." She caught sight of the Reverend Bird, who had been cornered by Roseabel Tress and had a glazed look in his eye. She said, "I'll tell you one thing. It never really seems to work if you try too hard with the young. I do believe the current generation are as shy and as fly as any we've ever produced. Look at Dicky Bird. He spends hours every day trying to gain their confidence and organize them and entertain them. But he hasn't persuaded a single one of the boys to sing in his choir."

"Maybe they haven't got voices."

"Then why do nine or ten of them go along once a week to Jonathan's house and sing songs there? They're talking of putting on a concert."

"Perhaps it's because Jonathan never bothers to be nice to anyone except small boys."

"Or maybe it's because he's got a guitar. He's a wizard performer with it."

"Oh? How do you know?"

"Someone told me," said Georgie vaguely.

"You should be out there dancing," said Jack Nurse. "When you're as old as your mother and me you can sit around and watch the others. Not when you're eighteen."

"Nineteen," said Sally automatically. She realized that she ought to be as fond of her father as she had been when she was nine, but she was finding it increasingly difficult to keep it up. "Besides, there's no one worth dancing with."

"Mickey Havelock."

"He's just a kid. And please don't suggest Harvey Maxton. A dance with him isn't a lot different from being mugged."

"It's a pity Peter isn't here," said Mrs. Nurse. "I think he's such a nice boy."

She had one eye on her daughter as she said this, but years of family in-fighting had rendered Sally proof against innuendos of this sort. She simply said, "He's all right, I suppose."

The waltz had finished and the band was striking up a tango.

"I'm not much of a hand at this number," said Billy Gonville, who had come up behind them unseen, "but if you're prepared to chance your arm—"

"Why not," said Sally. "You can only die once."

"Come on, then."

In common with other girls of her age and generation Sally was a much better dancer than most of the boys she met. She had never danced with Billy before. He was light on his feet and had a sense of rhythm, if not much expertise. But there was something more. She sensed—and it was a thing a girl is very rarely mistaken about—that he was interested in her. Nor, thank heaven, did he seem to want to talk.

"Billy's a nice boy," said Mrs. Nurse.

"He's in insurance," said her husband. "That's a good steady job. Not exciting, perhaps, but safe."

"When I was a young girl in India," said Roseabel Tress, "I was much attracted by the doctrines of Brahmanism. Brahma is the supreme being of post-Vedic Hindu mythology. I expect you know about all this, of course. You modern young clergymen are taught to be broad-minded."

"Well—" said the vicar.

"Brahma the Creator, with Vishnu the Preserver and Siva the Destroyer. They form the Trimurti, that is, the great Hindu Triad. An interesting conception."

"Yes indeed."

"I was particularly fascinated by the place they allotted to animals in their pantheistic mythology. The elephant, the tortoise, the bull and the snake. Does it seem absurd to you to worship animals?"

"Lots of people I know worship their dogs," said the vicar. "I think I must go and give my wife a hand. We're just coming up for the coffee break."

The coffee cups and lemonade glasses, the plates which had once contained tiny sandwiches, cakes and croissants and now contained nothing but crumbs, had all been cleared away. Outside it was growing dark. Walter Steelstock said to Lavinia, the oldest of the Havelock girls, "It's very stuffy in here, isn't it. What do you say we go outside and get a breath of fresh air?"

Lavinia looked at him thoughtfully. Walter was supposed to be the steadiest of the three Steelstock children, a nice boy, they said, and a great help to his mother.

"O.K.," she said. "It is a bit hot."

There was a curtained opening on the right-hand side of the stage, which led to the back door of the hall. To the left the path led back to Church Lane. To the right a gate gave directly onto the churchyard.

"Let's sit down for a moment."

It was a black night, with the rind of a new moon just showing over the church tower. The seat was set back between an ancient yew tree and an elaborate tomb. On the headstone of the tomb an angel was poised on one toe, ready to take flight at the sound of the last trump. Walter, as they sat down, slid one arm around the girl in a practiced sort of way. The angel looked disapproving.

Not quite as steady as people make out, thought Lavinia, who was nearly eighteen but not inexperienced. That was pretty smooth.

"There's something I wanted to tell you," said Walter.

"Now's your chance."

"You mustn't laugh at me."

"I'll do my best."

"The fact is, I haven't been able to take my eyes off you all evening. Last time I saw you, I was still thinking of you as a schoolgirl. Now you've changed—did you know it yourself, I wonder?—into someone quite, quite different."

A small shadow moved under the darkness of the yew tree. A twig snapped. Walter swung around and said fiercely, "Who's there? Come out of it."

"The same again, Sam," said Vigors. The round had reached him for the second time. Five drinks had inflated them all, but they were far from drunk.

"The real problem of today," said Mariner, "is mindless violence. The sort of violence that ruins football matches, breaks unoffending shopwindows and wrecks railway carriages. It'd be easier to forgive if there was some point to it."

"Like hijacking and kidnapping, you mean?" said Vigors.

"I don't condone that sort of thing, of course. But the people who do it do at least have an objective."

"Even if it's only money."

"Certainly. But they're *not* doing it because they're bored. And they're *not* doing it because they enjoy violence for its own sake."

"Doing it for kicks. Isn't that the modern expression?" said Gonville. "There was a case in the papers the other day. A girl of fifteen and a boy of twelve—*twelve,* mind you—got their evening's entertainment out of kicking an old woman to death. What can you do with people like that?"

"Half the trouble is our attitude," said Mariner. "The government positively encourages us to be weak-kneed.

That White Paper they put out, 'Children in Trouble.' What a load of drip! It's not the children who are in trouble, for God's sake, it's their victims. The women and old people they beat up and rob."

"It's not only the government. The newspapers play the same game."

"Some of them."

"Including," said Vigors, "that outstanding example of progressive pink journalism, the Hannington *Gazette.*"

"You mean the gospel according to Jonathan Limbery," said Gonville. "I thought that last article of his was practically contempt of court."

"I read it," said Mariner. His face, which was normally a placid and unrevealing mask, had sharpened into more than mere disapproval. Looking at him, Vigors thought, Something personal there, I fancy. "In my view, for what it's worth, that young man should have been prosecuted. Isn't it a crime to advocate the destruction of our existing institutions by force?"

"Sedition," said Vigors doubtfully. "You'd need a very strong case to carry a jury in these libertarian days."

"It was the savagery of the article that appalled me. The sort of gloating pleasure about the prospect of anybody with more money or position than him having their faces stamped on."

"He's a savage young man," agreed Gonville.

"A few years ago it wouldn't have been so dangerous, because people would have laughed at him. Now one isn't sure any longer."

"One can't be sure of anything these days," said Vigors. "Except that if the price of drink goes up much further we shall all have to take the pledge. Cheers."

"Cheers," said Gonville.

Mariner was still angry. He said, "Mark my words,

there could be trouble coming, and if it does come that young man and people like him will be to blame for it."

Noel Vigors was dancing with Katie. He was describing the strategy which had led the firm of Vigors and Dibden to an unexpected decision in their favor in the Reading County Court ("with costs") when Katie said, "I'm sorry, Noel. I've simply got to get out."

"Get out? Where to?"

"Out of this place."

"You're not feeling ill, are you?"

"No. I'm perfectly well. And all I've had to drink tonight is one glass of gin and lime—without much gin in it. Be a dear. I think this dance is nearly over. Steer me close to the door, so that I can slip out the moment it stops."

This was the main entrance and exit of the hall. The inner door led into a small lobby, with a gentlemen's cloakroom on one side and a ladies' cloakroom on the other, and then to the outer door, which gave onto Church Lane.

Noel said, "O.K. If that's what you want." The floor was now crowded. He timed his maneuver with precision, reaching the door as a roll of the drums marked the end of that bout of mixed wrestling. Katie awarded him a quick smile, picked up the bag off the chair beside the door, slipped through the door and was gone.

At least two other people saw her go. One was Tony Windle. The other was Sally Nurse. She never took her eyes off Katie for long. Katie represented her ideal. She admired the way she dressed and she modeled her own appearance unobtrusively on it. She admired the success Katie had made of her career, without much hope that she could do the same. It was selfless admiration, unspoiled by jealousy.

* * *

"For goodness' sake, Billy," said Mrs. Gonville. "Get your father out of that bar. He's been there for hours. I don't know why he bothers to come to these dances. It'd be much cheaper and easier for him to do his drinking at home."

"It's time all we oldsters were in bed," agreed Beaumorris. He had not stirred an inch from his chair during the whole evening and had enjoyed himself enormously.

Rosina, the youngest of the three Havelock children present, whirled past with Tony Windle in what they imagined was a Highland schottische.

Mrs. Havelock said, "I left Roney and Sim in charge at home. I tremble to think what they'll have been getting up to." She waved to Roseabel Tress, who wandered up in an absent-minded manner which suggested that her mind was more on Vedic Hindu mythology than on the Tennis Club disco.

"If you're ready to go," said Mrs. Havelock, "I'll give you a lift. I don't suppose the children want to come home yet, but they'll have to do what they're told, for once."

"Very kind of you," said Roseabel, staring around the room. "Very kind." The overhead lights had been dimmed and a zoetrope, operated from the stage, was throwing alternate jets of red and green light across the room. The tempo of the band had quickened to a jungle stomp.

"Quite, quite pagan," murmured Roseabel.

"Like demented traffic lights," said Mrs. Havelock, heaving her bulk out of the chair. "Are you coming, Olivia?"

"Walter will be driving me back," said Mrs. Steelstock. "I expect he'll be here in a moment."

"You're so lucky to have such a reliable child."

*   *   *

Joe Cavey had many jobs. His main one was running the boathouse, seeing that the private boats were looked after and club boats shared out equitably. Another of his jobs was keeping an eye on the Memorial Hall. When it was used for a function, as it was that night, he undertook to see the last people off the premises, to turn off the lighting, to see that all the windows were shut and finally to lock the door. He exercised a similar guardianship over the Tennis Club premises and ran the bar. He was paid a retainer for these activities and had the use of a cottage which stood at the point where Church Lane ran out onto the towpath.

On this evening, he was standing outside his back door listening to the sounds of dance music coming from the Memorial Hall at the far end of the lane. His own dancing days had been ended by a shell splinter through his right thigh at the crossing of the Santerno River. It had severed an artery and he had been lucky not to bleed to death. Fortunately the medical orderly had known his job and had clapped on a tourniquet in time. Joe could still see the bright red frothy blood which had pumped out at such an alarming speed. He sometimes dreamed about blood. His right leg was stiff and ached in the cold weather.

Mr. Cavey drew on his pipe and blew out a gust of smoke. His wife, who had objected to his smoking in bed, had been dead for fifteen years. He thought of her without regret. He preferred doing for himself. Most of his spare time was spent looking after his back garden, with its rows of early and main-crop potatoes, sprouts, onions and peas. He kept a shotgun in his kitchen and waged ceaseless war on the pigeons.

Out of the corner of his eye he thought he saw black shadows moving across the field beyond his garden hedge. The night was so dark that it was impossible to be certain. Dogs? Too big for dogs and the wrong shape. No. They were human, going fast and keeping low. Boys, he guessed. Or girls. Youngsters certainly. Mr. Cavey removed his pipe and bellowed out in his Army voice, "Oo's that?"

The figures checked for a moment, then accelerated. They seemed to throw themselves at the fence which bordered the towpath. No doubt about it, they were boys. Mr. Cavey heard the sound of ripping cloth.

"Young monkeys," said Mr. Cavey. "One of them'll need a patch in his breeks."

He stood for a few minutes more. The incident had disturbed him. The boys, whoever they might be, were clearly up to no good. Either they had been doing something they should not have been doing, or were intending to do something. Their flight had betrayed their guilt.

Mr. Cavey's mind did not move quickly. But, having thought the matter through, he came to a conclusion. The only place which concerned him where they could do any mischief was the boathouse. A window had been broken there a month or more ago. The culprit had not been discovered. Nor, now that he came to think of it, had the window been mended. Something must be done about that.

Mr. Cavey knocked out his pipe, leaving it on the window ledge to cool. Then he walked slowly back to his front gate, paused to enjoy the mixed smell of the honeysuckle and night-scented stock, emerged onto the towpath and set out for the boathouse, the bulk of which he could see dimly in the distance against the blackness of the western sky.

3

"You three can squeeze into the back," said Mrs. Havelock. "You come in front with me, Roseabel."

"It's very kind of you," said Miss Tress.

"*Why* have we got to go home?" said Rosina. She was fourteen and it was the first grown-up dance she had been allowed to go to.

"Don't argue with your mother," said Michael. "It's time all little girls were in bed."

"I was only just getting going."

"You were getting going all right," said Lavinia. "Who was that character you were dancing with? It was meant to be an old-fashioned waltz. It looked like all-in wrestling."

"It was Harvey Maxton. As you know very well."

"He's quite a useful rugger player," said Michael.

"He certainly tackled Rosina low."

"It's the new grip," said Rosina. "It's called the bear hug."

"Two minutes more and you *would* have been bare. He almost had your dress off your shoulders."

"Get *in*," said Mrs. Havelock. "Or walk." The three children climbed aboard mutinously.

Their mother drove as she progressed through life,

ponderously but steadily. The scattered lighting of the street ceased opposite West Hannington Manor. A few hundred yards farther on, at the point where Brickfield Road came in on the left, a narrow lane branched off to the right toward the river. The bungalow at the far end, as you approached the towpath, was a sprawling construction called "Heavealong." Here the Havelocks, all eight of them, contrived to lead their ramshackle lives. "Shalimar," the last bungalow, was smaller and neater. In it Roseabel Tress dwelt in lonely state. Both bungalows were built on brick piles and were regularly subject to flooding in the winter.

"Come in and have a cup of tea before you go to bed," said Mrs. Havelock. "Rosina can put the kettle on."

"I always put the kettle on. Why can't Lavinia do it for a change?"

Mrs. Havelock waved a massive arm at her children and they disappeared up the path, still arguing.

"It's very kind of you," said Miss Tress. "I think perhaps I would like a cup of tea." It was always a little daunting, the prospect of going back, particularly on such a dark night, to her empty home. Vishnu the Preserver might be there, but so too might Siva the Destroyer.

"I've had a lot of ups and downs in my life," said Mrs. Havelock, "and I've never known any circumstances where a good strong cup of tea with plenty of sugar in it didn't do me a power of good."

The tea had been made and Mrs. Havelock was on the point of pouring it out when she paused. In the silence they all heard the click of the lock.

"Someone at the kitchen door," said Rosina.

"Burglars," said Lavinia. "Go and see, Mike." Michael was sixteen and big for his age. He got up with a fair assumption of nonchalance and went out. There was scuffling; batlike voices were raised in protest; and he reappeared dragging the nine-year-old Sim by one ear. Roney followed, looking apprehensive.

"What on earth do you think you're doing?" said Mrs. Havelock. "You ought to have been in bed hours ago."

"Well, Mum, you see—"

"And what's happened to Sim's trousers?"

"It was old Cavey shouting at us. It startled us. Sim got caught in the barbed wire."

Roney was a very good-looking boy with an engaging smile which had extracted him from countless tight corners. He switched it on now. His mother seemed far from placated. She said, "It was very naughty of you. You know you were meant to be looking after the babies."

"They were all right," said Roney. "They were asleep. Snoring like anything. We didn't think you'd mind if we went out, just for a short time. After all, you were all enjoying yourselves."

"Well—" said Mrs. Havelock.

"You're letting him wriggle out of it, as usual," said Lavinia. "He ought to be on bread and water for a week."

"We'll talk about it in the morning," said Mrs. Havelock. "Take those trousers off, Sim, and leave them on my work basket. They'll need a patch putting in them."

The boys accepted this as dismissal with a caution. When he was safe in the doorway, with the door open, Roney said, "You've changed, Lavinia—did you know it yourself? I wonder—into someone *quite, quite* different."

"You little beast," said Lavinia, jumping up. "Just wait till I get hold of you."

Roney slammed the door, and they heard his feet scuttering down the passage.

"It's no good," said Michael. "He'll lock his bedroom door. If you want to do anything to him you'll have to wait till tomorrow."

"It's time someone took him in hand," said Mrs. Havelock. "He ought to be at boarding school, only the fees are so impossible nowadays."

"What exciting lives you do all lead," said Miss Tress wistfully. "I really must be going."

When she got home, she undressed slowly and climbed into her four-poster bed. It was a pity the night was so warm or she might have comforted herself with a hot water bottle. She looked at the bedside table and looked quickly away again.

What a difficult and expensive life Mrs. Havelock must lead. Seven children to feed and clothe and educate. The young ones, she knew, went to the secondary school at Hannington—that sweet little Roney—but the three older children were at Coverdales, the well-known Reading grammar school. A day school, but by no means cheap.

She looked at the bedside table again and her resolution weakened. One of the tablets would surely do no harm. The doctor had warned her. They're strong. Don't start to rely on them. It's much better to sleep naturally if you can.

She took one of the tablets. Might two work quicker? Better not. She was already beginning to feel drowsy when she thought she heard a car start up. It must have been parked actually on the towpath. She listened to it driving away, and as she did so was suddenly shaken by an uncontrollable fit of shuddering. It was as though a powerful electric shock had passed through her body. She reached out a hand, which was shaking so badly that she had some difficulty in unscrewing the top of the bottle, tipped out the tablets onto the bedside table and crammed two of them into her mouth. Her throat was so dry that they choked her. She grabbed the carafe of water that stood on the table and drank directly out of it.

Gradually the tremors ceased. Sleep came down like a gray blanket.

The dancers were thinning out now. The bandleader, looking quickly at his watch, saw that it was five past twelve. With luck, and a bit of stage management, he might bring the thing to an end soon. Then he and the boys could get to bed, which would be a blessing as they had an engagement for the following night, which was a Saturday; and Saturday engagements were always heavy ones. Like his fellow musicians, he worked by day and was beginning to feel the effects of trying to squeeze two jobs into twenty-four hours.

Tony Windle was dancing with a plain girl, a serious performer, whose name he had forgotten. His mind was not on her. He was wondering why Katie had been in such a hurry to get away. And he was wondering where Sally Nurse was. When Katie was not available, he found Sally an agreeable substitute. A self-created substitute. He had often laughed at her for her artless impersonation of Katie. But Sally was a very sweet girl. And where the hell *had* she got to? He was thinking so hard about this that he missed some comment his partner had made.

He said, "Sorry, I didn't get that."

"I said that this band had no real sense of rhythm."

"Perhaps they're getting tired."

Noel Vigors said the same thing to Georgie. "You look quite done up."

"Actually," said Georgie, "I'm feeling a bit sick."
"Sick?"
"Don't panic. I'm not going to *be* sick. I'm just feeling sick. Let's get up to that corner and sit down."
Noel steered her to the chair which had recently been occupied by Mr. Beaumorris. He said, "Do you think it might be . . . ?"
"I think it might. I missed at the weekend."
Noel sat down beside her, slipped an arm through hers and said, "Well. What do you know?"
"Which would you like it to be?"
"A boy, of course. He'll be articled in the firm. Third generation."
"Sometime next century."
"You realize we shall have to shift Dad out. The house is crowded enough now. Which reminds me. He's taken the car. How are we going to get home?"
"Walk, of course."
"Are you sure you can?"
"Fussing already," said Georgie. "A month or two and everything will be back to normal, I expect: 'Do you mind filling the coal scuttle and bringing some logs in. I've simply *got* to finish reading these papers.'"

Mr. Cavey came in and looked around the hall. About a dozen pairs of youngsters were still dancing. He walked over and said something to the bandleader, who nodded and brought the music to a firm conclusion.
Some of the dancers shouted out, "Encore."
Mr. Cavey was looking for someone in authority. The only person he could see whom he would have classified as belonging to the officer class was Tony Windle. He walked across and said, "I think we ought to finish now, sir. If you don't mind."
Tony said in some surprise, "You're packing us up

very sharp tonight, Joe. It's only a quarter past twelve. You usually give us half an hour's grace."

"I know, sir. But I think the band want to get home."

They were already packing up their instruments. The dancers started to drift slowly toward the door. Tony said, "You haven't seen Billy anywhere, have you?"

"Mr. Gonville? No, sir. I did happen to notice, when I was coming past the parking place, his car wasn't there."

"It's not the sort of car you could miss," agreed Tony. It was a blood-red Austin-Healey frog-eyed Sprite, ten years old and lovingly maintained.

The band had filed out of the back entrance and the last of the dancers could be heard claiming their belongings from the cloakroom.

"'After the ball was over,'" said Tony. "'After the break of day. After the dancers leaving. After the skies are gray. Many's the heart is breaking—' What's up, Joe?"

"Well, sir—"

"You've been looking like the ghost of Hamlet's father ever since you came in. George Mariner's driven into a lamppost? Old Mr. Beaumorris has fallen off his bicycle? Mrs. Havelock has run over a chicken?"

"It's not really funny—"

"I'm sure it isn't," said Tony, suddenly quite serious. "What is it?"

"It's our Miss Katie. I found her myself when I went down to check over the boathouse. Someone's smashed her head in."

4

Dr. Farmiloe was on the point of going to bed when the telephone rang. Being a methodical man, he noted the time. It was ten minutes to twelve.

He listened to what the telephone had to say, contributed one "Where?" and one "Right" and replaced the receiver. Without appearing to hurry, but without losing any time, he collected a small black bag, which lived in a cupboard in the hall, opened it and added one or two items to it from a shelf in the cupboard. Then he went out, leaving the front door carefully on the latch, extracted his car from the garage, which occupied the space between his house and the Beaumorris cottage, and drove off.

The whole of this sequence of actions took him less than five minutes. Before he had retired into private practice at West Hannington, he had spent twenty-five years as a police surgeon in the Clerkenwell area of South London.

He saw Cavey standing at the corner where Church Lane ran out onto the towpath. Cavey waved to him to stop and climbed in beside him. "It's two-three hundred yards along," he said. "Just before the boathouse."

"Who found her?"

"I did."

"Then it was you who telephoned Dandridge?"

"That's right. Straightaway I rang him."

The car had bumped on a hundred yards farther before Dr. Farmiloe said, "I suppose there's no doubt she's dead."

"I've seen plenty of dead people in my time," said Cavey. There was a note in his voice which might have been panic, or might have been bravado. "She's dead. No question."

"It's not always easy to be sure," said the doctor. A torchlight waved ahead of them. The doctor brought the car to a halt and climbed out. He said, "Better stay in the car. The less feet trampling about the better."

Cavey seemed glad of the advice. He was clearly more shaken than he chose to appear.

The man behind the torch was Chief Inspector Dandridge, who was, at that time, in charge of the Hannington station. He was a slow, heavy Berkshire man. His real name was Herbert, but people had called him Dan ever since he had joined the Berkshire County Force twenty-five years before. He said, "She's over there, Doctor. In the grass."

The girl was lying face downward, with one arm flung forward, the other arm doubled up under her body. Dr. Farmiloe knelt down beside her. He felt for the pulse in her neck and found nothing. Using his own torch, he examined the back of her head carefully and then shone its light into her wide-open eyes. He did all this quite slowly, because he wanted time to think.

He was in no doubt that Katie was dead. He had been sure of that from the moment he had seen the way she was lying: the disjointed, abandoned sprawl, as though the body, deprived of life, was hugging the ground from which it had come. Then shall the dust return to the earth as it was in the beginning. And the spirit—Yes, what had happened to the spirit of Katie, beloved of millions of people who had seen her picture on the small screen and had built their own image from it? The spirit, said the author of the book of Ecclesiastes, shall return unto God who gave it.

The problem remained.

How was he going to tell Dandridge what to do without upsetting his dignity? Because it was clear that he was out of his depth.

Thinking it out as he got to his feet, he said, "I shan't be able to make a proper examination before it gets light. But there are some things I've got to do at once. It's clearly going to be important to know exactly when she died. I can probably tell you that, but I shall need a bit of space to work in. Could you organize some screens?"

"Screens?" said Dandridge vaguely.

Detective Sergeant Esdaile, who had just arrived on his bicycle, said, "There should be a few screens and posts in the boathouse. They had them up round the Gents' at the regatta."

"Is the boathouse locked?"

"Cavey's got the key."

Hearing his name, Cavey climbed out of the car and shambled forward. He averted his eyes from the thing on the ground. Yes, he had a key of the padlock which held the big sliding doors, but it was back at his cottage.

"If he goes back to fetch it," said the doctor, "he could telephone for help. You're going to need all the hands you can get."

Dandridge turned this over in his mind and then said, "Right. Give McCourt a ring, too. He can get down here quick on his moped. And then get onto Detective Superintendent Farr, at Reading." He pulled out a pocket book and scribbled down the numbers.

"Tell him we've got a case of suspected murder. Will he please contact the Chief Constable and then get here as quickly as he can. After that, you might pack up the dance at the hall. Don't say anything about this, of course. The last thing we want is a lot of people coming down to have a look."

The doctor drew a line with his toe in the dust. "Screens here and here," he said. "And we ought to think about blocking the towpath altogether."

McCourt ignored the telephone as long as he could before stretching out a hand. He listened to Mr. Cavey, said "What?" and "Where?" and then "Right" and tumbled out of bed. By the time he got to the boathouse, progress had been made. Three hessian screens had been put up, one along the edge of the path and one at either end, forming three sides of a square inside which Dr. Farmiloe was at work. A long flex had been run out from the boathouse. The light he was working by was an incongruous string of red, white and blue bulbs which had last been used to adorn the rostrum at the annual regatta. White tapes marked off a further area of grass on each side of the screens.

Sergeant Esdaile said, "Now we've got Ian here, Skipper, couldn't he go and break the news to Mrs. Steelstock?"

Dandridge brought himself back from wherever his thoughts had taken him and said, "Mrs. Steelstock?"

"She'll have to know sometime. It doesn't hardly seem right just to telephone her. Ian's got his moped. He could do it easiest."

"Yes," said Dandridge. He moved across and peered over the top of the screen as though he was hoping that

Dr. Farmiloe might have brought Katie back to life. "I suppose that's right. You do that."

McCourt looked as if the job was one he would willingly have refused and started to say something. But Dandridge had retired into the hinterland of his own thoughts and was staring at him blankly as McCourt remounted his moped and bumped off along the towpath. When he reached the corner of River Park Avenue, he noticed that there were lights still on in Heavealong, but that Shalimar was dark. There was a little coolness in the air now and he was glad of it. He was not looking forward to what he had to do.

The front door of the Manor House was opened to him by Walter. He said, "Come in. You were lucky to find me up. The others are in bed. Is there some trouble?"

McCourt told him what had happened. Walter seemed to take in the information with deliberate slowness, absorbing it piece by piece, as though to cushion the shock. He said, "Have we really got to wake Mother up? She's probably just got off to sleep."

"The Superintendent thought she ought to know as soon as possible."

"Then I'd better do it. Peter needn't know until tomorrow."

He had himself well under control, the Sergeant thought. He said, thankfully, "I'll leave you to it, then." He was outside the front door when he heard Mrs. Steelstock cry out. It was a cry of pain and shock. But McCourt, who was an observant young man, detected another note behind the simple anguish: a note of outrage, a note of anger with fate for dealing her a foul blow.

Walter noted it too, and was relieved. He had braced

himself for tears and hysteria. He had not expected anger and resolve.

His mother threw a dressing gown over her shoulders, went across to a small davenport in the corner of her bedroom and took out an address book. She said, "I'm going to ring up Philip."

"Now?"

"Of course. At once." She was dialing as she spoke, picking out the numbers unhesitatingly.

When McCourt got back to the boathouse he found that reinforcements had already arrived. Detective Superintendent Farr, the head of the Berkshire C.I.D., was talking to a tall thin civilian whom McCourt placed, after some thought, as Sam Pollock, the Deputy Chief Constable.

"It'll be for the Chief to decide," said Pollock. "But I know what I'd do in his place. I'd get C. One in on the act from the start. No offense intended, Dennis, but this girl's a public character. As soon as the news breaks you'll have the press round your neck."

"Don't mind me," said Farr. "I've got enough on my plate already. So far as I'm concerned, the glory boys can have it and good luck to them."

"There's another thing. Agreed, this could turn out to be a local matter. But then again, it needn't be. The girl lived half her life up in London. There are bound to be inquiries to make up there."

"All right," said Farr. "Like you said, it isn't our decision. I can tell you one thing. Whichever way it goes, our chaps will have to do most of the work." He looked at his watch. "It'll be light in three hours," he said to Dandridge. "We want this section of the towpath blocked off at both ends. Put barricades at the end of Church Lane and River Park Avenue. Leave a man here to keep an eye on things. Right?"

"Right," said Dandridge. He seemed happy to be taking rather than giving orders. "You'd better stay here, Keep." This was to Police Constable Keep, who had been on night duty at the station and looked as though he would have been glad to get back there.

After sprinkling a few more suggestions and commands around, Farr walked back to his Humber and drove off. Dandridge said, "See you keep everyone off. Especially the newspaper boys." He then made for his car. Esdaile picked up his bicycle, which he had propped against the farther wall of the boathouse, and said, "I'll be seeing you."

McCourt thought, it was like the gradual emptying of the stage, the release of tension after the high point of the drama. He was perched on the rail of the landing stage which fronted the boathouse. He felt curiously wide awake.

Constable Keep, who had taken one cautious look over the sacking screen and then turned quickly away again, came across and joined him. McCourt got out a packet of cigarettes and they both lit up.

"Who could have done a thing like that?" said Keep.

"I expect we shall find out soon enough," said McCourt.

They smoked in silence. It was past the dead hour of the night. The pendulum had swung across the midpoint and was climbing toward morning. Soon light would be coming back into the world. A thin curtain of mist was beginning to rise from the water. In the intense stillness, they could hear the small sounds of life moving in the long grass and the bushes which fringed the riverbank. A white shape showed through the mist as a single swan sailed toward them breasting the current with easy strokes.

"Nasty brutes," said Keep. "When I was a kid playing

about on the river, I used to be terrified of them. They say they can break a man's arm easy."

"Is that right?" said McCourt. He had no wish to talk. If he had any sense, he thought, he'd have gone back to bed when the top brass left. They were going to be busy enough, in all conscience, when the sun rose.

It was as he was starting to get up that they both saw and heard something else. The growling of a car in low gear. The twin eyes of headlights dimmed by the mist. McCourt said, "I'd better stop them before they come too far."

He walked forward. It was a big black car with the stamp of officialdom on it. As he came up to it the lights flicked on inside and he saw the occupants.

The driver was a young man with a young and solemn face. The passenger, who had opened the door and was climbing out, was a small thick person with white hair and a nose which had been broken and badly set.

McCourt recognized him at once.

5

"My name's Knott," said the newcomer. "Chief Superintendent, C. One. And who are you?"

"McCourt, sir. Sergeant. Hannington C.I.D."

"Give me that torch, Bob." He returned his attention to Ian. "I understand you've got a body for me."

"It's behind those screens."

"Someone's had that much sense." He seemed to be in no hurry to examine the body but shifted the torch, not so that it shone into Ian's eyes but far enough for the side glow to light up his face. He said, "Haven't I seen you before?"

"I was two years at West End Central, under Watts."

"Thought so. Never forget a face. What took you out into the sticks? Looking for quicker promotion, or less work?"

"Neither, sir. My mother had folk in these parts. She wanted to get out of London and wanted me by her."

Knott grunted. He had, as McCourt remembered from the previous occasion on which he had met him, an orchestration of grunts which could mean anything. It was not clear whether this one implied disapproval of a mother who could stand in the way of a promising young man's career in the metropolis or contempt for a young man who could fall in with her wishes.

"When was she found?"

"I'm afraid I don't know, sir. I was in bed and asleep."

"Early to bed and early to rise, eh?"

McCourt said, with a smile, "I hardly got to bed at all last night."

"Then why the hell aren't you in bed now?" The torch shifted slightly. "You're not going to be much use to anyone if you're half asleep, are you? Push off. I'll see you at the station at nine o'clock. Not a minute before." As McCourt turned to go, he added, "And not a minute after."

As soon as he had gone, Knott moved across to the screen and peered over. He shone the torch down for a moment, then switched it off and turned to Constable Keep, who was standing impassively. Having discovered the constable's name, he perched himself on the rail which fenced the side of the boathouse slipway and sat there swinging his short legs. Then he said, "Tell me about yourselves, Keep."

"About ourselves, sir?"

"The Hannington Force."

"Oh. I see. Well, sir, it's not a big station. There's Chief Inspector Dandridge. He's in charge. On the uniformed side we've got Sergeant Bakewell. He's the Station Sergeant. And there're two other constables besides me—Coble and Mustoe. Then on the C.I.D. side we've got Inspector Ray, only he's not there just now, being in hospital at Reading."

"Serious?"

"Stomach ulcers. He's been there a month or more. Under observation."

Knott's grunt implied that he knew better than the doctors exactly what this could signify.

"And then there's Sergeant Esdaile and Sergeant McCourt. Him you were talking to. And Detective Arnold. He's away with a broken ankle."

Knott sat in silence for some minutes. He seemed to be counting up the numbers and estimating the caliber of the forces at his disposal. He said, "Has the doctor seen her?"

"Oh yes, sir. Dr. Farmiloe was here very quick."

"Farmiloe. Jack Farmiloe?"

"I believe that's his name, sir. He was up in London, doing police work, I understand, before he came down here. You may have met him."

"If he's the Jack Farmiloe I knew," said Knott, "we're in luck. It means that one job at least will have been done properly." He swung himself down onto his feet. "Keep your eyes skinned. We'll have both ends of the path blocked by first light. And if anyone comes past, keep them well away from the screens. *But get their names*. Right?"

"Right," said Keep. He thought, Cheeky bugger. One job at least done right. He, too, had recognized the squat white-haired figure. Charlie Knott, one of the self-appointed stars of the Murder Squad. His picture had been in the papers only that week. A case at Oxford. A man being led into the Magistrates Court by two detectives, with a coat over his head and Charlie Knott close enough behind to get himself into the picture. As per usual.

Knott was examining the boathouse. Solidly constructed out of good materials, it had been built nearly a hundred years before, in the heyday of Thames boating. It would last another hundred years, he thought, *if* it was looked after. But there were signs of deterioration. The paintwork needed redoing, and there was a missing pane of glass in the small door set into the left hand of the big swing doors which guarded the main part of the shed.

Knott shone his torch through and picked out the four-oar skiffs, the tub dinghies, the upended canoes and the lines of oars standing like guardsmen at the back.

The swing doors were fastened with a padlock. The small door was locked, too, with a Yale-type lock. Knott wandered around to the far side and found another door. Beside it a painted notice board said, "Hannington Boating and Aquatic Club. Committee Room." This door also was locked.

He completed his circuit of the building, past the lean-to at the rear, and came out again behind the point where Constable Keep was standing. He said, "Who runs this place?"

"Mr. Cavey, he's the caretaker. He's the one who found her."

"So I heard. What I meant was, who's the boss?"

"That'd be Mr. Mariner. He's the president of the club. Mr. Nurse is secretary."

Knott stood for a moment digesting this information. At the beginning of a case, like a careful hostess at the outset of a party, he liked to memorize names and fit them to faces. He walked back to his car. The driver was lying with his eyes shut. He looked absurdly young.

Knott said, "Wake up, Bob. Take the car back to that pub—the one we telephoned—can't remember the name."

"The Swan," said Sergeant Shilling sleepily.

"Right. Drop our stuff there. Tell them we'll want an early breakfast. Then get round to the station. There'll be someone on night duty. Tell him to get hold of Dandridge. I'll meet him there in half an hour. Then you can go to bed."

"How are you going to get back?"

"When I've finished here, I'll walk. It isn't far. Don't try to turn the car. Back it until you reach the turning we came down. And don't go into the river."

"Do my best," said Shilling.

Knott followed the car as it backed. It was a tricky maneuver in the mist but deftly accomplished. He watched the car turn down Upper Church Lane. The cottage on the corner, which he knew belonged to Mr. Cavey, was in darkness. He wondered about Mr. Cavey. The first person on the scene of a crime was always important. He must find an early opportunity for a word with Mr. Cavey.

Turning about, he walked slowly along the towpath, keeping to the metaled portion in the center. On his right the river ran black under its quilt of curling mist. On his left was a strip of rough grass, backed for the first fifty yards by a barbed-wire fence, and after that by a hedge of what looked like thorn bushes and alder. The sunshine of the past fortnight would have baked everything rock hard. But it would all have to be searched, because it was the path down which Katie Steelstock had walked to her death.

He continued on past the boathouse. Here there was a change. No hedge on the left, but a row of fenced building plots. Then a shed. Then a bungalow—"Shalimar" in Gothic script on the gate—and here was the turning he had expected. River Park Avenue. If he went along it, it must bring him back to the main road. Twenty minutes' brisk walk would get him through West Hannington and back into Hannington town.

It would also restore his circulation and give him time to plan his strategy. He had been long enough at the game to know that the first twenty-four hours could make or mar the outcome.

In this case, the fact that important people were involved had given him a flying start.

Mrs. Steelstock had telephoned her brother, Philip, at twelve forty. Philip Frost was the Deputy Director of Public Prosecutions. He had immediately contacted his friend and professional colleague of long standing, Terence Loftus, Assistant Commissioner of the Metropolitan Police. Two telephone calls had followed, the first to the Chief Constable of Berkshire, who had already been alerted by the Deputy Chief Constable and who was not only wide awake but had been on the point of telephoning Loftus himself; the second to Detective Chief Superintendent Knott, who was sleeping the sleep of the just in a small hotel outside Oxford, having that day brought to a successful conclusion the hunt for the killer of two Somerville students. One more jump forward in the rat race. A real possibility that he might make the coveted and difficult step up to Commander. It was a two-horse race really. Himself or Haliburton. And, as a result of the Oxford case, he fancied that his own nose was in front.

Success at Hannington could make a certainty of it. And success should not be too difficult. When a girl was killed you started with the 90 per cent probability that the killer was one of her boyfriends. In this case there was the extra possibility that it was a casual crime. The girl might have disturbed someone who was up to no good. A wild blow, not meant to kill. A panic-stricken flight. That would be much more difficult.

Could the missing window in the boathouse door be significant? How long ago had it been broken? He would have to ask Cavey about that. As the outlines of the investigation formed themselves in his mind, he began to consider what help he would need. He would have the two detective sergeants: McCourt and—what was the name?—think—Esdaile. McCourt had struck him as a cocky type who would be inclined to strike out a line on his own. He would want watching. For immediate purposes he would need more men. A lot more. The first step would be to contact Dennis Farr at Reading. He had met him in the course of the Oxford investigation and had got on well with him. Farr would help.

West Hannington merged into Hannington town. The change occurred quite suddenly. One moment he was in a village. The next moment in a suburb of small houses. Ten minutes more took him to the central point, where he turned left for the bridge over the river and the railway station and right up the main shopping street, near the far end of which was the police station.

Here he found Chief Inspector Dandridge waiting for him.

"Sorry to keep you up, Dan," he said. And if Dandridge was surprised that he should know, and use, his nickname he managed not to show it. "There's one or two things we've got to arrange before we all go to bed. First we've got to block both ends of the towpath. Trestles and a notice will do for the moment. One lot at Cavey's cottage, the other lot where River Park Avenue comes out. But notices won't keep the press out. We'll need a constable on duty at each end."

"I've only got—"

"Limited manpower, I know. That's the next thing. I'm going to give Farr a buzz and borrow a dozen men."

"A dozen?"

"For one day. Maybe two. After that we can rely on the men we've got here. With a little help from time to time. Next point: Who does your photography here?"

"That's Sergeant Esdaile."

"Christian name?"

"Everyone calls him Eddie."

"Is he O.K. with a camera? We don't want any slip-ups."

"He took a course at Roehampton."

"All right. Have him down there at first light. When he's done his stuff we can shift the body. We can probably arrange to have it taken straight down to Southampton for the autopsy. Not that I imagine they'll find out anything we didn't know already." He looked at some notes he had been scribbling on a scrap of paper. "Last point: Can you tell me where Dr. Farmiloe hangs out? I want a word with him. Then we can all get a bit of shut-eye."

Dandridge gave him the address and directions for getting there. After Knott had gone he stood quite still for nearly a minute. In the same way that the recoil mechanism of a gun will nullify the shock of a shell's discharge, he seemed to be absorbing the impact of Detective Chief Superintendent Knott's personality.

As he went out through the charge room he looked at the clock over the Station Sergeant's desk and saw that it was exactly five o'clock. In an hour's time it would be fully light. He said goodnight to Sergeant Bakewell and went out into the street. He doubted whether he would get any sleep now, but he would go through the motions.

By nine o'clock Dandridge's office had quite a few people in it. Reading was represented by Chief Superintendent Oliphant of the Uniformed Branch and Detective Superintendent Farr of the C.I.D. McCourt and Esdaile were making themselves inconspicuous in the background. Shilling had set up a blackboard and was drawing a plan on it. Knott was standing beside the blackboard in a schoolmasterly attitude. Dr. Farmiloe was seated on the edge of the table with a sheaf of notes in one hand. Sergeant Bakewell had squeezed in and was effectively blocking the door. The window was wide open. It was going to be another scorching day.

"You've heard Dr. Farmiloe's report, gentlemen," said Knott. "It was extremely fortunate that he was able to be on the spot so quickly. And knew what he had to do when he got there."

A murmur of assent. All the senior officers present had suffered at one time or other the frustration of delayed or incompetent medical work.

"We shan't know for certain until we get the results of the autopsy, but it's fairly clear that Kate died at once, as the result of this single blow. Dr. Farmiloe has given us, as limits of the time of death, ten minutes to eleven and twenty minutes to twelve. He stressed that these were *outside* limits. A more probable time of death would be sometime between ten past and half past eleven."

He paused and then said, "It's a narrow time span. Geographically the area we have to consider is small, too."

He turned to the blackboard on which Shilling had finished his plan.

"We know that Kate left the Memorial Hall . . . there. At the point where Church Lane—Upper Church Lane, I think they call that bit—turns off and runs down to the river. Presumably she went straight down the lane. No evidence of that, but I can't see why she should have done anything different. The area on the left of the lane is Tennis Club property. All locked up. And there's a thick bramble hedge on the right. So let's assume that she made straight down the lane to the river."

"Distance?" said Oliphant.

Knott looked at Shilling, who said, "Two hundred yards, near enough."

"When she gets to the river she turns left, onto the towpath. That square at the corner is a cottage. It belongs to a bloke called Joe Cavey."

"The one who found the body?" said Farr.

"That's the man. The distance between his cottage and the boat shed is about twice the length of the lane, so call it four hundred yards. Say six hundred yards in all. It could have taken her around ten minutes to walk it."

"It was pitch dark," said Farr. "She couldn't have hurried. I'd say all of ten minutes, maybe a bit more."

"Agreed." Knott turned back to the plan. "There are no buildings between Cavey's corner and the boathouse. After the boathouse the path goes on again without buildings for about three hundred yards. It's not a large area. If we put enough men onto it we can comb it thoroughly."

"What are we looking for?" said Oliphant.

"Anything that's there," said Knott. The half smile that went with the words took some of the sting out of them. "But principally we're looking for a weapon. Something short and heavy, like an iron bar or a light axe. And here is where we've got to consider two different possibilities. Was it a planned killing, or was it just a hit-and-run job? If it was planned, we're not likely to find the weapon. There are too many places the killer could have hidden it. He could have buried it or thrown it into the river five miles away. On the other hand, if it was a panic job, the man will have slung the weapon away as quickly as possible. Into the bushes."

"More likely straight into the river," said Oliphant.

Knott helped himself to a piece of chalk and drew two lines across the Thames, one about fifty yards upstream from the boathouse and another a hundred yards downstream. He said, "I've laid on a team of divers from the

Marine Commandos at Portsmouth. They're coming in later this morning. I've given them that piece of the river to search. If they don't find anything there, it'll be a waste of time to extend the search."

"You'll have to keep the pleasure boats away while that's going on," said Oliphant. "It won't be easy."

Farr agreed. He said, "If you stop the press boys coming down the towpath, first thing they'll do is hire boats and come down the river."

"I had thought about that," said Knott. "We can't keep people off the river altogether, but the Thames Conservancy have agreed to lend me one of their launches, with a crew and a loudspeaker. They'll see that no one gets too close. I'd like to borrow every man you can spare, Dennis. Make the search a saturation job. Get it finished in one day. Then we can lift most of the restrictions."

Oliphant said, "That certainly sounds a practical way of tackling it. Anyone got any comments?"

No one had any comments.

Knott said, "So much for search. When it comes to inquiry, we can take that a bit more deliberately. I'd like two experienced men from you, Dennis, to help Sergeant Esdaile and Sergeant McCourt in a house-to-house routine covering the area between Brickfield Road and the river." He was drawing further boundary lines on the board as he spoke. "I should guess that's about two hundred houses in all. Doing it carefully, we should be able to cover it in two or three days."

"Asking what in particular?" said Farr. "Apart from the obvious question of where people were between eleven and twelve last night, I mean."

"I'd be very interested in the movements of cars. If this was a planned job, the chances are the man came most of the way by car and did the last bit on foot."

Ian McCourt was aware that it was an occasion on which sergeants spoke little, or kept their mouths shut altogether. He ventured to say, "I think that almost all the people who knew Miss Steelstock well were at that dance at the Memorial Hall."

"The point had not escaped me," said Knott. "And the first job today for you and Esdaile will be to get round to everyone who was at the dance—and I mean everyone—and ask them to be present at eight o'clock tonight at the hall. If they ask why, tell them that they will be helping us to find out who killed Kate. If any of them won't cooperate, take their names and I'll talk to them later. And another thing. Tell them to come the same way they came last night. If it was by car, leave their cars in the same place."

"They'll all cooperate," said McCourt.

"All right. We've all got a lot to do. Anything else?"

"There's a crowd of men outside want to talk to you," said Sergeant Bakewell. "I think they're from the papers."

"I'll deal with them," said Knott.

As he stepped out into the High Street, bulbs flashed and cameras clicked. Knott had arranged his face into a noncommittal expression. Some years before, when he had been investigating a child murder, a photographer had taken a picture of him grinning. What he was laughing at was, in fact, a comment made by the local superintendent about the Chief Constable's wife. The paper, which was indulging in one of its anti-police crusades, had printed this picture alongside a picture of the small victim's mother in tears.

Knott said, "You'll understand, boys, that it's early days and I can't tell you anything much yet. I've always gone on the principle of working with the press, not against it. Anything I can tell you, I will. I'm staying at the Swan Inn, and if you care to come round at six o'clock this evening I'll see what I can do for you. One other thing. For today, you'll have to keep clear of that part of the towpath. We're planning to take it to pieces and put it together again. Right?"

"Any leads yet, Superintendent?"

"I've been on this job for six hours, son. If you care to say that I'm baffled, help yourself."

This produced the expected laugh. The reporters began to disperse. They recognized an old hand when they encountered one.

Knott caught Dandridge as he was leaving the station and said, "Somewhere I can have a quick word with you?"

"In my car. It's in the yard at the back."

He led the way around and they climbed in. Knott said, "This evening I'm going to meet a lot of the local characters. One thing I always like to find out first is, who are the nobs?"

Dandridge didn't pretend not to understand him. He said, "The biggest man round here, by a long chalk, is George Mariner. He's chairman of the local Bench, a District Councilor, president of the Boat Club and the Tennis Club and any other club you care to mention. Not only in Hannington. He's vice president of the Reading branch of the British Legion and patron of a boys' club in the East End of London."

"Married?"

"Wife, no children."

"Any particular reason?"

"Meet his wife."

Knott laughed and said, "Anyone else?"

"There's Group Captain Gonville, D.S.O., D.S.C.

Retired now. A very nice chap. He's on the Bench, too. Our third J.P.'s a woman. Mrs. Havelock. She lives in a bungalow near the end of River Park Avenue, with a pack of tearaway kids."

Knott thought for a moment and said, "'Shalimar' or 'Heavealong'?"

"'Heavealong.' You certainly seem to have picked up the local geography."

"I happened to notice them as I was walking back last night. That's one of only two places where you could get a car down onto the towpath. Who owns 'Shalimar'?"

"Roseabel Tress. Artistic."

Knott grunted.

Well before eight o'clock that evening there was a sizable crowd outside the Memorial Hall. They watched the cars drive up, turn into the car park and station themselves carefully in their remembered places around one car that was still there, the cynosure of all eyes.

Katie's scarlet mini-Cooper.

Mr. Beaumorris, who had pedaled up on his ancient bicycle, said to Mrs. Havelock, "I feel like one of the minor guests at a royal wedding. A groom, or gardener, or some other humble functionary who has been invited and hides himself bashfully away behind the important guests." He did not look either bashful or humble. He looked rather pleased with himself.

Inside the hall the crowd tended to coalesce into the sort of groups they had formed on the previous evening. The chairs had been left undisturbed, and Mr. Beaumorris took possession of the one in the corner. Rosina Havelock and Harvey Maxton started to dance, but no one else thought this funny and they stopped at once when Mrs. Steelstock came in accompanied by Walter.

Eight o'clock struck from St. Michael's Church. The side door behind the stage opened and Detective Superintendent Knott stumped up the steps onto the stage and stationed himself in the center of it.

All eyes were on him. The silence was absolute.

6

Knott said in his gravelly voice, "I have been informed by the representatives of the press that what I am doing here tonight is reconstructing the crime. That's journalistic imagination. What I'm doing is quite different. I'm asking *you* to help *me*."

There was a slight relaxing of tension. Was the man human after all?

"Most of you knew Katie and most of you, I guess, were very fond of her." His eye rested for a moment on Mrs. Steelstock sitting at the back of the hall. There was evidence of a sleepless night in her gray face and a livid smear under each eye, but her mouth was set in an uncompromising line.

"Our first job in a case like this is to establish times and places. Then we can do some elimination and get down to facts. It seemed to me that the quickest way of doing this was for all of you to write down—Sergeant Shilling here has got plenty of paper—as accurately as you possibly can, *when* you left the hall last night and *who* left with you and *where* you went. That's the reason I've got you all together. If one can't remember, the chances are someone else will be able to help him out. If you were in a party, discuss the matter. Someone will be sure to have looked at his watch. Someone will have said, 'We promised the baby sitter we'd be home by eleven,' or 'We wanted to get back to see the late night film on the box.' Talk about it. Argue about it. And when you've got the best answers you can, write your name and address on the top of the paper and give it back to the Sergeant. And let me assure you once more. There's no trick about this. All we're doing, in a manner of speaking, is to clear away the undergrowth. When that's done, we may be able to see a few of the trees."

As he said this he shifted his weight slightly, in a movement which seemed to throw his head forward. His eyes scanned the blur of faces in front of him. They were eyes which had seen a lot of brutality and stupidity and evasion and guilt.

"I believe he's trying to hypnotize us," said Mr. Beaumorris loudly to Mrs. Havelock. The audience was breaking up and re-forming into groups. A murmur of voices broke out and increased in volume. Suddenly everyone seemed to be talking at once.

"Like a cocktail party," said Georgie Vigors.

"A slow start," agreed Mr. Beaumorris, "but getting nicely under way with the second round of gins."

He had taken a fountain pen from his pocket and was staring at the sheet of paper which Sergeant Shilling had put into his hand.

"Not bad," said Knott as he shuffled through the papers. "Really not bad at all."

He was seated behind a big table in the room behind the courtyard at the back of Hannington police station. It had been cleared and equipped for him. The wall facing the window was papered with an overlay of map sheets of West Hannington. These were from the Land

Registry Map Section at Tunbridge Wells and were on a scale of twenty-five inches to the mile, large enough to show individual houses and gardens. There was a smaller-scale map of the surrounding area, with the new M4 running like a yellow backbone down the middle of it, from Exit 12 south of Reading to Exit 13 on the Newbury–Oxford road.

"We've got three estimates of the time Kate left the hall. Young Vigors, who was dancing with her, says it was about eleven o'clock. He says she slipped away quietly, saying she didn't want to attract attention. Tony Windle confirms that. Another person who saw her go was Sally Nurse. She says it was a few minutes after eleven. Why she noticed the time was that she was surprised to see her go so early. Our Katie was usually one of the last to leave a party."

Shilling said, "That puts her at the boathouse between a quarter and twenty past eleven. Always supposing she went straight there. And that fits in well enough with the doctor's timings. He said most likely between ten past and half past eleven."

"Yes," said Knott. He thought about it, screwing up his eyes, as though he was looking into the sun. "It doesn't give them a lot of time for romance, does it?"

"Romance?"

"Kate and the chap she'd gone off to meet."

"How do you know she went to meet a chap?"

"When a girl cuts away from a dance on a warm summer night and goes down to a rendezvous on the riverbank, I'd be surprised if she'd gone to meet her stockbroker and talk about investments. Maybe that's because I've got a dirty mind."

Shilling, who had been turning over duplicate copies of the papers on his desk, said, "If you're right, it cuts out almost everyone who was at the dance."

"That's what I was thinking," said Knott. "What we've got is a lot of nice interlocking stories. Here's the score to date. The Mariners left, by car, just after Kate. Mr. and Mrs. Nurse a few minutes later. Then that old pansy. What's his name?"

"Beaumorris."

"Right. Frank Beaumorris. Used to work in the manuscript department at the Victoria and Albert."

Shilling looked up for a moment and said, "Did you run into him by any chance?"

"I did," said Knott. He seemed disinclined to pursue the subject. "He pedaled off at around ten past eleven. Old Vigors went off by car shortly after that. He put it at a quarter past. Then we've got a foursome, the Gonvilles and the parson and his wife. They went together to the Gonvilles' house for a cup of coffee and stayed there nattering until around midnight. Mrs. Steelstock and her son, that po-faced boy—name?"

"Walter," said Shilling. He had a list of names in front of him and seemed to have been memorizing them. "Works in an insurance office in Reading."

"Right. They were away by eleven twenty. The last to go was the big woman—"

"Mrs. Havelock. J.P. Seven children. Three of them at the dance."

"She took her three kids with her. And that dotty character—wait for it—Tress. Roseabel Tress. Lives next door to her in a bungalow called 'Shalimar.' If anyone came that way, she'll have heard them. A real nosey old virgin."

"If you take the latest possible time of death, eleven forty," said Shilling, "it's *just* possible, I suppose, for any of those people to have driven their cars to the end of River Park Avenue, walked along the towpath and been in time to kill Kate."

"It's possible," said Knott. "But I don't believe it. I don't think anyone who was at the dance killed her. I think they're all as innocent as they sound. No. Someone was there waiting for her. Someone who'd planned to get her to just that spot and meant to kill her."

Shilling had worked with Knott on a number of cases. It had not taken him long to realize that the Superintendent was not an intellectual man, was not, in most senses of the word, clever. But he had one faculty which was based partly on shrewdness and partly on experience. He could grasp the shape and outline of any crime he was called on to investigate. He could sense whether it was a professional job or an amateur job, whether it was motivated by greed or fright or frustration, whether it was the outcome of careful premeditation or thoughtless fury. It was an instinct which had very rarely let him down and had brought him to the eminence he enjoyed.

"I can tell you something else, too," he said. "You can forget about passing tramps or interrupted burglars. When I said that, I hadn't seen her bag. That spells premeditation. No question."

The bag had been found by the searchers. It was an evening dress bag, a pretty little thing with a pattern of roses woven in silk on the outside. The contents were laid out on the table beside it: a running-repair kit, a double folder of oiled silk with a sponge in one pocket and a box in the other labeled "Toasty Beige"; a cylinder labeled "Pearl Spin Eye Glaze"; a lipstick labeled "Mulberry"; a couple of tissues; and a folded pound note.

"If she'd been knocked on the head by some toe-rag who happened to be passing, first he'd have been too scared to stop and search her bag. Second, if he *had* searched it, he'd have taken the money."

"Someone did search it," said Shilling.

There was a photograph of the bag lying where it had been found in the long grass a few feet from the body. The contents were scattered beside it and the silk lining had been ripped half out.

"Right," said Knott. "Someone opened it in a hurry and took something out of it. And I guess we know what he took, don't we?"

Shilling smiled and said, "No marks for guessing. He was looking for the note he'd sent her, asking her to meet him at the boathouse."

"That's for sure."

"And if there was a note in the bag," said Shilling, smiling in the shy way that made him look a lot younger and more defenseless than he really was, "it wasn't the only thing the killer took. Where are her car keys?"

Knott shot a sharp look at his assistant and then said, "Full marks for that one, Bob. I'd missed it. Do you think they could have fallen out somewhere?"

"If they had, I guess the searchers would have found them. They didn't miss much."

The search of the previous day had produced a mass of curious articles. The obvious rubbish and anything at all old or rusty had been put in a basket under the table. On the table were spread the more promising finds. They included a scout's knife, a small compass of the type used by escaping prisoners of war, three twelve-bore shotgun cartridges, an old-fashioned collar stud, a new type tenpenny piece, an old type half crown and a torn shred of gray flannel.

Knott said, "That came off the barbed wire in the field next to Cavey's cottage. And from what he told us, I can make a good guess where it came from."

Shilling was still looking at the contents of the evening dress bag. He said, "I suppose all these things have been dusted." When Knott nodded he picked up the cylinder labeled "Eye Glaze" and drew a line on the back of his hand. Then he repeated the process with the lipstick and regarded the result critically.

He said, "Not such a terribly with-it girl, our Kate."

"What do you mean?"

"They're top-class stuff all right. But blue eye shadow rather went out last year. The fashionable shade this year is blue-brown. It's called "Livid." And I don't think a blonde who was really giving her mind to it would have used mulberry lipstick. Much more suitable for a brunette."

"I can see you haven't been wasting your evenings off," said Knott. "Maybe it was all part of the pose. The simple village girl sporting with the yokels. We don't really know much about her yet."

He paused for a long moment, standing hunched and still in front of the side table, looking down at the odd collection of exhibits but not seeing them. His mind was moving over the information he had collected; over the statements and the photographs and the impressions he had gathered while talking to people. Already he could see the killer. He was standing in the shadow of the boathouse waiting for the girl he had summoned. The girl who must have thought he was in love with her, or at least harmless, or she would not have come tripping so boldly down that dark path to meet him.

He said, "There's one mistake we mustn't make. She didn't spend all her time down here. She had two lives. One of them was lived up in London. We'll have to divide this. Get back to London first thing on Monday and see her agent. I've got his name and address here somewhere." He searched through a bulging wallet and extracted a card. "Mark Holbeck, 22a Henrietta Street, Covent Garden. He'll know as much as anyone about her. Don't be too long about it. I'll want you back down here. I've a feeling we should be able to clear this one up pretty quickly."

He picked up the internal telephone and said, "Eddie? Would you and Ian come in for a moment, please." He used their Christian names with a slight hint of irony, as if it was all part of man management and he knew it and they knew it. To Metropolitan officers, country policemen were swedes. Men who checked the rear lights on bicycles, dealt with sheep-chasing dogs and could recognize a Colorado beetle when they saw one, but knew nothing about the realities of serious crime.

"One of them took some nice photographs," said Shilling. "That must have been Eddie."

They were good clear color prints, taken from directly over the object so as not to distort its dimensions, with a yard rule lying alongside each. They showed the body of Kate as it lay face down clasping mother earth. There was a close-up of the deep fractured wound in her head above the right ear, as though someone had been standing directly behind her and she had half turned her head, perhaps sensing at the last moment that there was someone there.

"Right," said Knott. "Here's how we split it up. Ian, you tackle the Havelocks and the Tress woman. Eddie, you take the Nurses. The one I'm interested in is the girl, Sally. She seems to have gone for a midnight spin with young Gonville. Interesting to compare their stories. That's why I want them taken separately. Then you can have a word with the parson and the Group Captain and their trouble-and-strifes."

Esdaile said, "Is there anything in particular you want us to find out? I mean, they all seem to be—"

"They're all as white as driven snow," said Knott. "What I'm interested in is two things in particular.

Whether they saw, or heard, anyone else on the move around that time. And what they knew or thought about Katie. What sort of girl she was. What her interests were. Who were her special friends. They may be a bit shy of talking about that, but if you go about it the right way you'll probably get there in the end. All those people should be available, being Sunday." He paused, then added, "There's one other thing. Don't rely on your memories. Take these with you. They'll save you a lot of trouble afterwards."

He pushed toward each of them a contraption the size of a small camera. "Put it in your side pocket. It will pick up a voice speaking normally at five paces. Don't forget to switch it on."

Esdaile had picked up the box and was fingering it lovingly. He was a man with a passion for mechanical devices. He said, "That's a great little machine."

McCourt said, "I take it that these tape recordings will be in place of written statements."

"Wrong," said Knott. "I want both. I want the tape *and* your transcription of it. And I want them both by six o'clock every evening."

"The thoughts of all of us present here today," said the Reverend Bird, "must be focused on the tragedy which has struck our happy community like a bolt from the blue. It would be idle to pretend otherwise. It is in times like this that we have to ask ourselves reverently, but seriously, why God should permit such things to happen."

Matins at eleven o'clock was the popular service in West Hannington. It allowed the men to get to the club for their pre-lunch drink and the women time to cook the lunch for which the men were going to be late coming back from their pre-lunch drink. On this occasion St. Michael's Church was unusually full.

("It's the cohesive effect of shock," Mr. Beaumorris had explained to Georgie Vigors when he met her in the porch. "How it does bring people together!")

"Katie was not our private possession. She belonged to the whole country. Nevertheless, having been born here and living here, she had a very special place in our hearts."

There was a stir at the back of the church, as of an animal moving.

"In spite of her public fame we all knew her for a simple, natural, lovable girl—"

"Stop it," said a loud and angry voice. "Stop it at once. Leave Katie alone. Get on with your preaching."

All heads jerked around. The rector seemed to be paralyzed by the interruption.

Jonathan Limbery was on his feet. His face was scarlet. "You none of you knew anything about her. And now she's dead, so for God's sake let her lie."

The two churchwardens, George Mariner and Group Captain Gonville, were moving down the aisle toward him.

Their advance seemed to provoke Jonathan. His voice rose to a cracked shout. "All right, you pious hypocrites. You can throw me out, but it's not going to stop me telling the truth."

"Come along, old man."

"She was a bitch."

"Take his other arm, Gerry. You can't make scenes like this in church."

"Leave me alone. I'm going. I wouldn't want to stay here and listen to a lot of drip like that."

Jonathan stalked to the door, shepherded by the churchwardens. When he reached it he swung around as though to say something else, but the Group Captain pushed him kindly but decisively through the door and followed him out. He said to Mariner, "I'll look after him, George. You get back and stand by the rector. I thought he was going to pass out."

Mariner went back into the now completely silent church. The rector was standing motionless in the pulpit gripping the rail in front of him, his face white. Mariner plodded back to his seat, his footsteps sounding loudly on the tiles of the floor. As he reached the pew the rector came to life. He said in a loud clear voice, "And now to God the Father, God the Son and God the Holy Ghost we ascribe as is most justly due all might, majesty, dominion and power, now, henceforth and for ever more." The liturgy of the Church of England swung back onto its course.

It was during the singing of the last hymn that the Group Captain returned and made his way back to his seat. In response to the raised eyebrow of his wife he mouthed at her, "Gone home."

"*Well*," said Mr. Beaumorris to Mrs. Havelock, "what are we supposed to make of that?"

"Nothing we didn't know already. Limbery is unbalanced. Some regulator inside him isn't working."

"Whatever he may have thought about Katie's character and—um—disposition, church was hardly the appropriate place to voice it."

"It wasn't very tactful."

"Although actually, strictly between you and me and with all deference to the feeling about *nil nisi bonum de mortuis*, it has to be admitted that there were times when our Katie did behave rather bitchily."

* * *

“Isn’t it a crime, or a felony, or something?” said Mariner.

“Sacrilege? Yes. It’s still on the statute book,” said Vernon Vigors. “It’s usually breaking into churches and smashing or defiling the sacred ornaments, something like that. There were those ultra Protestants who used to smash up altars.”

“You don’t think that interrupting the sermon comes into the same category?”

“It’s a moot point,” said Vigors.

7

When Knott had asked Ian McCourt if he knew how to take a plaster cast, McCourt had said nothing but had simply nodded. One reason for this was that he was beginning to find Knott's manner irritating and he felt that the less he said to him the better. The other reason was that he thought he did, in fact, know how to set about it.

The reason for his confidence was that he had recently read in an old copy of the *Police Journal* an article entitled "Traces of Footwear, Tires and Tools" by Detective Constable Douglas Hamilton of the City of Glasgow Police.

He had the journal with him as he pored over the faint marks in the sandy patch between the end of Roseabel Tress's garden and the first of the building plots. A car had been driven a few yards up the towpath and then backed onto this patch, but not very far. The prints had been made by a small portion of both rear tires, rather more by the off side than the near.

"An impression in moist firm earth can be reproduced without any preliminary treatment. But when impressions are found in loose earth or sand it is advisable to 'fix' the surface before pouring in the plaster, since with-

out this the weight of the plaster will distort the formation of the loose surface."

McCourt looked at the sand. It was totally dry and friable. The sharp edges of the tire marks had already started to smooth out. Clearly they would have to be "fixed." What did Detective Constable Hamilton say about that?

"A *solution of shellac in methylated spirits or a cellulose acetate solution may be used with excellent results.* A *very light coating only should be applied.*"

Fine, thought McCourt. No doubt the Glasgow central police station was equipped with shellac, methylated spirits and acetate solution. But how was he supposed to find them in Hannington on a Sunday?

A shadow fell across the sand.

"Something troubling you, son?" said Knott.

McCourt scrambled to his feet. Knott stooped down and picked up the journal which had been open on the ground beside him. He studied it for a long moment and then said, "You ought to keep up to date in the techniques of your profession. You're not married, are you?"

"No."

"Got a girlfriend?"

"Well—"

"Or a mother or an aunt or a landlady. Someone who'll lend you a hairspray?"

"Every now and then," said Roseabel Tress, "I do take a little sleeping pill. It's not my regular habit, you understand. They're fairly mild, not what you'd describe as knockout drops. Helen Mariner put me onto them. She gets them from her doctor. So you see, I shouldn't be a very effective witness. But it's true, yes. I did hear a car."

"About what time might that have been?" said McCourt.

"Let me think. We got away from the dance before half past eleven and came straight back here in Constantia Havelock's car. She asked me in for a cup of tea. Then there was that business about Roney and Sim—"

"I heard about that."

"I don't suppose I was more than twenty minutes in their house. When I got back I went straight to bed."

"Then it would have been soon after midnight when you heard the car."

"That's right. Five or ten minutes after."

"Was it coming, or going?"

"Oh, going. I'm sure of that. It would have been parked on the path, I imagine. I heard it start up. And I heard it drive off, down the avenue. I—yes, that's right. I heard it drive away."

McCourt's ear picked up the change of tone in her voice, the note of panic, and looking down saw that her hands, which had been lying loosely in her lap, were now clasped so tightly that her knuckles were white and the bones at the back were standing out.

He said, "What is it, Miss Tress? Is something wrong?"

"Nothing," she said. "It's nothing. I'm sorry. I was stupid." Her self-possession was coming back slowly. "I just remembered something. It was rather unpleasant. I hardly know how to explain it."

"Try."

"It was just that . . . well, the fact is that I'm a seventh child of seven. All my life I've known that I have these powers. I read a most interesting article about them the other day. I understand that they are now known as extrasensory perception. There's quite a scientific basis for them."

The word "scientific" seemed to reassure her. She looked at McCourt to see how he was taking it. He smiled and said, "Science is explaining a lot of things we used to call miraculous. What exactly was it that you felt when you heard the car driving away?"

"Evil, Sergeant. Naked evil."

"Yes, I heard it go," said Mrs. Havelock, "a little after midnight. That would be right."

"Could you tell from the noise it made what sort of car it was?"

"I'm afraid all cars sound the same to me. If one of the boys had heard it, they'd probably be able to tell you. But they sleep at the back."

McCourt opened his briefcase and produced a torn scrap of gray flannel. He said, "This was found on the barbed wire of the field by Cavey's cottage."

"And I can tell you *exactly* where it came from," said Mrs. Havelock. She opened her sewing basket and produced a pair of boy's flannel shorts. "You can match it up if you like."

"Aye, that's where it came from, no doubt," said McCourt. "Which of them was it?"

"Sim. He's the nine-year-old. Roney's eleven. They're as bad as each other. Beyond parental control, Sergeant. They need a father's hand."

"I'll have a word with them in a moment. There are just the one or two things I'd like to clear up first. You all drove home between twenty and half past eleven?"

"About then."

"Which way did you come?"

"Straight down the street and turned right into the avenue."

"Did you pass anyone?"

"No one at all. I'm pretty sure of that. You could ask Roseabel Tress."

"I have," said McCourt. "She agrees with you. She doesn't remember passing anyone. Tell me, Mrs. Havelock, what did you think of Katie?"

"That's a fast ball."

"A fast ball?" said McCourt, with the hesitation of someone who had been educated in a school which regarded cricket as a game played by southerners to fill in the awkward gap between two football seasons. "You mean it was an unfair question? I'm sorry."

"Not unfair. Unexpected. What *did* I think about her? It's a difficult question. She was two quite different people, of course. When she was here she liked to play the simple home-loving girl who went out with the boy next door—or one of the two or three boys next door—lived with Mum and went to church on Sundays."

"You said 'play'?"

"Oh, I think so. After all, that was the character she put over in her television appearances. She can't really have been as simple as that. If she had been, she'd never have got where she did. I don't know what goes on behind the scenes in television, but I should imagine it's one of the toughest rat races there are. And working in London's not the same as working down here."

"When I was in London," said McCourt, "everything seemed to go twice as fast and sound twice as loud as it does in the country. I'd like to have a word with the boys."

"With me here?"

"Certainly. I don't want to frighten them."

"I sometimes wish," said Mrs. Havelock, "that I'd found some way of doing it."

Roney and Sim were waiting outside the door. They

bounded in looking excited and important but not at all apprehensive.

"Well, now," said McCourt, "what were you up to on Friday night?"

Roney told him. McCourt had found that boys usually made good witnesses. They stuck to the facts. He said, "This question of timing is becoming rather important. When exactly did you leave the dance?"

"When we saw Mum driving off. That's why we ran. We wanted to get back ahead of her. We might have done, only old Cavey shouted at us and Sim got caught up in that barbed wire. After that we went more slowly."

"In that case," said McCourt, "you must have been walking down the towpath at around twenty-five to twelve."

"That's right," said Roney. He shot a look at Sim, who was bouncing gently up and down on the edge of his chair, looking like a kettle coming to the boil. He opened his mouth to say something but Roney cut him off with the firmness of two years' seniority. He said, "From what we read in the papers, she must have been dead by then, wouldn't you say?"

In his Saturday evening briefing, Knott had given out the presumed time of death. It had been done quite deliberately, weighing advantage against disadvantage.

"It seems possible," said McCourt cautiously.

"Then," said Roney, "she must have been lying there on the grass when we went past."

Sim could contain himself no longer. He said, "We might have met the murderer coming away."

The two boys looked at each other with an equal mixture of horror and excitement.

"It's lucky you didn't," said McCourt.

When he had gone, Mrs. Havelock said, "What are you two keeping back?"

"We're not keeping anything back, are we, Sim?"

Sim said, "No. Honestly, we're not, Mum."

Mrs. Havelock looked at her sons. She was thinking, In about two years' time I shall have to start treating Roney as though he was grown up. It wasn't too bad with Michael. He was pretty reasonable. Roney's different.

The two boys stared solemnly back at her. In the end she said, "If there *is* anything else, it must be told. This isn't a game."

"I can't tell you a great deal," said Tony Windle, "because I was almost the last away from the hall. Old Cavey came in looking like death and started clearing people out and I asked him what was bothering him and . . . well . . . he told me."

"Can you remember what he said?"

"Not the exact words. But I do remember I was surprised."

"Why?"

Tony thought about it. Then he said, "He didn't wrap it up at all. It was something like 'She's dead. Someone smashed her head in.' As if he was talking about someone he didn't really know."

"But he did know her?"

"Of course he knew her. Everyone knew Katie. He'd taught her to punt when she was eight and picked her out of the river when she fell in."

"And everyone loved her."

"Is that a question," said Tony coolly, "or a statement?"

"I suppose it was a sort of question."

"When she was a little girl with a snub nose and pigtails, certainly everyone loved her. Everyone loves little girls. When she grew up, naturally things got a bit more complicated. Either you loved her, or you liked her, or you didn't care one way or the other."

"And which category did you fall into?"

"Something between two and three. I think we both regarded each other, in a different sort of way, as an asset. If I took Katie to a function, I could be sure that everyone else there was envying me. That was the plus as far as I was concerned. From her point of view, I was a useful attendant-cum-door-opener-cum-chauffeur. With a kiss last thing instead of a tip."

"And nothing more?"

"I regret to say, Sergeant, nothing more. Just a convenience. Give you an example. I'd have been expected to pick her up in my car and take her to that dance on Friday night. Despite the fact that she was within walking distance of the hall, and if she hadn't wanted to walk, her own car was parked in the stableyard outside her flat. But it would have been a bore to have got in and started up the engine. Much better to rely on good old Tony."

"But she *did* take her own car."

"Only because mine was out of action, being minus its distributor head. And there wasn't really much time to ask anyone else."

"You're making her out to be rather a heartless sort of girl."

"All girls are heartless," said Tony, with the accumulated wisdom of twenty-five years. Then he corrected himself. "Heartless is the wrong word. Katie had a heart buried deep down. Given the right sort of man, she'd have gone overboard like any other girl. I wasn't the right type, that was all."

"And what do you think would have been the right type?"

"You're fishing."

"Aye," said McCourt placidly. "I'm fishing."

Tony thought about this and then said, "All right. I'm only telling you what anyone else who knew her would tell you. She wanted two different things. From a man she wanted passion. She wanted someone who could really let himself go. An out-and-outer. But even while she was letting herself go, the dispassionate part of her would have been saying, 'I wonder whether he couldn't be some use to me, do something for me, help me in my career.'"

"How can you be sure of that?"

"I'm sure of it," said Tony, "because on one occasion she actually told me so. I remember it, because normally she didn't talk about herself. I think she'd had one drink above her ration; which was unusual, too, because she kept as firm an eye on her drink intake as she did on every other aspect of her life."

Tony seemed to have lost track of what he had started to say. McCourt prodded him gently back. He said, "And what was it she told you?"

"Oh, we'd had a bit of a quarrel. I think I started it by implying that she relied too much on my services and if she wasn't a bit nicer to me I might think twice about doing things for her and so on. That annoyed her. She said, 'The trouble with you, Tony, is that you don't amount to anything and never will. The most you'll ever end up as is "something in insurance." That's no good to a girl like me. What I need is people with influence. People who can help me out when I get into trouble. I've got friends like that up in London. And I've got at least one *very* useful friend down here.' I asked her who it was and she wouldn't tell me. I pulled her leg about it when we next met up. I asked her who Mr. Big was. She denied having said anything about it. I think she was sorry she'd opened her mouth. And I think I'm talking too much."

"On the contrary," said McCourt, "you've been most helpful. One other question. When you got home, did you go straight to bed?"

"Actually, no. It was too bloody hot. I sat up and waited for Billy. I wanted to find out what he'd been up to."

"With Sally Nurse?"

"Yes. It didn't seem to amount to much. We had a bit of a natter and split a bottle of beer out of the fridge. It must have been half past one, or even later, before we finally went up. Oh, and I remember we heard Jonathan coming back. He'd been out on some job for the paper. A fire or something, wasn't it?"

"I believe it was," said McCourt.

"Everyone seems to think," said Billy Gonville, "that if you take a girl out for a midnight spin in your car your intentions are dishonorable."

"And they're wrong, of course."

"Not necessarily. What they're overlooking is that your intentions are unimportant. It's the girl's intentions that matter. With some girls you don't have to think twice. They've started undressing before you've got the car into second gear."

"But with Miss Nurse it was different?"

"Sally's a nice girl. A very nice girl." McCourt wasn't certain whether admiration or regret was the predominant note in young Mr. Gonville's voice. "The trouble is, she's been too much under Katie's shadow. Following her round, imitating her getup, all that sort of thing. She'd buried her own personality. I thought it was time it was unburied."

"Then you regarded this midnight run as a sort of therapy?"

Billy looked at him suspiciously and said, "Look here, Sergeant, you're meant to be inquiring into a crime. Not exploring my sex life."

"I'm sorry," sad McCourt. He always found it difficult to maintain an official attitude with Windle and Gonville. They were all much of an age. Off duty, they used each other's Christian names without embarrassment. "Could you tell me where you went?"

"No difficulty. We started along the by-road, took the A329 as far as Streatley and then went straight on, until we hit the north-south road between Newbury and Oxford. Went down it a few miles to that junction with the M4."

"That's Access Point Thirteen."

"Right. Up to then we'd had to take it easy. Still a lot of traffic about. When we got onto the motorway, I let her rip. We must have damn near made a ton."

"Please remember I'm a policeman."

"So you are. I'd forgotten. Anyway, luckily I'd eased off a bit when we were stopped."

"You were stopped?"

"At Access Fourteen, south of Reading. The police had the road blocked. A lot of cars queuing up. Took everyone's names and addresses. Surely you know about it. They had a ring round the whole area. Trying to catch the people who did Yattendon House."

"I haird something about it; we weren't directly involved. I gather they didn't catch anyone."

"Total flop. They kept it up until three in the morning and netted one or two men out with other people's wives. The burglars were too smart for them."

"After Access Fourteen?"

"We went home. I had Sally back at her house about

one fifteen. Both parents still up. Rather a frosty reception."

"So I should imagine," said McCourt. "Could you be a bit more definite about some of those times?"

"Let's think." Billy Gonville pressed his lips together and wrinkled his brow to demonstrate thought. "When we were all asked by Superintendent Dracula to write down our times, I had a word with various other girls I'd been dancing with and the general opinion seemed to be that we cleared out around ten forty-five."

"And up to that point you'd been dancing continuously?"

"Non-stop. I can't tell you all the girls' names because some I didn't know. A pity we didn't have those old-fashioned dance cards. Anyway, if you asked anyone living in Lower Church Lane they'd have been bound to have heard me. Coming and going."

McCourt was inclined to agree. Gonville had modified the fishtail exhaust on his Austin-Healey Sprite so that it now boomed like a bittern. He said, "Going at a reasonable pace"—he was studying the local ordnance sheet which he had brought with him—"it took you how long to get to Access Thirteen? I make it about fifteen miles."

"All right. Say thirty minutes."

"And from there to Access Fourteen?"

"No time at all. When you give that car her head she practically takes off. You can see why they call her a sprite."

"All right. Ten minutes. That gets you to Fourteen at twenty-five past twelve."

"We were held up there answering questions for five minutes."

"But," said McCourt, "if you left there at half past

twelve, how did it take you three-quarters of an hour to get home?"

"We stopped for a bit. For a talk."

"For a talk?"

"For a talk," said Gonville firmly. "I told you I thought she needed bringing out." He started to laugh. "She's an odd kid. Do you know what her real ambition is? She wants to be adopted."

"By anyone in particular?"

"No. Just by someone. She feels she's picked the wrong parents."

Roney and Sim were squatting among a pile of deck chairs and punt cushions at the short end of the L-shaped balcony which screened the front and side of their bungalow. It was their favorite place for private discussions, and this discussion was both private and important.

Sim said, "Don't you think we ought to tell someone?"

"No," said Roney. He said it quickly but firmly, as though he'd been thinking about it a lot and had come to an irrevocable decision.

"Well, I don't know," said Sim.

"You promised."

"I know I promised, but—"

"There aren't any buts about it. You promised, and if you don't keep your word I'll . . . I'll skin you alive."

They were sitting so close together that their noses were nearly touching. Sim said very seriously, "You know what Mum said. This isn't a game. It's murder."

"Why should it have anything to do with murder?"

"Well, Johnno used to meet her there. More than once. *We* know that."

"All right. He used to meet her there. Just because

people meet each other it doesn't mean they kill each other, does it?"

"I suppose not," said Sim unhappily.

"Then promise you're not going to say anything about it."

"I've promised already."

"Promise again."

"Well, *I* think he ought to tell the police," said Rosina. She had been standing out of sight around the corner, listening.

The two boys scrambled up. Roney was bright red in the face. He said, "Sneak, sneak, sneak. You've been listening."

"Certainly I've been listening. And lucky I was listening, because otherwise I suppose nobody would ever have heard about this."

Roney took a step toward his sister. He was almost as tall as she was. He said in a voice which was rising out of restraint, "You filthy little cow. Sneaking round. Listening. If you say a word to anyone I'll kill you."

"Don't be daft."

"If you don't promise, I'll kill you."

"Of course I'm not going to promise—"

Roney jumped at her, his hands groping for her face. He was sobbing with fury. Rosina gave a cry as his nails scored her cheek. Sim said weakly, "Roney, don't. Don't."

And at that moment Mrs. Havelock appeared in the doorway. She said, "Leave Rosina alone."

"I'm going to kill her," said Roney. He had hold of her hair with one hand and was scrabbling at her face with the other. Mrs. Havelock took one step forward and hit him. She was a big, strong woman. The blow knocked him down and knocked most of the breath and all the fight out of him. Sim was crying. Rosina was mopping the scratch on her cheek with a handkerchief.

Disregarding Roney, Mrs. Havelock said, “Will one of you now tell me what all that was about?”

Rosina said, “I heard them talking. About the boat-house.” She hesitated for a moment, as if conscious of what she was going to do.

“Well?”

“They knew that Jonathan used to meet Katie there at night. They used to creep along and spy on them. Just like they did on Lavinia in the churchyard. Beasts.”

Mrs. Havelock said, “Is that true?”

Sim gulped out, “Yes. I knew we ought to say. Roney made me promise.”

“Why on earth did you do that, Roney?”

Roney said nothing.

“I expect he was in love with Jonathan,” said Rosina spitefully.

8

The Boat Club and the Tennis Club shared a bar which was part of the Tennis Club pavilion. This was a convenient arrangement, since most people belonged to both clubs.

On that Sunday morning it was crowded and Mr. Cavey was busier than usual serving gins and tonics with ice and pints of warm beer.

"We have carried out our religious duty," said Mr. Beaumorris to his confidante, Georgie Vigors, "by going to church and vowing to love our neighbor as ourselves. We can now perform our social duty by dissecting our neighbor's character."

"If you're talking about Jonathan," said Georgie, "I can't say I was entirely surprised. He's been working up for an explosion for months. Actually, I had a certain amount of sympathy for him. I think Dickybird could have left Kate out of his sermon."

"Oughtn't you to be sitting down?" said her husband.

"Hullo, hullo," said Mr. Beaumorris, "are you pregnant, woman?"

"It's on the cards. Noel's in the fussing stage. I'm told it lasts for quite a week."

"Husbands suffer terribly over their first child," said

Mavis Gonville. "I thought Gerry was going to pass out when I told him. He had to be revived with a large brandy."

"I've never touched brandy since," said the Group Captain. "It would bring back memories. Have you had a visitation yet?"

Noel Vigors looked blank. Gonville said, "The buzz is that the fuzz—I say, that's rather good. Buzz-fuzz. Fuzz-buzz."

"Get on with it."

"Well, they're said to be going round to everyone who was at the dance asking a lot of questions. Sergeant McCourt was in Riverside Avenue grilling Roseabel Tress and the Havelocks."

"As long as it's just McCourt or Esdaile," said Mavis. "That little white Superintendent gives me the creeps."

"He's a dangerous man," said Mr. Beaumorris. "As I have every reason to know." He had raised his voice sufficiently to receive the attention of everyone near him.

"Come on, Frank."

"Tell us the worst. What episode in your murky past did he have to investigate?"

"It wasn't my past," said Mr. Beaumorris. "It was when I was at the V. and A. It was some years ago. Knott wasn't on the Murder Squad. He was a detective inspector at the local station. The auditors had unearthed a rather serious discrepancy in the imprest account of the Far Eastern Section. One of the cashiers was suspected. An old man called Connington. Bill Connington. Knott really took him to pieces. He was grilling him for most of the day and part of the evening."

Mr. Beaumorris picked up his glass of shandy and

finished it while his audience waited. Then he got to his feet and picked up his walking stick.

"Really, Frank," said old Mr. Vigors. "You can't leave us all in suspense. What happened? Was Connington guilty?"

"It was never *completely* established. He cut his throat that same night. With an antique Malayan kris." He pottered to the door. "My young lady will have my luncheon ready. She gets very cross if I'm late."

Mavis said, "I sometimes wonder if Frank isn't the biggest old humbug in the whole village. *Could* you cut your throat with a kris?"

"You can cut your throat with anything if you give your mind to it," said her husband. "I remember one young pilot officer—"

"Not before lunch," said Georgie Vigors firmly. "And who is Frank's young lady? I didn't know he had one."

"It's a girl called Myra," said Mavis. "Don't know her surname. Her sister's Polly. The one who does for the Mariners."

"So *that's* where he gets all his gossip from," said Georgie.

It was Polly who opened the front door of the Croft to Superintendent Knott. She was back on her Jeeves impersonation and paced in front of him to the study. Mariner, who had a sense of protocol, kept him waiting for only two minutes. This compared with the five he would have allotted to Inspector Dandridge and anything up to twenty for Sergeant McCourt, whom he disliked as much as the Sergeant disliked him.

"I can't tell you much more than I put down on that paper," he said. "My wife and I left at about eleven o'clock. A lot of people seem to have seen us go. My wife doesn't like to be up late. She sleeps badly. She went to bed immediately we got home."

"That young personage who let me in. Does she live here?"

"Polly? No. You can't get residential staff nowadays. Not in West Hannington anyway."

"Difficult enough in London," agreed the Superintendent.

"She's willing, under protest, to stop in while we're out at night. In return for suitable reimbursement. She was sitting in for us on Friday night."

"But she took off as soon as you got back?"

"As soon as she heard our car in the drive. The young haven't much sense of duty these days."

"They like to live their own lives," said Knott. The making of trite remarks like this enabled him to divorce his mind from the conversation and devote it to taking in impressions. Impressions of his surroundings, of the man he was talking to, of tension or relaxation. Mariner seemed to be easy enough. A cock on his own dunghill.

"So what did you do then?"

Mariner looked surprised and said, "Well, I didn't go to bed at once. I had a whisky and soda. In here, actually. Which reminds me—"

"Not at the moment, thank you."

"I finished reading the local papers. Put out the dog. Locked up the house. I expect it would have been midnight before I went up."

"I imagine that one of your reasons for hanging about would be to allow your wife to get off to sleep?"

"Actually we sleep in different rooms."

Knott said, so casually that the thought might only just have occurred to him, "I meant to ask you. What did you think of Kate? You knew her quite well, I imagine."

"Not particularly well." Mariner thought about it. "She was a nice unspoiled kid. When she made such a success of her television career, it might have turned her head. Perhaps it did, a little. But not nearly as much as you might have expected. Mind you, we only saw the Hannington side of her."

"And the outside of the London side."

"I don't follow you."

"The side that came over on the television screen."

"Oh yes. Well, my wife and I aren't great television watchers."

"But you have a set," Knott said with a smile. "The great detective demonstrates his methods. I saw the aerial."

Mariner said, "Yes, we have a set. It's kept in the kitchen. We have it brought in here if there's something we particularly want to watch. Wimbledon or a test match."

"I imagine she didn't lack for admirers," said Knott. He had often found this simple technique surprisingly useful. Let the conversation drift, then pull it back with a jerk. On this occasion the result was surprising. Mariner flushed, started to say something, changed his mind and then grunted out, "Of course she had. Dozens of them. Round her like flies."

"Anyone in particular?"

Mariner was recovering himself. He said in a more normal voice, "Her accepted squire was young Tony Windle, but I don't think he meant anything more to her than a free taxi service."

"But there's someone else?"

"There *was* someone else. Until about a month ago. The general impression was that the only serious proposition was Jonathan Limbery."

"And what happened to Jonathan?"

"Katie and he had a flaming row. In public. In the Tennis Club bar."

"I'd like to hear about that."

Mariner thought about it. Knott was watching his face. He said to himself, Even if I hadn't asked him, he was going to tell me about it. There's some sort of personal involvement here. Either he dislikes Limbery, or maybe he was after the girl himself. You can never tell with these middle-aged men.

Mariner said, "It was early in the evening. There were only five of us there. Kate and her brother Walter. They'd been playing in a foursome against Noel and Georgie Vigors. I'd looked in on my way back from our Reading office. Holst and Mariner. I retired last year, but I still go in occasionally. As I was saying, I dropped by as the game was finishing and we all went in together for a drink. I gathered that Katie had intended to play with Jonathan, but he'd let her down at the last moment, and Walter had stepped into the breach. She was still annoyed about it. She didn't like people letting her down. And Walter isn't much of a hand at tennis, so they'd lost the game badly, which didn't improve her temper."

"She had a temper?"

"Oh yes. *De mortuis* and all that sort of thing. But she certainly had a temper."

"Please go on."

"All things considered, it was a bit unfortunate that Jonathan should have turned up at this moment, and not only turned up but turned up wearing flannels and looking as hot as if he'd been playing tennis himself. Katie said something like 'What's all this? I thought you were so busy putting your paper to bed that you couldn't play tennis,' and Jonathan said, 'That's right. It didn't take as long as I thought it would,' and Katie said,

'Wouldn't she cooperate?' and when Jonathan looked a bit blank she said, 'Your paper, I mean. When you put her to bed.' Everyone thought this funny, except Jonathan. He's not a young man who likes being laughed at. He said something fairly rude. I can't remember exactly what it was. Then they went at it hammer and tongs. It ended with Katie saying to Walter, 'You might run me home. I don't think I can stand much more of this ill-bred lout.' That broke the party up. We were all feeling pretty embarrassed, actually."

Knott seemed to be visualizing the scene, turning it over, shaking out any possible implications. He said, "Can you remember anything specific that was said when they were slanging each other? It might be important. You often get a lot of truth out of people when they're angry."

"I can't remember anything that was actually said."

"Who was angrier?"

"They were both angry, but Kate was definitely more in control of herself. She was able to pick her words and make them sting. Jonathan was out of control altogether."

"He sounds an unusual type."

Mariner drew a deep breath. O.K., here it comes, thought Knott.

Mariner said, "In my opinion, Limbery is a dangerous and unpleasant young man. You heard about the scene he made in church this morning?" Knott nodded. "That was absolutely typical. He has no control over his temper and very little sense of what is right and wrong. If you want an example of his outlook on life and morals I advise you to read some of the drivel he produces for his local rag. I've got some back numbers here. To me they're futile nonsense, although I suppose very young and immature people might be taken in by them, in which case I suppose they might be dangerous. Anyone with any sense just laughs at them." But Mariner wasn't amused, Knott noted. He was angry.

He said, "If you'd lend them to me I'll look through them. Do you think his violence is confined to words? Could it come out in actions as well?"

"Certainly it could. Last Christmas at a local dance Tony Windle was pulling his leg about one of those effusions of his and he took a swing at him. He picked the wrong man there. Tony's twice as quick as him and a bit of a boxer, too. He put him on his back."

"So what happened?"

"He scrambled up shrieking out a lot of filth and went for him again, quite unscientifically. But a lot of people had rallied round by then and he was pulled off and told not to be a bloody fool. I believe he apologized next morning. On the face of it, he and Tony are quite good friends. But I've noticed that Limbery hasn't graced any of our social gatherings since then—and thank goodness for it."

"He wasn't at the dance on Friday, I believe."

"That's right. Something about an article he had to finish. Though why there should have been any hurry for it I can't imagine. The Hannington *Gazette*'s a weekly rag, and comes out on Thursdays."

Knott said, "You don't like him very much, do you?"

"I don't like him at all," said Mariner. "There's no secret about that."

"So it's fair to assume that he doesn't like you."

"He dislikes everybody who's older than he is, or better off."

"Quite so. I wondered whether he might have been responsible for those stupid practical jokes I was hearing about. Letting down tires and emptying radiators and so on."

"Now that you mention it," said Mariner, "it's quite on the cards. When it started, we assumed it was kids playing jokes. But it could have been Limbery. That's his mental age."

"And one of his victims was Tony Windle."

"That's right," said Mariner thoughtfully. "So he was."

Old Mr. Beaumorris had once laid it down that, of all unnatural associations, the one to be most avoided was association between a parent and his married children. Since Mr. Beaumorris rarely made any statement without a personal angle to it, it was assumed that he was talking about the household at Limpsfield, the ugly red brick house next door to the Croft, shared by the widowed sixty-one-year-old Vernon Vigors and his married son, Noel.

The house had been informally divided. Mr. Vigors senior regarded the rooms on the left of the front door as his private domain. He had furnished them to bursting point with pieces from a much larger house. The shelves were full of leather-bound books, and every available flat space held photographs and mementos of married life.

Knott had not found the old man informative. Forty years of solicitordom had accustomed him to asking questions, not to answering them. He agreed that he had left the dance at a quarter past eleven. He had driven straight home and had gone to bed. He had been practically asleep before his son and daughter-in-law had got home. He had no particular views about Katie. He thought she was a nice girl and failed to understand how anyone could have done such a thing to her, but supposed that they had to resign themselves to the fact that they lived in a violent age.

After twenty minutes of this sort of thing, Knott crossed the hallway to talk to the younger generation. The distance between them and the old man was three yards and thirty years. He found Noel and Georgie sitting together on the sofa in front of the open French windows which gave onto a small tidy garden. Since they had not left the dance until after half past eleven and could neither of them have had anything to do with the crime, he decided to question them together. In that way they would be able to supplement each other's impressions. He was particularly interested in the quarrel at the Tennis Club.

"I've been told how it started," he said. "Katie thought Limbery had stood her up. No girl likes that. But it doesn't sound like a reason for a public row. Particularly with someone you'd been rather attached to."

Noel and Georgie looked at each other. They could sense without difficulty the implications of what the Superintendent was saying.

Georgie said, "Jonathan never minds his rows being conducted in public. It adds spice to them."

Noel said, "I think the heat was self-generating. One said one thing and that provoked a sharp answer. Both of them had saw-edged tongues, when they chose to use them."

"Can you remember what they did say? I don't mean the actual words. What line did they take?"

Noel said doubtfully, "It was a month ago—"

Georgie said, "Come on, Noel. You can do better than that. I remember perfectly well. When Katie got down to brass tacks, towards the end, she kept accusing Jonathan of being a schoolmaster manqué. A man among boys, a boy among men. That sort of thing. Immature. Trying to impress the kids but making a laughingstock of himself in the eyes of anyone who was adult. She said, 'You ought to rename that rag you run *Beezer* or *Tiger Tim's Weekly*.'"

"Yes. That's right. And he said that just because she couldn't understand anything more than the leading article in *Peg's Weekly* it didn't give her the right to sneer at *his* work."

"Something you said a moment ago, Mrs. Vigors. Schoolmaster manqué. Meaning he'd have liked to be a schoolmaster? Or that he'd tried it and failed?"

"Actually he did teach for a few terms at Coverdales. That was soon after he left school himself."

"Do you know why he stopped?"

Before Georgie could answer, Noel said, "Not really. No." He said it very firmly.

Knott's mind seemed to be running on schools. He said, "Coverdales. That's at Caversham, isn't it? Just outside Reading. Boys and girls? Or boys only?"

"It was boys only when I went there," said Noel. "Now they take girls in the sixth form, for 'A' level subjects."

"Did Katie go there?"

"Good heavens, no," said Georgie. "That wouldn't have been nearly grand enough for the Steelstocks. She went to—What's the name of it? Princess Anne went there."

"Benenden."

"Right. I expect that's where she made a few friends who were useful to her when she got up to London."

"Friends are always useful," said the Superintendent.

While this was going on, Detective Sergeant Shilling was making an examination of the boathouse. The exterior of the doors had been dusted and had produced the expected number of fingerprints. The legible ones had been photographed. There was no reason to suppose that the murderer had touched the doors, but it was the taking of routine precautions, unnecessary in nineteen cases out of twenty, that characterized good police work.

The boathouse, he noticed, was built in two pieces. There was the main part, which housed boats and gear, a roomy single-story construction with an open penthouse at the back. On the west side, looking as though it might have been added as an afterthought, was a two-story annex. The big sliding doors which gave onto the ramp in front of the main section were padlocked, but there was a smaller door cut into the left-hand sliding door. It was in this that one of the panes had been broken. The jagged pieces had been carefully removed, and it was not easy at first glance to realize that the glass was missing.

Shilling put his hand through, reached downward and found the catch of the spring lock. He could just touch it with his fingers. He took off his coat, rolled up his sleeve and inserted his bare arm. This time the catch was in reach. He turned it gently and the door opened inward.

Not very secure, he thought. But since the most valuable items inside were the boats and since you would need to open the main doors to get them out, perhaps not dangerously insecure.

There were three smart-looking four-oar skiffs. The nearest, which had been recently varnished, had the letters G.C.M. in black paint on the stern. George Mariner? Alongside them, two tub dinghies and two rather shabbier skiffs. The rudders had been lifted out of their pintles and were stacked in a rack against the back wall. Just inside the door was a school desk, at which, no doubt, Mr. Cavey sat to record bookings. Behind this lay two canoes which looked as though they had had a hard life. The punts were moored along the landing stage, but would live under the penthouse at the back in winter. Punt and boat cushions were stacked in a neat pile under the window in the left-hand wall. Oars along the back wall, paddles, punt poles and boat hooks across the rafters. Everything shipshape and a credit to Mr. Cavey. The whole place smelled of hot varnish and creosote.

After a look around which produced no surprises, Shilling went out again, leaving the door ajar, and walked around to the side. The door of the annex was locked. Who would have a key?

Shilling went back into the boathouse and used the telephone which stood on the booking desk to call the Hannington police station. McCourt answered. He had spent two sweltering hours transcribing the tapes of his interviews with Roseabel Tress and the Havelocks.

He said, "Boat Club offices? Mariner will have one key. But if I ask him for it he'll keep me waiting for at least half an hour. Jack Nurse is a better bet. He's secretary of the Boat Club. I'll nip up to his house on my moped and borrow it for you."

"I could do that," said Shilling. "I've got the car."

"No trouble," said McCourt. He welcomed the excuse to get out of the police station.

Sergeant Esdaile, realizing that Sunday was the rector's busiest day, had timed his movements so that he arrived at the Rectory at exactly two o'clock. He calculated that lunch would be over and Sunday School not yet begun. He had watched McCourt at work and was not looking forward to the labor of transcription. He planned to keep *his* interviews as short as possible. The rector had very little to tell him and seemed more interested in discussing Limbery's outburst in church. Esdaile headed him firmly back. He and his wife—Would the Sergeant like to have her in, too? Not necessary, said Esdaile—had walked back with the Group Captain and his wife to their house, the Old Rectory. He couldn't help thinking it odd that of all the money the Church Commissioners had made by selling these fine old buildings and housing the incumbents in bungalows, none had gone into increasing stipends.

"Scandalous," said Esdaile. "What happened next?"

"We had a cup of coffee. All except my wife, that is. She can't drink coffee at night. It keeps her awake."

"And what time did the party break up?"

"It must have been after midnight. You know what women are like when they start talking."

"And you walked home?"

"Certainly. It's only a very short distance. Past the Memorial Hall and the church. We noticed that Katie's car was still parked outside the hall and I think I commented on it. My wife would remember. But of course, we neither of us had any idea—"

"Of course not, sir. Did you meet anyone? Did any cars pass you?"

"Let me think. No. We met no one and I don't think anyone passed us. The Street is very quiet at that time of night. I do remember that we heard a car coming down Brickfield Road. I said to my wife, 'I wonder who that is.' Just idle curiosity. And we stopped to have a look. You can see Brickfield Road from the Street. It's less than a hundred yards away."

"And did you recognize the car?"

"It was much too dark to recognize it. But we noticed one odd thing. It was driving on its sidelights. Dangerous, I should have thought. It was a dark night and there are no streetlamps in Brickfield Road, although it's not for want of asking. Young girls don't like walking down it at night . . ."

At this point Sergeant Esdaile slipped his hand into his coat pocket and switched off the tape. He had heard the rector more than once on the perils of Brickfield Road and knew that he was good for at least ten minutes on the subject of Youth in Dark Streets. He judged that if he got away by a quarter to three that would be about right for his visit to Jack and Sylvia Nurse.

"Nothing," said Sally Nurse. "Nothing happened at all. We went for a drive."

"Your mother and I were dreadfully worried."

"I've said I'm sorry. There wasn't the least need for you to be worried."

"A quarter past one! We were on the point of ringing up the police."

"They wouldn't have thanked you. They'd got other things to think about by then."

"*Anything* might have happened."

"The worst that could have happened," said Sally in an effort to lighten the discussion, "was that we might have turned the car over. Billy drives like a maniac."

Mr. Nurse was not to be diverted. He said, "In my young day, if girls went out for midnight drives with young men people knew what to think."

"Then people in your young day must have had filthy minds."

"Really, Sally. You mustn't speak to your father like that."

"Why not?" said Sally mutinously.

"Because he is your father."

"And I'm his daughter. And I'm nineteen, not nine."

"You're living in our house—"

"A*nd* paying for my keep."

"As long as you're living here, you've got to behave yourself properly."

"For God's sake," said Sally, her voice going up, "this is the twentieth century, not the reign of Queen Victoria. And it's England, not the Arabian Gulf. If you don't want me in the house, say so. I can find somewhere else to live—"

"Don't shout at me. I'm not deaf."

"I'm sure your father didn't mean—" said Mrs. Nurse and broke off.

Two policemen were coming up the front path.

9

"There's no need to be alarmed by this invasion," said McCourt pleasantly. "Sergeant Esdaile was on his way round to ask you a few routine questions. Lucky he's found you all together." He was looking at Sally as he spoke. He had heard the shouting as he came up the path. He thought that Jack Nurse must be a trying parent.

"All I'm here for," he went on, "is to borrow the keys of the Boat Club. Sergeant Shilling asked me to get hold of them."

"The keys," said Nurse vaguely. "Why?"

"I expect he just wants to have a look round."

"I suppose it's all right. I'll fetch them." He came back with two keys, each with a label attached. When McCourt had taken them and departed on his moped, Nurse said, "Do you want to question us together or alone?" He felt awkward about it. Sergeant Esdaile was a family man. He knew him and his wife well and had made their wills for them.

"You and your wife were together after the dance, so I gather," said Esdaile. "Save time if I had a word with you two first."

Sally took the hint and departed into the garden.

"There's not a lot to tell," said Nurse. "My wife and I

left the hall soon after the Mariners. A minute or two after eleven, I should say. We walked straight home."

"Not a long walk," said Esdaile.

In fact their bungalow, *Syljack*, was almost directly across the road from the hall.

"Then we sat up and talked for a bit."

Mrs. Nurse said, "We watched the end of the film on television and had a cup of coffee to pass the time."

"To pass the time?"

"We never like to go to bed until Sally's back."

"When one o'clock came, we were very anxious. We thought we ought to do something. Then Sally came back, with Billy Gonville."

"That terrible car of his," said Mrs. Nurse. "You can hear it half a mile away. We asked her where she'd been and she said—"

"I'll ask her about that myself," said Sergeant Esdaile firmly.

One key said "Outer Door" and let them into a tiny hallway with a door on the left labeled "Committee Room" and a wooden staircase straight ahead. The air was heavy with stored heat and undisturbed dust. Like a forgotten attic in an old house, thought McCourt as he followed Shilling.

The committee room was unlocked. It was furnished with a table and chairs and two old-fashioned wooden filing cabinets. On the walls hung rows of framed photographs of regatta events. One was a photograph of a man with a large mustache, with the legend "Alfred Butt. Single Sculler. Oxford to London. Five hours, forty minutes." Mr. Butt had a thoughtful look on his face, as though he was wondering why he should have done such a thing. One of the cabinets held files of correspondence, membership cards and minute books.

The other was empty. A moth flew out as Shilling opened it.

"No wonder they don't bother to lock it up," said Shilling. "Let's try upstairs."

The room upstairs was labeled "Chairman's Office." This was locked. The second of the two keys opened it. It had a square of carpet on the floor, a rolltop desk with a swivel chair in front of it, a small table and three wicker chairs. There was a triangular cupboard in one corner with glasses in it, a nearly full bottle of gin, a half-empty bottle of whisky and some unopened bottles of tonic and soda water.

"Quite a snug little den," said Shilling. "I suppose this is George Mariner's hideaway."

"He's a man who likes to do himself well," said McCourt.

This room had signs of recent use. There were three cigarette ends in a glass ashtray on the desk. They looked new.

"When was the last Boat Club Committee meeting?" said Shilling.

McCourt, after some thought, said, "I imagine it would have been in connection with the regatta. That was on July fifteenth."

"More than a month ago. They don't look a month old."

"He could have been up here dealing with correspondence. Something like that."

Before Shilling could pursue the matter they heard the telephone. It was ringing down in the boathouse.

"Wonder who that can be," said Shilling. "The Super's the only man who knows I was coming down here. Something must have turned up."

He made his way with no undue haste down the stairs. McCourt, left to himself, took a look around the room. The first object which struck his eye was the calendar on the wall beside the desk. The picture of the girl on it, if not actually obscene, came close to the borderline. McCourt's lips wrinkled in distaste. Two years as a policeman in London and three in the quieter backwater of Hannington had eradicated some, but by no means all, of the puritan ethos bred into him by his upbringing.

At that moment a small spotlight flicked across the room. It seemed to come from behind the desk. McCourt went across to examine the phenomenon.

He saw what had happened. When Shilling had opened the door to let himself back into the boathouse the sunlight, reflected off the glass, had shone directly onto the opposite wall. It had not only shone onto it. It had shone through it.

McCourt went down onto his knees behind the desk and found the hole. Originally a knothole, it looked as though it had been enlarged with a knife. As he knelt, it was on eye level and gave him a view of a section of the boathouse below. To the left he could see the legs of Sergeant Shilling, who was sitting at the chair behind the booking desk talking into the telephone. To the right the ends of the two canoes. Straight ahead, across the tops of the skiffs, he could see the flat punt cushions stacked in line under the window in the wall.

As he stared down through this peephole, other matters were circling through his mind, not settled yet into a definite pattern. The wheel marks of the car which had been parked farther along the towpath. The car which Roseabel Tress and the Havelocks had heard driving away at around midnight. The car which had aroused such a strong presentiment of evil in Roseabel's curious mind.

There was something else that one of the women had

said to him. He felt sure that it was important. No need to trouble his mind about it. He could play back the tapes and listen. As he heard Shilling coming back up the stairs he scrambled to his feet.

"I've got to get back to the Steelstock house," said Shilling. "And pick up something on the way. At once, if not sooner. You'd better jump onto your moped and come too. Things are beginning to move."

"And I hope you're not going to be like Dad about this," said Sally Nurse.

"I've got two girls of my own," said Sergeant Esdaile. "They're only eight and ten. When they're a bit older, I expect I'll be exactly like your father. At the moment, I'm broad-minded."

"There isn't anything to be broad-minded about. Billy asked me if I'd like to go for a drive. You remember how hot it was on Friday night. I thought it was a chance to get a breath of fresh air before I went to bed." She smiled and suddenly looked much younger. "Oh, boy. Did I get some fresh air. We must have gone over a hundred down that bit of the motorway."

"Better give me a rough idea of where you went and what the timings were."

"Do my best," said Sally.

Esdaile let her talk, only interrupting her to say, "Yes. I heard about the police check. They had a lot of men out that night. It was organized from Reading. We weren't involved."

And later: "What did you talk about?"

"What people always talk about, of course. We talked about ourselves."

"Did he . . . ?"

"If you're getting round to asking me if he tried to rape me, the answer's no. All he did was kiss me, in a brotherly way. Well, perhaps a bit more than brotherly. But he didn't paw me. He really is a very nice person."

"I'm sure he is," said Esdaile.

They had moved down to the far end of the garden but could hear the telephone when it rang. Mr. Nurse appeared and said, "It's for you, Sergeant. Superintendent Knott. He says it's urgent."

Knott's voice at the other end of the line was deliberately flat. He said, "Is Sally there?"

"Right here."

"Ask her to check if her evening bag's there."

"To check—"

"Just to check it. Not to open it. Not even to handle it. The bag she had with her at the dance."

Sally said, "What on earth! Why should he want that?"

"No idea," said Esdaile. "Suppose you go and look. He's hanging on."

"I expect it'll be in your bedroom," said Mrs. Nurse. She and her husband were listening to the conversation. "I didn't see it when I made your bed that morning."

"That's right. I remember I just threw it into one of the top drawers when I got back. There's nothing much in it."

"Could you see if it's still there. Don't open it. Just look."

"What does he think's in it, for goodness' sake?" said Sally. "A bomb?"

Mr. Nurse said sharply, "Don't be absurd. Just do what he asks."

Esdaile, still grasping the receiver, said, "I've no idea what it's all about. But could you just check on it."

Sally departed. The others stood in silence until she came back. They noticed she was looking upset.

"It's there all right. Where I said."

"Miss Nurse says the bag's here, sir. Just where she left it."

Knott's voice came over the telephone so clearly that everyone in the room could hear it. He said, "Good. Now listen. Do you know where Shilling has got to?"

"I expect he's still down at the boathouse. McCourt went down there with the keys for him. Less than half an hour ago."

"Is the boathouse on the telephone?"

Esdaile looked at Mr. Nurse, who nodded. The excitement was beginning to get hold of them.

"Right. I'll ask him to pick up the bag himself on his way past. I'm at Mrs. Steelstock's house."

He rang off. The four people in the room stood staring at each other.

10

The next person on Superintendent Knott's visiting list after he left Mariner's house had been Mr. Beaumorris, but, on reflection, he had decided to leave the old gentleman alone, for the time being at least. He could not really visualize him as having taken any part in the murder, since he had bicycled straight home from the dance and had sat until well after midnight in the bow window of his cottage in the street, seeing and being seen. He might be useful later as corroborative evidence of other people's movements.

There was a stronger reason for leaving him alone. The Superintendent knew that he disliked him and knew the reason for his dislike. He had not forgotten Bill Connington. He would certainly not be helpful and might even be obstructive. Knott therefore decided to go straight on to the Manor and talk to Mrs. Steelstock. She ought by now to have recovered from the initial shock and should be able to give him evidence on a number of points which were beginning to interest him.

West Hannington Manor was the oldest and incomparably the most handsome house in the village. Built in the reign of Queen Anne, it lay well back from the road, protected on three sides by an old brick wall and by ornate iron railings along the front. Matthew Steelstock, who had hated all modern inventions and had preferred a horse to a motorcar, had often expressed the intention of building a fourth and higher wall along the Street, but this had proved to be beyond even his purse and the project had died with him.

As the Superintendent walked up the drive he noted on his left, at right angles to the main building, the stable block, the end part of which Katie had converted into her private living quarters. He knew from his study of the plan that it had a private exit onto the lane on the east side of the property. It would have to be searched. He proposed to do this important job himself.

The door of the Manor was opened by a boy in corduroy trousers and a blue and white checked shirt. Peter Steelstock, said the card index in the Superintendent's mind. Sixteen. At Coverdales School. Wasn't at the dance. An immature nose, a band of freckles above it and the sullen look which seemed to be fashionable with boys of that age; it lightened when he smiled, as he did now. It was a smile which flicked on and off again as abruptly as a sky sign. Advertising something, or nothing? Difficult to tell at that age.

"You must be the Murder Squad," he said. "Mother's been expecting you. She's in the drawing room with Walter."

He led the way down a paneled passage into the big room at the back of the house which looked out over a wide stretch of lawn. It had been furnished with a real taste for its period, a taste which came from the widow, Knott guessed, and not from her late and unlamented husband, who seemed from all accounts to have been a Philistine as well as a bully.

Mrs. Steelstock was sitting upright on a wooden-framed tapestry-covered armchair. There was bone and character in that face. A lot of it had gone into Katie. Some of it into Walter. By the time they reached Peter, maybe the wells had been running low?

She said, "I expect the Superintendent wants to speak to me privately. He may want to talk to you afterwards."

When the boys had removed themselves, she indicated a chair for Knott to sit in and composed herself for questioning. A little too composed, perhaps, for a mother whose only daughter had been savagely killed less than forty-eight hours before?

She said, "Yes. Walter drove me home. I'm told by various people who have been busy checking other people's movements"—a slight smile touched her thin lips—"that we left at eleven twenty. I have no exact recollection of the time myself. When we got here I went straight to my room. Walter stayed up. He usually makes himself responsible for locking the house up."

"Would he have been waiting up for Kate?"

"No. Kate lived her own life. We didn't interfere with her in any way."

Lived her own life. Died her own death.

"I only wondered whether you could see her windows from this house. I mean, so that you would know, seeing lights go on, whether she got back."

"No. Her house is the far end of the old stable block. It used to be the coachman's cottage. It's completely hidden from the house. She preferred it that way."

"Was Peter up when you came back?"

The sudden switch did not disconcert Mrs. Steelstock. She said, "Peter was in bed. He had told us he had a headache. I think it was only an excuse. He's not of an age to find dances amusing."

"And you didn't wake him up when Sergeant McCourt came round with the news?"

"I discussed it with Walter. But there seemed no point in doing so. We told him next morning."

The Superintendent was not really interested in Peter. He had been devoting most of his mind to the question he had really come to ask. It had to be put in exactly the right way.

He said, "You'll understand that in a case of this sort —a girl being killed—the very first thing we have to consider is men who were . . . well . . . interested in her. In particular, I wanted to ask you about one of them. Jonathan Limbery."

"Yes?" said Mrs. Steelstock, her mouth set in a tight line.

"He was friendly with her?"

"At one time he was round this house so much that I got the impression he considered himself a member of the family. I appreciated that Kate didn't fancy entertaining him in her own little place. That would have been altogether too intimate. So she used to bring him in here. I really didn't know what to do with him. He hardly seemed to fit. Of course, there were things he could talk about. The firm Walter is articled to in Reading, Holst and Mariner, they happen to be the accountants for his paper. And he knew Peter. He'd taught him at one time at Coverdales. And he sometimes even condescended to talk to me, but since it usually developed into a lecture on politics or economics I can't say I found it very entertaining."

"But it was Kate he really came to see?"

"So I assumed."

"I'd be interested to know how he first got to know her."

"Sooner or later, Superintendent, in a place like West Hannington, everyone gets to know everyone else. In this particular case, of course, there was the song he wrote for her."

"Song?"

"'What Are They Like in Your House?'"

"Good heavens! Did he write that?"

There had been a time, two or three years earlier, when you could hardly cross the street without hearing someone humming or singing or whistling the curiously seductive lilt: "What are they like in your house . . . your house . . . your house. Rich house . . . poor house."

"Kate used it as a sort of theme song when she started on television. I imagine the music publishers took most of the profits. They usually do, don't they?"

"So I understand."

"But it made a bit for both of them. I don't suppose Jonathan gets paid much for that stupid paper he plays at editing. I doubt if it sells a hundred copies outside this area. He uses it as a sort of pulpit for his views."

"Not very popular views?"

Mrs. Steelstock considered the point coldly. She was a curiously dispassionate woman, the Superintendent decided.

"Since they were mostly attacks on older people who were doing responsible jobs, they must have had a certain attraction for the young, I imagine."

A very faint echo flicked through the Superintendent's mind. Something he had overheard. It would come back if he didn't chase it. He said, "You'll have heard all about the quarrel Kate had with Jonathan at the Tennis Club."

"Certainly I heard about it. From the people who were there, and from a lot of people who weren't there but wished they had been."

"I'd appreciate your view of the reason for it."

"The reason?"

"People don't indulge in a public slanging match on the spur of the moment. They must have been building up for it."

"I think the reason was very simple. Kate had moved ahead of him. The fact that he was unsure of himself might have a certain appeal to young people who are unsure of themselves. But Katie was growing up. She was meeting people in London with adult minds. People who had really done something, not just talked about doing it. It was bound to alter her perspective."

"Anyone in particular?"

"If there had been some man, she would not have discussed him with me. We hadn't that sort of relationship. Of course there were girlfriends. People she was at school with, people like Venetia Loftus. Not Loftus now, of course. She's married. I forget the name."

Mrs. Steelstock smiled again as she mentioned this. She knew, and she knew that Superintendent Knott knew, that Venetia's father was the Assistant Commissioner in charge of Criminal Investigation at Scotland Yard: the man most directly responsible for Knott's professional future, the man whose influence had brought him so quickly to West Hannington and who would be watching the progress of the case with more than superficial interest.

Knott said, "Any men friends at all?"

"The only name I can remember being mentioned more than casually was Mark Holbeck."

"Her agent?"

"Yes."

"But he might have known if she had other close friends."

"He might," said Mrs. Steelstock. "But I think it was simply a business relationship." As the Superintendent got to his feet she added, with the first hint of personal feeling she had shown, "You will find the man who did it, won't you?"

"Yes," said Knott. "I'll find him." He opened his briefcase and took out the evening dress bag. "This was in the grass near Katie. I've no doubt it was hers, but I'd like you to identify it formally, please."

He stopped. Mrs. Steelstock had opened the bag and had started to examine the contents. Now he saw that her hand was shaking. He said, "I do apologize. I realize it must be painful for you—" and was interrupted.

Mrs. Steelstock said, "*This isn't Katie's bag.* She's never used lipstick of that color in her life. She couldn't. Anyway, I know the bag well. I gave it to her. I think I can tell you who it did belong to. Sally Nurse. She had a crush on Katie. Copied her clothes and everything." She stared at Knott, the horror beginning to build up in her eyes. "Do you think . . . Is it possible . . . My God, how cruel."

Knott, who was still trying to grapple with what had happened, stood staring at her. Then he said, "What do you mean?"

"That he made a mistake. That he killed the wrong girl."

"No," said Knott. "I don't believe that. But he certainly made a mistake. And if he did, he's going to pay for it a lot sooner than he expected. I'll have to use your telephone, please."

"Of course they think it's Jonathan," said Walter.

"Why should they?" said Peter furiously.

"Because he's the obvious person. He was keen on her. She turned him down flat. He's not the sort of person to stand for that."

"It's not true."

"How can you possibly know?"

"Because . . . because I know Jonathan better than you do. *And* I liked him. You and Mother hated him."

"That's a stupid thing to say," said Walter. "Why should we hate him?"

"No more stupid than saying Johnno would have killed Katie."

"All right," said Walter pacifically. Whenever Peter flew into a rage he found it easier to back down. "I'm not saying I thought he did it. I'm saying it's what the police will think."

The bags looked very similar, but when they were placed side by side on the drawing-room table in the clear afternoon sunlight, the small differences in the beading and metalwork were clear enough.

"I gather," said Shilling, "that Sally came home about one in the morning, had a flaming row with her parents, went up to her room, hurled this bag, which she thought, of course, was her own, into the drawer of her dressing table and hadn't touched it or thought about it again until you telephoned."

Knott seemed to be in no hurry to open the bag. He said, "You've read all the statements, Bob. And you can help us here, too, Mrs. Steelstock. I seem to remember that Katie had a chair fairly close to the main exit door. The one on the west side of the hall."

"I think that's right, sir."

"And that Sally Nurse had a chair close to hers. But even nearer to the door."

Mrs. Steelstock said, "Her chair would be as close to Katie's as she could possibly get it."

"So that it's perfectly possible that when Katie left in rather a hurry she picked up the wrong bag and took it with her. It partly explains one point that had been puzzling us. When we examined the bag we found near the boathouse we did notice"—Sergeant Shilling grinned at the use of the royal "we"—"that there were no keys in it. Since Sally had no car she'd need no car key. But she ought to have had a house key, surely?"

Shilling was about to say, "You don't know her parents," but realized that this was not a moment when comments would be welcome. Knott was talking deliberately because he was thinking deliberately, feeling his way step by step along the new and promising path which had suddenly opened in front of him.

He said to McCourt, who was standing unobtrusively near the door, "Find out, will you?" McCourt backed out into the hall and shut the door. Knott picked up Katie's bag, still without opening it, and said to Mrs. Steelstock, "I take it you identify this as your daughter's property?"

"Of course I do," said Mrs. Steelstock impatiently. "I told you. I gave it to her. Less than a year ago."

Knott clicked open the catch and upended the bag so that the contents slid out onto the table. Items of makeup, a handkerchief, some money and a ring with three keys on it. There was something else. Knott inserted a finger and thumb and drew it out delicately. It was a plain white envelope, which had been folded to get it into the bag.

Knott said, a note of savage satisfaction in his voice, "So *that's* what he was looking for."

"Then that's a note from . . . from a man . . . the one who got her to go down to the boathouse and—"

"That's right," said Knott.

"Aren't you going to look at it?"

"For the moment, what I'm going to do is label it." He took out a thin silver pencil and wrote on the envelope, "Taken from a bag identified by Mrs. Steelstock as belonging to Miss Steelstock." Then he initialed it, handed the pencil to Mrs. Steelstock and said, "You saw me take it out. Would you mind initialing it too."

She did so. Her fingers were clearly itching to extract whatever secret the envelope held. Knott took it back, still folded, placed it carefully in his wallet and put the wallet in the breast pocket of his coat.

McCourt reappeared. He said, "Sally did have a house key. And it was in her bag that night. But she didn't have to use it, because her father had the door open before she was halfway up the front path."

Knott considered this information, fitting it into the pattern which was forming in his mind. He said, "I take it your daughter was careful about locking up her house when she left it?"

"She's been careful since the burglary. Before that I don't think she bothered so much."

"Burglary?"

"About two months ago," said McCourt. "The man was actually in the house when she got back. Mairci-fully he seems to have been as frightened as she was. When he haird Katie coming through the front door he bolted out of the back. All she could tell us was that it was a man and youngish."

It was one of the difficulties of an investigation of this sort, thought Knott. Too much information. Important issues could become clouded by irrelevancies. As he thought about it he realized that everyone was looking at him. He smiled.

"Well," he said, "we'd better go down and have a look at her place ourselves. I'd like a word with Walter when we've finished. I wonder if you'd ask him to wait." Mrs. Steelstock nodded, but coldly. She was still angry that the Superintendent had refused to show her what was in the note. It had been found in her daughter's bag. It probably contained the name of her daughter's killer. Who had a better right to see it than her mother?

If Knott was aware of her displeasure he gave no sign of it. He led the way out of the house. His mood had changed. He was easy and, for once, talkative. It was the period of relaxation which follows a successful orgasm. He strode fast down the drive, toward the stable block, the sergeants almost trotting to keep up.

"It's making a lot of sense now, isn't it?" he said. "He was looking for that note. That's why he ransacked the bag. He didn't find it, of course. Because it was the wrong bag. *But he wasn't to know that.* His next idea must have been that Katie had left the note behind her in her house when she came out."

Shilling said, "I'd just about got that far myself."

"Right. So what does he do? He's a careful planner. But bold and quick when he has to be. I guessed that much almost as soon as I saw the body. *Now he thought he'd been given a second chance.* He'd take the key that was in the bag, thinking it was Katie's house key, and he'd come up later that night to have another look for the note. He'd be in a hurry, maybe a bit nervous. That's when mistakes are made."

Shilling said, "Let's hope so." McCourt said nothing. His deliberate Scottish mind was trying to keep up with this new and unexpected version of the Superintendent.

The coachman's cottage had been converted with tact. The only apparent addition was a two-story annex at the back. The rustic porch had been taken down and replaced by a plain strong door and the old windows taken out, the openings enlarged and modern frames put in.

Of the three keys on the ring from Katie's bag one was clearly a car key, one was a tiny cylinder of steel of the type known as a "Bramah." The third was an ordinary Yale. And it opened the front door for them.

Knott said, "He couldn't have opened the door with Sally's key. So let's try to find out how he *did* get in. Have a look round, Bob."

They waited, standing in the sunlight outside the open front door. Shilling reappeared. He said, "There's a window open at the back. It looks as if it's been forced. And I could see a chair that had been kicked over."

Knott grunted. He was trying, unsuccessfully, to see into the front room. He said, "We don't want three of us trampling about inside there. You go in, Bob. And open the curtains. Then we can see in."

They were heavy lined curtains and had been pulled right across the window. When they were drawn back, they could look in from the outside into what was evidently the living room. Shilling opened the window and said, "What do you make of that?" Against the wall, to the left of the window, was a desk. It was a solid affair, with drawers on either side of the kneehole and a cupboard on top of it. A masculine piece of furniture in a feminine room. The door of the cupboard had been forced. There was a gash in the woodwork beside the lock and a crack right across the panel.

"Rough work," said Knott. "Try the key."

He handed the key ring to Shilling, who moved across the room. McCourt noticed that he avoided standing directly in front of the desk, keeping over to the far side. The smallest of the three keys fitted the tiny keyhole.

"Not a lock he could pick," said Shilling. "So he bust it open. Using this, I shouldn't wonder." He pointed at the heavy steel poker lying in front of the fireplace, but he made no attempt to touch it.

"All right," said Knott. "Let's start the routine. Get

Dandridge up here and warn him he's going to need help from Reading. We'll have the whole place dusted and photographed. Particular attention to the carpet in there, Bob. We want holograms of any footprints. When that's been done, have them take that cupboard door off its hinges, fit it up with clamps and a facing of cardboard or plywood—You see what I mean?"

"To protect the front surface."

"Right. And when you've got it rigged up, put it in the car. Tomorrow you can take it up to London when you go and hand it over to the boys at Hendon. And tell them not to take a month of Sundays about it."

"Quickest if I use the telephone here."

Knott thought about it and said, "Should be all right to use it. You come with me, Ian. We're going back to the house."

As they walked up the drive, McCourt could contain himself no longer. "Surely," he said, "the man would be careful not to leave prints. He'd likely be wearing gloves."

"Likely he would," said Knott with ferocious good humor. "And likely they'd be thin cotton gloves. And likely he wouldn't realize that on a hot night his hands would be sweating. You can sweat a fingerprint through cotton gloves. Did you know that?"

"I did not."

"It's not infallible. The camera has to screen out the mesh of the glove. But it can be done. And let me tell you something else, Ian, which may be useful to you later on." They had reached the doorstep of the house and the Superintendent paused with his hand on the knocker. "In a case like this you do *everything*. You take *every* step laid down in the book. Even when you know who the killer is."

McCourt gaped at him. During the last hour he had

seen two different superintendents. This was a third. The father figure, dispensing wisdom to his children.

He said, "Did I hear you say, 'Even when you *know* who the killer is'?"

"Certainly. It was pretty clear all along what sort of man it had to be. We'll be putting a name to him in a few minutes. Knowing *who* it is doesn't really matter. It's a help, of course. But it's not the important point. We've got one problem and one problem only now. We have to put together a case that'll stand up in court." On the word "court" he thumped down the knocker. It was the full stop at the end of the sentence.

It was Walter who opened the door. Knott said, "Let's go in somewhere quiet." He indicated the dining-room door, on the left of the hall. Walter and Sergeant McCourt followed him in. He took his wallet out of his jacket pocket, opened it and extracted the folded envelope. He said to McCourt, "You've been with me, Sergeant, ever since I took this from Mrs. Steelstock and put it in my wallet."

"Aye."

"Then you are able to state that I haven't touched it until this moment." He turned to Walter. "And you can watch me open it."

"Certainly," said Walter. "But why—"

"Because," said Knott, "sooner or later, some snotty-nosed barrister is going to get up in court and say"—here Knott adopted a horrifically upper-class accent—"'Naow, Superintendent, perhaps you will tell the court just haow you intend to prove that you faound this letter in the handbag of the deceased.' That's why I'm going to get both of you to initial this piece of paper which you see me extracting from this already identified envelope. Right?"

Walter said, "All right." McCourt said nothing. He felt breathless.

The Superintendent spread the paper delicately on the table, holding it by the edges. It was a plain sheet of white paper. They craned over Knott's shoulder to read the words which had been typed on it.

> Darlingest Kit Cat. I can't keep this up a moment longer. I don't believe you want to, either. If I'm not wrong about that, come to our usual place. I'll be there at eleven. LYPAH.

The Superintendent read it out loud, pausing on the last word, which was in capital letters. He said, "'LYPAH.' That's an odd word. Do you think it's a name?"

He became aware that Walter was scarlet in the face. He was struggling with a mixture of embarrassment and laughter, in which embarrassment predominated. He said, "What's up, son? Something tickle you?"

Walter said, "It's LYPAH."

"You understand it?"

"It's just a stupid thing. It used to be a sort of catchword with some of the boys round here. I think it started at Coverdales, actually. You put it at the end of a letter —a letter like this—making a date with a girl."

"Why?"

"You put it there so that she'd ask you what it meant."

"I'm asking you."

"It meant 'Leave your pants at home.'"

The Superintendent considered this, but could think of no appropriate comment.

11

"Then you're sure it came from Limbery," said Dandridge.

"Almost sure enough to prove it in court," said Knott. "Quite sure enough to make it a working hypothesis. The Steelstock boy confirmed to us that 'Kit Cat' was Limbery's pet name for Katie. He hadn't heard anyone else use it. The first part of the note indicates that they'd had a quarrel and he wanted to make it up. Well, we know all about that. And LYPAH. He'd have picked that nonsense up no doubt when he was teaching at Coverdales."

"In our part of the world," said Shilling with a grin, "we don't put LYPAH, we put—"

Knott said, "That's quite enough, Bob. We don't want any reminiscences of your lecherous past. There's a lot to do." He considered it, standing squarely on his stubby legs in front of the map in the operations room. Then he swung around on Sergeant Esdaile. He said, "I want a proper case book set up, Eddie. An hour-by-hour log of everything we've done and everyone we've questioned so far. Transcripts of what they said. A timetable showing people's movements that night. Copies of the photographs you took at the boathouse. Good photographs, by the way. I congratulate you. Photographs of the fingerprints on the boathouse door. Copies of Dr. Farmiloe's report and the report of the pathologist from Southampton. Also, as soon as it's available, a second report that I've asked for from Dr. Summerson, checking both of them. Not that I think there's anything wrong with them, but you can't be too careful with medical evidence. Then there'll be photocopies of this letter and a written statement, which I'll give you, of how and where it was found. You get the general idea?"

Esdaile looked dazed but resolute. He said, "You want everything we've got so far organized into one file."

"That's right. Next, we'll extend the search for the weapon. Have two men cover every yard of the way between the place where the body was found and Limbery's house. Search all drains, culverts, ditches and wasteland. We'll assume he wouldn't risk coming home via Upper Church Lane, because that would have taken him straight past the hall. He'd have stuck to the towpath, turned off it up Eveleigh Road and crossed the end of the street into Belsize Road. His house is number seventeen. That's just beyond the Brickfield Road crossing. It's the part they call Lower Belsize Road."

Dandridge said, "Windle and young Gonville share digs at number thirty-four Upper Belsize Road. They both say they heard Limbery's car coming back at sometime between half past one and a quarter to two. If he'd been out in his car, isn't it possible that he'd dumped the weapon miles away?"

"Extremely possible," said Knott placidly. "Even probable. Or he may have thrown it into the river five miles downstream. But killers do odd things. So we'd better make sure." He turned to Shilling. "You're going back to London. You know the points I want you to cover. You'll have a full program and I want you back tonight, so I suggest you take McCourt with you. He can do the checking at the Documents Division. It's in Lambeth Road. You can explain the form to him as you're driving up. Right?"

This seemed to be a signal for general dispersal.

The offices of the Hannington *Gazette* were fifty yards down East Street, on the south side. They occupied the ground floor and the yard of what had once been an undertakers' establishment. The editor before Jonathan Limbery had been an absent-minded man with a passion for wild flowers, on which he had written a number of booklets.

With the arrival of Jonathan, wild flowers had given way to wilder polemics, without noticeably changing the circulation figures. When Knott was announced, Jonathan was in his shirtsleeves, talking on the telephone. He said to the boy who had brought the news, "Find him a chair in the outer office. I'll give you a ring when I'm free," and continued with the call, which was to the news editor of the Reading *Sun*. It was a bad-tempered conversation, at least on Jonathan's part, which finished with him saying, "Even if you didn't use it, I think you ought to pay for it," and banging down the receiver.

After which he sat for a full minute, apparently deep in thought, before stretching out his hand and ringing the bell.

"I can see you're busy," said Knott, "so I won't take up more of your time than I have to. As you probably know, we've been questioning everyone who was at the dance on Friday night when Miss Steelstock was killed. Now we're widening the scope of our inquiries to take in people, like yourself, who weren't at the dance but who were her friends . . . and acquaintances." Knott paused slightly before adding the last two words, then said, "Which category would you place yourself in, Mr. Limbery?"

"A friend," said Jonathan shortly.

"A close friend?"

"If you like."

"It's not what I like, sir. I'm just a poor dumb copper asking questions. Do I gather that you *were* a close friend?"

"Yes."

"A friend of the family?"

Came the faint flicker that Knott was trained to recognize. Without meaning to do so, he had touched a nerve. Follow it up.

He said, "I gathered from Mrs. Steelstock that you were quite a frequent visitor at their house—at one time."

"If she told you that, why ask me about it?"

"We like to have everything confirmed."

"Even though they haven't got a damned thing to do with the crime you're supposed to be investigating."

"You must leave it to us to judge that, sir."

"I can't stop you asking impertinent questions. I'm not bound to answer them."

"That's your privilege," said Knott. "Then perhaps we could deal with something which might be more relevant. You weren't at the Tennis Club dance?"

"No."

"Why not? All your friends were there."

"I don't have to account to you for my movements. Just take it that I don't like dances."

"A lot of us don't, sir. But wasn't there some other reason in your case? Some work you had to finish for your paper."

Jonathan looked up sharply, as though it had occurred to him for the first time that the Superintendent really had been doing his homework.

He said, "I don't know who told you that, but it happens to be true. There was an article I had to finish. And it was bloody lucky I did stay in. Otherwise I might have missed the fire."

"The fire?"

"Quantocks Paper Mills. Just outside Goring."

"Oh yes. I think I read about it. I didn't realize you'd covered that."

"I do a certain amount of local work for the Reading *Sun*."

"I see, sir. A stringer."

"If you use technical terms, you should use them accurately. A stringer is an amateur. I am a whole-time professional newspaperman."

"My mistake," said Knott. "However, I take it you got a call from the *Sun* and volunteered to do them a piece."

"That is correct."

"At about what time?"

"It would have been around ten o'clock. I know that I was there by half past ten. When you're doing a piece for a daily, you have to keep an eye on printing times."

"Of course, sir."

"They put the paper to bed at one o'clock, so anything I did give them would have to be dictated over the telephone."

"And that's what you did, sir?"

"Yes."

"At what time?"

"Around midnight. Perhaps a little later."

"And where would that have been from?"

"From a call box on the Oxford road. Come to think of it, it must have been a little before midnight, because I had time for a quick drink and a sandwich at the King of Clubs. That's that big roadhouse between Goring and Whitchurch—"

"I know it well," said Knott, with a smile. "I've often dropped in there myself. A nice place. Broad-minded about closing times, too, I found."

"I think they had a Friday night extension." Knott noticed that Limbery was much easier now. "Anyway, they weren't in a hurry to turn me out. It must have been nearly half past twelve before I left."

"And came back home the same way."

"Actually, no. There's not a lot in it, but the King of Clubs is a bit closer to Whitchurch than it is to Goring. So I came back that way."

The Superintendent seemed to be visualizing the map. He said, "Wouldn't that mean you had to go all the way back to Reading to cross the river?"

"Certainly not. There's a bridge between Whitchurch and Pangbourne."

"Of course. Stupid of me. So that's the bridge you used?"

"Right."

"And were home by when?"

A shade of caution was observable in Jonathan's voice as he dealt with this question. He said, "I wasn't keeping one eye on my watch the whole time, Superintendent."

"Naturally not, sir. But we can work it out roughly, can't we? I take it you came straight back. You didn't stop for any reason?"

"No."

"And you'd left the roadhouse by half past twelve."

"Now I come to think of it," said Jonathan slowly, "it must have been even later than that."

"What makes you think that?"

"I remember now. When I was driving through Pangbourne, I saw the clock on the Town Hall. It was a few minutes before one."

"Then it's about twelve miles to Hannington. Say twenty-five minutes. That gets you home at twenty past one."

"I don't drive fast at night. It might have been any time between half past one and two."

If the Superintendent observed the way in which the timing was stretching, a little implausibly, toward two o'clock, and so matching itself with the statements made by Windle and Gonville, he gave no sign of being disturbed by this. He said in his smoothest voice, "Quite right to be careful at night. Why did you stop visiting the Manor, Mr. Limbery?"

Jonathan's head jerked around. There was a moment of silence. Then he said very softly, "Would you mind repeating that?"

"I asked, Why did you stop being a regular visitor at Hannington Manor?"

"I thought that's what you said. I've no intention of answering the question."

"Was it because you'd quarreled with Miss Steelstock?"

Jonathan said nothing.

"I was referring, of course, to that little tiff you had with her at the Tennis Club—about six weeks ago, wasn't it?"

Jonathan had started breathing deeply, taking in great gulps of air. It reminded Knott of a diver charging his lungs with oxygen before a deep plunge. He said, "I only mention it because it seems to have been fairly common knowledge. After all, if you conduct your quarrels in public, people are bound to talk about them.

But what puzzled me was why it should have made you drop Mrs. Steelstock and her boys. Like I said, you were a friend of the whole family."

Again that flicker. Keep at it.

"That's right, isn't it, sir?"

"I realize now," said Jonathan, in a voice so thick with fury that the words had some difficulty in forcing their way out, "exactly what people mean when they talk about police harassment."

"Oh, come, sir. A perfectly straightforward question."

"You've no more right to question me about my personal relationships than I have to question you about yours. Suppose I started asking you impertinent questions about your wife and your girlfriends—"

"There's a difference. My girlfriend, supposing I had one, doesn't happen to have had her head smashed in."

But Jonathan was hardly listening to him. A dangerous and explosive mixture was building up inside him, a mixture of which he hardly understood the elements himself. Contempt for his father and resentment of his authority. Building from that, resentment of the authority of old people over the young, of employers over employees, of the conventional over the unconventional, of the state over its subjects—all personified in this sly and bullying policeman.

The lava belched out, scalding and stinking, but pleasurable to the god of the volcano. He said, "I loathe you and I despise you. You're a puffed-up nothing. A sadistic little bastard. We've all heard about you. How you like tormenting helpless and frightened people. I'm not helpless and I'm not frightened of you, or twenty like you. And I'm glad to answer for everyone you've trampled over in your filthy bullying life who've been too timid to answer for themselves. I've only one message for you. And that is Fuck off. Crawl back down whatever hole you came out of and leave us alone."

Knott said, without a flicker of expression, "I ought to warn you, sir, that everything you say is being recorded."

Limbery hardly seemed to hear him. He was still inflated by the passion of his own rhetoric. He said, "Tell your superiors. Tell the world. The sooner people realize what they're up against, the better. We point our finger at other countries, but we can't see what's happening here. This is a police state. A filthy fascist police-ridden autocracy."

"Well now," said Knott, "all countries have got to have policemen. After all, there has to be someone to direct the traffic."

If Jonathan had been less exalted by the wind of his own oratory he might have detected the purring note of satisfaction in the Superintendent's voice.

12

During his service in the Metropolitan Police, McCourt had visited the headquarters of the Forensic Science Laboratory at 109 Lambeth Road on a number of occasions but had never before penetrated as far as the Documents Division, which occupied part of the fourth floor.

A notice beside the lift regretted that it was temporarily out of order "owing to maintenance work" and he resigned himself to climbing the flights of stone steps.

It was three years since he had quit the shabby, crowded, jostling streets of London for the peace of Hannington.

He was a country boy. His father was a Scottish Unitarian minister and his mother the daughter of an Oxford don, so he and his two sisters had been brought up in a house where intellect was treasured and integrity was more than a catchword. It had been planned for him that when he left Glasgow High School he should go to the university and study law. The death of his father when he was eighteen had killed this project. His mother had uprooted the family and moved back south to be near her own folk. It was at this point that Ian had made up his mind. If the academic study of the law was now out of his reach, he would pursue it on its executive side. He had joined the Metropolitan Police as a constable.

The stairs he was plodding up now were no harder than some of the steps he had climbed in those years, but serious application to the job in hand, backed by his educational standards, had won him a place at Bramshill and the early promotion to sergeant for those who survived the course there.

It was an unhappy chance that his first C.I.D. posting should have been to West End Central.

Ian McCourt was a natural puritan. Some of the sights he had seen and some of the things he had to do in London's square mile of vice had sickened his simple soul. When things had come to a head and he had been offered the chance of transfer to the Berkshire Force, he had jumped at it. He would not only be back in the country. He would be closer to his mother, who needed him now that her daughters had married and gone.

One more flight. He was glad to note that he was hardly out of breath.

It was the arrival of Superintendent Knott which had upset him. He had recognized in him a hard professionalism, an ideal which he had once held himself and which was now slipping out of his reach in the backwater of Hannington.

Mr. Mapledurham, the head of the Documents Division, had been warned to expect him. He examined the photocopy of the letter with expert attention, scratched the back of his neck and said, "A Crossfield Electric, I should say. Not a golf ball, though. The earlier mark."

Ian tried to look intelligent.

"A lot of machines are turning to the golf-ball type now. It might be an Olympia or a Hermes, but I don't think so. We can easily find out. Let's see what we've got. Short 'm' and 'w.' Serifs at top *and* bottom of the 'I.' Lateral at the bottom of the 'T.' That should be enough to be going on with."

Remembering Knott's instructions, McCourt said, "How long will it take?"

"Ten minutes, if the line's clear."

"Ten minutes?"

"That's right. We'll put it on the computer." He was scribbling out a message as he spoke and said to the young man who sat at the other desk, "Feed this into the magic box, would you, Les. Gent wants an answer quickish."

"I'd no idea," said Ian. "I imagined these things took weeks to work out."

"Some things take months. Some things take minutes. That's science for you. If it'd been a Ransmeyer we'd have had a lot more trouble. That's a communal type face, used by a lot of different machines. I'd guess this is a PLX face, which generally means a Crossfield."

"Will it make it easier, or less easy, if it does turn out to be an electric machine?"

"It won't make any difference in identifying the machine. Make it more difficult to peg it down to any one typist. With a manual machine you get variations in pressure. An electric machine smooths them out."

"But if I got hold of another letter typed on this machine, you'd be able to say for certain that they both came from the same machine? Sorry. That was a bit confused, but you see what I mean."

"I see what you mean and the answer's yes. Provided the two samples were typed reasonably soon after each other. Machines develop different peculiarities as they grow older."

"Like people," said Ian.

Soon after that Les came back and said, "You're right. It was a Crossfield Mark Four Electric."

Mr. Mapledurham was consulting a large book. He said, "Crossfield Mark Four. Ex-factory at the end of 1973. Available in the shops early in 1974. I'll make one guess about your machine. It doesn't come from an office. If it had been bashed by an office typist for several years the type face would be a lot more worn. Anyway, this letter wasn't typed by a professional."

"How can you tell?"

"Spacing and alignment. If you wanted a guess, I'd say a private owner. Someone who did a fair amount of typing, but not a professional."

"Thank you," said Ian. "That's going to be very useful."

"Do you want a written report?"

Ian thought about Superintendent Knott and said, "Yes. I'm afraid we shall want a written report. I'll give you the address."

Mark Holbeck's agency occupied the third floor of an eighteenth-century house in Henrietta Street, Covent Garden. It looked across at the Tuscan portico of St. Paul's Church, designed by Grinling Gibbons, from which Samuel Pepys had watched a Punch and Judy show and in which Professor Higgins had met Eliza Doolittle.

Mark Holbeck was a young-old man with a sunburned and freckled bald patch in the middle of an outfield of sandy hair. If you asked what he did for a living he would tell you that he dealt in words and flesh, which meant in the jargon of his trade that he promoted both books and people.

The books were all around him, new copies in bright jackets. They filled every shelf in his office, spilled over onto the floor, occupied the window seats and trespassed onto his table. He shifted a couple off a chair and waved to Shilling to be seated.

"Of course I read all about it," he said. "It was in the later editions of the Saturday papers, and the Sunday papers made a meal of it."

First surprise. Lack of any real evidence of distress.

Shilling said, "She was your client. I imagine it must have come as a considerable shock to you."

Holbeck looked at him with the suspicion of a smile. "Sorry, Sergeant," he said. "No crocodile tears. Naturally I don't approve of people who kill my clients. It costs me ten per cent of their annual earnings. And in Katie's case that was beginning to add up to a very respectable sum of money. But no personal involvement."

"I wasn't suggesting anything of that sort, sir. I was just surprised that you didn't seem to mind much. On a personal level, I mean."

The two men looked at each other. Each was sizing the other up. Holbeck said, "What are you after, Sergeant? An analysis of her character or a list of her friends?"

"Both might be helpful, sir."

"I'll do what I can for you, on one condition."

"Yes, sir?"

"That you stop calling me sir. It's a habit policemen seem to have picked up from watching television."

Shilling grinned and said, "O.K. It's a deal."

"All right then. I first met Katie when she was eighteen. She had just left a top-line girls' school and wanted to behave like all the debby friends she'd made there, but she realized that she hadn't quite got the money to do it. Only two choices. She had to make money or marry it. And there were quite a few men—old men"—Holbeck's mobile mouth wrinkled at the corners—"who were prepared to buy her, even at the price of matrimony. She was sensible enough to say no. And she started out on the other route. She had no acting experience, so it was tough going. She got a job as a researcher with one of the independent television companies. A producer who liked her looks—correction, who liked her—wangled her a spot in one of their advertising quickies. And it *was* a wangle. He'd have had to get round Equity rules, but he did it. That was the beginning."

Holbeck stopped. He was looking back seven years, and some of the things he was seeing seemed not to please him.

He said, "You need just one quality to succeed in that field. It isn't beauty and it isn't brains, though both are useful. It's a rock-hard, chilled-steel determination to succeed. You asked me just now if I liked Katie. I didn't like her. But I respected her. One day—it was after she'd been working for about two years and making peanuts out of it—Rodney Ruoff the photographer made an approach. Through me, of course. I'd been half expecting it. Katie was playing down her age in those early commercials. Down to fourteen or even younger. Girls with small bones and unextravagant figures can go on doing that for a surprisingly long time. Rodney was very interested in young girls. And boys. He's known in the trade as 'Rod the Sod.' He's also a brilliant photographer and really has got some sort of pull with the television studios. Katie knew all about him. She asked my advice. I said, 'Steer clear of him. He's dangerous.' She said, 'If I was able to handle you, Mark, I ought to be able to handle him.' And off she trotted to his studio near the Kings Road."

Holbeck paused again, then said, "I'm damned if I know why I'm telling you all this. It must be because you've got such a disingenuous sort of face. You don't look like a policeman at all. When you first came in, I thought you were another hopeful pop star. Sorry."

Shilling was unoffended. He said, "It is a fact that people do talk to me. But not often as usefully as you're doing. So please go on. How did Ruoff get on with her?"

"I'm not sure. He certainly took some wonderful photographs of her—dressed, half dressed and undressed. And peddled them round the studios. Whether he got anything else out of her, I rather doubt. In fact, I'm pretty certain, if anyone got anything out of anyone it was the other way round." He smiled. "I remember I ran into Ruoff at a party about a year ago. Katie was a big property by then and, knowing he had an interest in her, naturally I was ready to talk about her. As soon as I mentioned her name, Ruoff went the color of a beetroot. I thought he was going to burst into flames. He squeaked out, in that funny high-pitched voice of his, 'Don't talk to me about her, Mark. Don't mention that bitch to me. She's a criminal. She's a thief. Why did you ever send her to me?' I had to remind him that it was the other way round. He'd sent for her himself. But he wasn't listening. He was too bloody angry."

"Did you gather what he was angry about?"

"Not exactly. I gathered that she'd lifted some of his property, but done it so cleverly that he couldn't go to the police. You'd better ask him. I imagine you'll be wanting a word with him."

"I'll be seeing him next. Will you tell me something else. That is, if you don't mind. It's rather a personal question."

"You alarm me."

"When you were talking to Katie about this photographer chap, she said, 'If I was able to handle you, I ought to be able to handle him.' Did she mean anything in particular by that?"

"I knew I was talking too much," said Holbeck gloomily. He thought about it. Outside, a motorist tried to go around the Covent Garden piazza the wrong way and got spoken to by the driver of a vegetable lorry.

At last Holbeck said, "All right. Confession is said to be good for the soul. I made a fool of myself. Mind you, I was seven years younger then. And you can take that smirk off your face, Sergeant. This isn't going to be a sex story. No. It was Katie's contract. I've got a standard form, drafted by my own lawyer. When I showed it to Katie she opened those innocent eyes wide and said, 'Oh, we don't need anything like *that*, surely. It's much too legal for poor little me. I wouldn't understand a word of it. If we must have something in writing—you know, about the ten per cent and all that—just give me a bit of paper. I'll jot down what I think we've agreed and we'll sign it here and now." And she sat straight down and did just that. Ten lines of school-girl handwriting. I've got it in my safe over there. Any time I feel I've been smart I take it out and read it. It's an excellent corrective to self-esteem. Because she'd slipped in a final sentence which said, 'Agreement to be firm for two years and then renegotiable.'"

"And that wasn't a good idea?"

"As far as I was concerned it was a lousy idea. When these kids start out, it's make-or-break and it usually takes a year or two to show which it's going to be. If they're a flop, they want to get out anyway. If they're a success, that's when you begin to get back some of what you've put into them. In fact it took Katie almost exactly two years to make the grade. It was that song that helped. Remember it? 'What Are They Like in Your House?'" He hummed the well-known tune.

"I was at school when it came out," said Shilling. "We used to sing a rather coarser version of the second line."

"Any song which can be perverted is halfway to success. It was short-lived, but it was dynamite while it lasted. It blew Katie up into stardom almost overnight. That's when I hoped she'd forgotten what was written on that paper."

"But she hadn't?"

"She'd made a copy and she'd kept it. She showed it to me sitting where you are now, with a wide smile on her face. She said, 'You realize I can walk away whenever I like, Mark. There are plenty of people would be glad to have me now.' And she trotted out the names of some of my rivals. And that's the way it was from then on. Whenever we had an argument; she'd say, 'All right, Mark. If you don't like it, I'm off.' And then, of course, I'd have to knuckle under. I don't think she actually meant to leave. She just liked having the whip hand. And cracking the whip every now and then."

Shilling thought about this. It opened up a rather startling line of thought. He said, "Are you telling me she had a sadistic streak?"

"That's rather overstating the çase. You don't call a kitten sadistic when you see it playing with a ball of string or chasing a leaf."

"No. But I might when it grows up and becomes a cat chasing a mouse. Do you think she tried the same game on with Ruoff?"

"You'd better ask him," said Holbeck. "Only keep upwind of him. When he gets excited he's inclined to spit."

Ruoff's house-cum-studio was in Chelverton Mews, which lies north of the Kings Road. It had three tubs of hydrangeas in front of it and a big white metal knocker in the shape of a bull's head on the scarlet front door. Shilling seized the bull by the horns and knocked. When this produced no response he tried the door, found it unfastened and went in.

A notice on the wall of the entrance hall said, "Studio Upstairs. Excelsior." An enlarged photograph of a human hand pointed upward. Shilling went up. It was one of those tall thin London houses which have their living rooms on the second floor. A further hand pointed up a further flight of steps. Bedroom floor. Further steps—scrubbed and uncarpeted. Above him a murmur of voices. A notice on the door at the top said, "Pray Enter." He went in. It was a small room and was empty.

The wall opposite the door was entirely covered by a photomontage made up of heads, bodies, arms and legs. Some of the heads were upside down. The arms and legs had been arranged into groups in a floral pattern. The effect in that small brightly lit room was hypnotic.

He was staring at it when a door in the left-hand wall opened and a boy came out. He was wearing gray flannel shorts and a cricket shirt. Shilling guessed his age as twelve or thirteen. He said, "Excuse me. I was wondering if your father was anywhere about."

"About what?" said the boy.

"I mean, could I have a word with him."

The boy said, "You'd have to shout pretty loud to do it from here. He lives in Southwark."

"Then I take it Mr. Ruoff's not your father."

"That's right. And I'm not his son."

"Who are you?"

"Me? I'm one of his favorite models. If you've come to have your photograph taken, Rod's in there. Got to be off. Got another engagement.

"How old are you?"

"Ninety-nine," said the boy. "Next birthday. Goodbye for now." He departed and his footsteps went clattering down the stairs. Shilling stood looking after him.

The murmur of voices which he had heard as he was coming up broke out again. It was louder now and came from behind the door in the left-hand wall. Shilling opened it cautiously and looked in. The first impression he got was of blinding light, directed not at him, but toward the far end of the room. Light and heat. The room was overpoweringly hot. It stank vilely of sweat and of some scented stuff which had been splashed about, presumably to hide the smell of the sweat.

On a low stage, bathed in the full glare of the lamps, two young men were engaged in a wrestling match. He thought at first sight that they were naked, but then saw that they were wearing flesh-colored tights. A squeaky voice from behind the lamps said, "Hold it," and the wrestlers froze into immobility. "Left hand a little higher, love. Pull his wrist up behind his back. You aren't really hurting him."

"He bloody is."

"Hold it."

"For Christ's sake, Rod, I'm getting cramp."

"That's it. All right, relax. And shut that bloody door."

Shilling, who could already feel the sweat running down his face, backed toward the door. The voice said, "See what he wants, Louie. But outside. For God's sake, this isn't a public waiting room."

A paunchy man, wearing off-white trousers and a singlet, followed Shilling out into the anteroom and slammed the door. He said, "Mussen come barging in there, chummy. Rod gets very up-tight when he's working. He's artistic, see."

"I'm sorry," said Shilling, mopping his forehead with his handkerchief. "It's very hot in there, isn't it?"

"It's the lamps. You'll get used to it. Turn sideways a moment."

"Why?"

"Profile, lad. That's the important thing. Not bad. Not bad at all."

"You've got it wrong," said Shilling. "I haven't come here to have my photograph taken."

"Then what the hell have you come here for?"

"To talk to Mr. Ruoff." Shilling took out his warrant card and slid it across the table.

The man looked down at the card without touching it, looked up again at Shilling and said, "You could have fooled me. I'll tell him." He departed into the studio, closing the door carefully behind him. Then a murmur of voices, which went on for a long time. Shilling composed himself to wait. He was determined on one thing. He was not going into that stinking hothouse again. Minutes ticked by. Then the inner door opened and a small man bounced out. He had pink cheeks and a gray beard which jutted from his chin as though it had been trained in espalier. It waggled when he spoke.

He said, "I've got nothing to say to you. This is a respectable establishment. Regularly inspected. Licensed by the London County Council. Passed by the health authorities and the fire authorities."

"Do the authorities know that you employ juvenile models?"

"I've no idea what you're talking about."

"That boy who just came out of your studio."

"A relative. Paying me a visit."

"He might have been a relative, of course. What he said was that he was one of your favorite models."

"Joking, Sergeant. You know what boys are. They say the first thing that comes into their heads."

"The first things people say are often the truth," said Shilling. "Actually, I didn't come here to talk about your studio. Or only indirectly. The person I wanted to ask you about was Miss Steelstock."

Up to that point Ruoff had been standing. Now he came across and sat down, very slowly, at the table opposite to Shilling. He said, "You're referring to Katie Steelstock, of course."

"Yes."

"Who was killed two days ago."

"Yes."

"Apart from the fact that I took a number of publicity photographs of her some years ago, I can tell you nothing about her at all."

"You did a little more than that, didn't you?"

"Meaning?"

"Using your influence to get her a start in television."

Ruoff's babyish mouth opened in what might have been the beginning of a smile. A tip of pink tongue looked out. He said, "Who have you been talking to?"

"I had a word with her agent, Mark Holbeck."

"You mustn't believe all that agents tell you. The only way I influence anyone is by taking beautiful, beautiful photographs. The eye of the camera, Sergeant, which never lies, but seldom tells the whole truth."

The inner door opened and the two young men came out. They had put on track suits. They looked incuriously at Shilling and one of them said, "Anything more, Rod?"

"I'll tell you when this lot come out," said Ruoff. "If they're as good as I think they're going to be, there'll certainly be more." As the door closed behind them he said, "An interesting pair. Cousins. They both have beautiful bodies. Did you know that it was Michelangelo who first exploited the full potentiality of the male body?" He got up. "I'm afraid I can't help you any further, Sergeant."

Shilling got up, too. He said, "What did Katie steal from you?"

He saw the color rising like a tide from the veins of the neck into the cheeks, turning pink to dark red and red to crimson.

"Who said anything about stealing?"

"Actually it was you. Something you said to Mark Holbeck at a party." Shilling was watching him closely.

"Did I say that? I'd forgotten. It can't have been very important, can it?"

"Possibly not."

"And in any event, if such a thing did happen, it happened years ago. It could hardly affect your inquiries."

"Mark Holbeck said last year. And until I know what she took from you, sir, I'm in no position to judge."

If his forehead was made of glass, thought Shilling, I swear I'd be able to see those brain cells working. He knows damn well what Katie stole. He's thinking it out, in all its aspects. Will it be to his advantage to tell me or not? Will it damage him in any way? Dare he tell me? Dare he *not* tell me?

In the end Ruoff evidently came to some sort of conclusion. He said, "If I do happen to remember, Sergeant, I'll let you know."

And Shilling had to be content with that.

13

Mrs. Havelock came into the operations room at the Hannington police station like a very large liner towing a very small tug. The tug was Sim. She had him fast by one hand.

Knott said, "Please sit down. You too, lad. I gather you've got something to tell me."

"It's Sim here who's got to do the telling." She looked down at her son, who was very pale. "It should be the older boy, Roney, but he wouldn't come, so Sim's got to do it alone."

It took ten minutes of patient questioning to get the story into some sort of shape.

"Just those two occasions you and your brother saw Jonathan and Katie by the boathouse?"

Sim nodded.

"And when you got there they were lying on the grass together?"

"Yes."

"Could you see what they were doing?"

"Not really."

Knott paused. He knew only too well with what delicacy a nine-year-old witness had to be handled.

"O.K.," he said. "They were just lying there. Then what happened?"

"Then they went into the boathouse."

"How did they do that, when the door was locked?"

"Oh, everyone knows how to do that. You just put your hand through that place where the glass is gone and turn the handle. The one on the little door."

Knott nodded. He had read Shilling's report. He said, "What then?"

"There was no point hanging around. We came home."

"Did that happen both times? I mean, going into the boathouse?"

"No, that was only the second time."

"How long ago was the first time?"

"I can't exactly remember."

Mrs. Havelock said, "Was it holidays or term, Sim?"

"Holidays. Last holidays. Just before term started."

"That makes it early May," said Mrs. Havelock.

"And the second time?"

"I can't exactly remember. It was before the regatta."

"Long before?"

"Not very long before."

"That would make it early July," said Mrs. Havelock. She had one eye on Sim. He was going to be sick and she wanted to get him outside before it happened. Knott picked up the warning in her eye. He said, "That's fine, Sim. You've done very well. Only one more question. You're nine. Right? Nearly ten. Old enough to know what telling the truth means."

"Oh, yes."

"Because you may have to stand up in court and say all this to a judge."

"Outside," said Mrs. Havelock.

She got him into the courtyard in the nick of time.

*   *   *

Knott had kept Dennis Farr at Reading informed about the progress of the investigation. He had telephoned him each evening and sent him copies of all the interrogation reports. He took this extra trouble because he knew that it would be repaid in cooperation.

As he drove over to Reading he could already see the bones of the Crown case. There were gray areas, to be sure, and shadowy corners, but that was the way with murder investigations. Some points of detail were never cleared up. There were questions which remained unanswered even after trial and conviction. Why should a man who had poisoned his wife with lead arsenite and watched her die in agony keep more than twenty photographs of her pinned up around his bedroom? Why had the college porter who had murdered two girl students wasted long minutes after each killing smashing up their bicycles? These were problems for psychologists, not for policemen. They needed investigation only if they were going to form part of the defense case.

"Not much doubt who did it," said Farr. "The difficulty is going to be proving it."

"As bloody always," said Knott. "Did you fix things for me?"

"Both sound men. And very willing to help. I could see the point of having a word with Cowie, of course. But why the schoolmaster?"

"I want to find out why Limbery was sacked."

"Resigned by mutual agreement was what I heard."

"I don't believe he'd have left the school unless he was forced to. Remember what Katie called him when they had that slanging match? A schoolmaster manqué."

"You might be right. I certainly got the impression he enjoyed working with kids."

"Too thoroughly perhaps?"

Farr said, "I shouldn't have thought there was anything like that. You never can tell, of course. Is it important?"

"It would give us a motive. He's unbalanced. I don't mean mad. But he's got a hair-trigger temper. And Katie had a saw-edged tongue. Suppose she said something to him like, 'You're no good to a girl. Small boys are your scene.' He'd lash out without thinking twice about it."

"He'd lash out," agreed Farr, "but that doesn't mean he'd plan a cold-blooded killing days or weeks later."

"That's what I thought, at first," said Knott. "*But suppose we've all been jumping to conclusions*. Suppose that note was genuine. Suppose he really did want to make things up and put things back on their old footing."

"Rolling round on the punt cushions to prove he could do it."

"Right. *But suppose Katie had quite different ideas*. Suppose she planned to spend a few enjoyable minutes telling him exactly what she thought of him. You great big poof, go chase a choirboy. What then?"

"He'd blow his top, no question. But do you think you could make a jury understand it?"

"Twenty years ago—even ten—I wouldn't have cared to try. Nowadays I think they'd take it."

"I suppose you might call that progress," said Farr, "of a sort. Look in on the way back and tell me how you got on."

"It's all right," said Roney. "I told him you didn't want to do it. I told him Mum made you."

"Good," said Sim. They were sitting on the fence at the bottom of the garden. Since Rosina had sneaked up on them they had avoided the veranda. "What did he say?"

"He said O.K. He understood."

"Good."

"What I can't see is why everyone thinks it must be him who did it."

"It could be anyone."

"That's right."

"It could be the rector."

"Or old Mr. Beaumorris."

They considered them. Neither of them seemed plausible murderers. Roney said, "I'll tell you what. What about Mr. Mariner? It could easily be him. He was always hanging round the boathouse."

"I'd rather it was him than Johnno."

"I'll tell you something else. Johnno isn't going to let them arrest him."

"How's he going to stop them?"

"He'll fight them."

"He couldn't fight them all."

"He could. He's got lots of weapons. He showed them to me. He's got a saber and a kukri."

"What's a kukri?"

"It's a thing the Gurkhas have. A sort of curved knife. They used them to cut off Japs' heads."

Sim tried to visualize a row of decapitated policemen.

"And a swordstick. And a pistol."

"Did he show you the pistol?"

"No. He's got that hidden somewhere. But I saw the swordstick. It's got a catch just under the handle and you pull it and it comes out—*wheesh*."

Not decapitated. Impaled. It seemed tidier somehow.

Mr. Ferris, headmaster of Coverdales, was a distinguished scientist, a fact evidenced by the string of initials after his name. He was small and squat and his iron gray hair stood up from out of his head like a crown of thorns. It was clear at first encounter that he was a man you did not take liberties with.

He said to Knott, "I accept your authority to ask me questions. I have an equal right not to answer them."

"That is so, sir."

"I am prepared to answer them on the understanding that anything I say is off the record. That I shall, if necessary, deny that I said it and shall not be asked to give evidence in any court proceedings."

"Quite so, sir," said Knott easily.

"Totally off the record, Superintendent."

"Totally, sir."

"Then suppose you switch off whatever gadget it is you've brought with you."

Knott had noticed the curious object on the desk between them. It was made of black metal and was about the size of a cricket ball. The top was opaque milk-colored glass. Behind the glass a yellow eye moved and flickered.

"It's called an 'Encore,' Superintendent. It records any instrument receiving or emitting electric impulses within a range of about a hundred feet. There are larger instruments with much longer ranges. This is what you might call a pocket model."

"Interesting," said Knott. He slipped one hand into the side pocket of his jacket and switched off his tape recorder. "To tell you the truth, I'd forgotten I had it switched on." He told this lie without embarrassment.

The yellow eye centered in the glass and stood coldly still.

"Very well, Superintendent. What is it you want to know?"

"I'd like to find out why Limbery was sacked from this school."

"Sacked?"

"So I was told."

"The person who told you that was using an inaccurate piece of shorthand to describe a complex situation. It is quite true that Limbery did not take the initiative in the matter. He was happy here and got on well with the boys. Less well with the girls, but since he did no sixth-form teaching he didn't come across them much. And our pay here is good. Above Burnham Scale."

"Then," said Knott, "if he was happy here . . ."

Mr. Ferris was not to be diverted. He had an explanation to make and he proposed to offer it in the same logical way that he would have explained any natural phenomenon.

"When I said that he got on well with the boys, it would have been more accurate if I had said that he got on too well." Although Knott had not tried to speak, Mr. Ferris held up one hand as though rebuking an importunate student. "And when I say that, I do *not* mean that he made advances to them or interfered with them. Had he done so, he would indeed have been sacked. No. It was more subtle and more difficult. I think the truth of the matter is that he was the same age, mentally and emotionally, as the boys themselves. That is perhaps why he got on with them and not with the girls. Girls become adult more quickly."

Here he paused so long Knott ventured to say, "That hardly seems any reason for getting rid of him."

"You might not think so. But it had one unfortunate result. If any difference or difficulty arose, regardless of the rights or wrongs of the matter, he *always* took the side of the boys as against constituted authority. This did not make him popular with other members of the staff, who had more old-fashioned ideas about discipline. It came to a head over one particular boy. Another member of the staff wished to punish him. Limbery, I am told, threatened to kill him if he did so."

My God, thought Knott, I wish I could get the tape recorder turned on. His hand was actually in his pocket when he saw the yellow eye on the desk looking at him. He took his hand out again.

"That wasn't something I could overlook. And it was the culmination of a number of smaller instances of this sort of disloyalty."

"Sticking up for the boys against the staff?"

"*Trahison des clercs,*" said Mr. Ferris. "Uncommon in schools, but the bane of our newer universities."

Knott thought about it as he drove back into Reading. He could subpoena Mr. Ferris and despite any promises would have done so without a scruple if he thought it would assist the Crown's case. But he had had some unhappy experiences with witnesses dragged into court against their will. They might not tamper with facts, but they managed somehow to put a different slant on them.

What did it demonstrate, anyway? That Limbery had a violent and uncontrolled temper. They knew that already.

"Frankly," said Arnold Cowie, news editor of the Reading *Sun*, "it just wasn't good enough. A lot of descriptive stuff. Flames leaping sky-high. Smoke billowing. Readers don't want that sort of thing. They can imagine it for themselves. They want *facts*."

"And Limbery's account was a bit thin on facts?"

"I could have done it without leaving my house."

"You mean that, literally?"

Cowie thought about it. It had suddenly occurred to him where the questions were leading.

"No," he said. "Perhaps not literally. He reported

something the skipper of the local fire brigade said to him. That could have been checked, so he wouldn't have made it up. He was there, all right. But I don't think he stayed very long."

"What makes you think that?"

"Did you read our account—the one we did publish?"

"No. But I'd like to."

"I'll get you a copy." Cowie spoke into the telephone. "It's good stuff. It was sent in by a local stringer. The roof of part of the factory collapsed and trapped two of the firemen inside. The brigade lowered one of their ladders down to horizontal and used it as a battering ram. Smashed a way in through the side of the building. Just got them out in time."

"And none of this was in Limbery's account?"

"Not a word. Nothing but flames and sparks and hot air."

"I see. I wonder if you could give me a few timings. For instance—when did the fire start?"

"I don't know when it started. We heard about it around a quarter to ten. I'd just got back from dinner and the news was on the blower as I got here."

"And you telephoned Limbery at once?"

"Right."

"And he answered the telephone at once?"

"Not at once. He was in his bath."

"But within a few minutes?"

"Right. He said he'd finish getting dressed and go straight out."

"Let's say he left at ten o'clock. How long would it take him to get to Goring?"

"Twenty minutes, if he hurried. A few minutes to get over the bridge and through Goring. The paper factory's half a mile out, on the Oxford road."

"I suppose you don't know exactly when the roof collapsed?"

"I might be able to tell you that." Cowie had the stringer's report in front of him by now, three sheets of foolscap slashed by the editorial blue pencil. He said, "We didn't use it all, of course. But I'm sure there was something. Yes. That's right. The rescue effort I was talking about was put on by the Streatley and Goring brigade. Here's what I was looking for. 'The Wallingford contingent, who must have turned out with remarkable speed to be there on the stroke of eleven, were able to help with the latter stages on this courageous rescue.'"

"Then we can place the collapse of the roof at some minutes before eleven. Say between ten and five to eleven."

"That's a fair assumption."

"In other words, Limbery must have left the scene by a quarter to eleven. Having arrived at about a quarter past ten."

"It certainly looks like it."

"And when did he let you have his report? I gather he dictated it over the telephone."

"That's correct. We got it sometime after midnight. We were going to set it up when this other chap steamed up on his motorbike with his much better account. So we scrapped Limbery's." Mr. Cowie smiled thinly. "He still wants us to pay for it."

"Did he say where he was speaking from?"

"From a public call box. It cost him fifty pence. That's one of the things he was complaining about."

Knott thought about it. It was clear that Limbery had told him less than the whole truth. But a man could lie about some things and tell the truth about others.

The news editor was looking at him curiously. He said, "I hope what I've told you has helped."

"It's been most helpful."

"Then if you could—"

"All right," said Knott with a grin which showed all his teeth. "When I'm ready to charge someone you shall hear about it first."

Back at the Reading police station he told Farr what he had found out, skipping most of what Mr. Ferris had told him and concentrating on the timings.

Farr said, "It was a fluke, of course, the fire happening when it did, but he grabbed the chance to give himself an alibi. He could have been back in Hannington by eleven. Easily. The difficulty's going to be to prove it. Everyone round that factory would have been too bloody busy to notice when people came and went."

"I thought about that," said Knott. "And here's where I'll want a bit of help. Limbery told me he phoned in his story from a public call box on the Oxford road. We know he was telling the truth about it being a call box. I had a word with the shorthand typist at the paper who took it down. She heard the tenpenny pieces going in and Limbery cursing every time he had to find another one. At night you get four minutes for tenpence. So we know he was in that box more than sixteen minutes, maybe twenty."

"If his account was any length he'd need all of twenty minutes. You know what these girls are. He'd have to spell all the names for her."

"I'm not questioning the length of time he took," said Knott. "What I was wondering was just where he found a public call box on that bit of the Oxford road. I know it quite well. There are two A.A. boxes, but he's not a member of the A.A. and anyway he said quite clearly a *public* call box. So what I'd like you to do for me is this. Find out from the Post Office what public call boxes there are between, say, Streatley on the east and Pangbourne on the west." Farr got out a map and they studied it. "No. Spread it a little further. Make it a square. Moulsford, Yattendon, Pangbourne, Whitchurch. Then take those two men of yours off the house-to-house inquiry they've been doing at Hannington and put them onto the call boxes."

"Hoping," said Farr, "to find an indignant member of the public who wanted to use a particular box and was kept waiting for twenty minutes."

"Right," said Knott. "The *Sun* can provide you with a photograph. They had one in connection with a personality piece they did about that song he wrote. And I'll bet you a level quid that if we locate that call box it'll be a damned sight nearer Hannington than away out on the Oxford road."

"I don't bet on certainties," said Farr. He said it with such conviction that Knott's head jerked up. He said, "Come on, Dennis. You've got something for me."

"Maybe," said Farr. "Maybe not. I won't know for sure unless you happen to know the make and number of Limbery's car."

Knott thought for a moment and then said, "It's an old Morris Traveller. And the number is ABB 9190 G."

"What a memory!"

"It's not a question of memory," said Knott. He was watching Farr turning over the pages of a police logbook and thinking, I wonder if he really has got something. He's looking very pleased with himself. He said, "Whenever I've got my eye on someone, someone I may want to pull in, I naturally get the number and description of his car. If he makes a break for it, ten to one he'll take his car."

Farr had found the page he wanted and was running his finger down it. He had stopped listening to Knott, who continued placidly. "Then I can put out an all-stations call without wasting any time. Minutes can be precious at a moment like that."

"ABB 9190 G, you said?"

"Right."

"And Limbery drove back across the Pangbourne bridge at some time between twelve and one?"

"Right."

"You're sure about the time?"

"He said he noticed the time on the Town Hall clock."

"Then he's a liar."

Knott said, "Ah-h-h." It was like a letting out of long-held breath.

"That was the night we had a dragnet out to try and pull up the villains who did Yattendon House. Remember? We had blocks on every bridge over that stretch of the Thames. They went on at eleven and didn't come off until three. Here's a list of the cars they checked, Pangbourne bridge. Makes. Registration numbers and times. No ABB 9190 G. No Morris Travellers either."

"Beautiful," said Knott softly.

14

The Coroner said, "You are Charles Knott of 56 Albany Street, St. John's Wood, N.W. 8, a Detective Superintendent in the Metropolitan Police Force, and you are in charge of the police inquiries into this case?"

"I am, sir."

"Have you concluded your inquiries?"

"No, sir."

"I understand it will assist your inquiries if I adjourn the case."

"Yes, sir."

The Coroner directed his gaze on the five men and four women in the jury box and said, "This is an inquiry into the death of Kate Louise Steelstock at a point adjacent to the West Hannington Boat Club premises on the night of Friday, August fifteenth, in circumstances suggesting murder. I shall adjourn the inquest for fourteen days, that is to say until Tuesday, September second."

"Witnesses in this case may leave the court," said the Coroner's office.

The jury, and the members of the public who had packed the room to suffocation, looked baffled. The press, who had expected nothing more, looked bored. A reporter caught Knott as he was making his way out and said, "How's it going, Superintendent?"

"Not too bad, son."

"An arrest imminent?"

"Well now, you'd hardly expect me to be as definite as that, would you?"

This was accompanied by what could have been a wink. The hint could hardly have been more deliberate. The reporter, who had been a long time at the game, said, "Knott's got his teeth into something. Won't be long now."

Back at the operations room Knott settled into his chair and started to leaf through the brown-covered green-laced folder that Sergeant Esdaile had strung together for him. From his smaller table, Shilling looked across at him. He was remembering like moments in other cases.

"Well," said Knott at last, "so what have we got? We know that Limbery and Katie used the boathouse as a rendezvous for lovemaking. We know that the note found in Katie's bag probably came from him. There's no direct evidence. We haven't traced the typewriter. But there's evidence in the wording of the note itself. We know it was sent by the man who killed her, because he searched for it. First, in her bag. Then, when he couldn't find it there, at her house."

"Sound nerve," said Shilling.

Knott accepted this remark as a criticism. He said, "All right. I agree. It doesn't fit in with the picture we've got of Limbery. But remember, he was desperate. He had to have that note. If it was found, he was finished. Next point, he lied about where he was and what he did that night. Why?"

"Obvious answer, because the whole trip was set up to give him an alibi."

"Obvious answers can be right."

Shilling knew what his job was. He was critic. He was counsel for the defense. He said, "You're building up two quite different characters, aren't you? One's a man with no control over his temper who flies off the reel because of something spiteful Katie says to him, hits her on the head too hard and finds himself with a corpse on his hands. The other's the sort of man who could make a plan to get her to that particular spot, taking care to fix himself up with an elaborate alibi first. They don't match."

"I think there's an answer to that," said Knott. "We know, now, that Katie had another side to her character. She liked to have people on the end of a string. So that she could give it a twitch from time to time and watch them dance. There are women like that. Remember Mrs. Huntingdon?"

"Yes," said Shilling with a grimace, "and I remember what her husband did to her when she twitched it once too often."

"Right. Now suppose Katie had something on Limbery."

"What sort of thing?"

"Anything. Going too far with a boy, most likely. Her brother was at Coverdales. He could have known about it. And told Katie. She'd have enjoyed tweaking Limbery."

"All right," said Shilling. "But here's another point. If he did send her that note, just how and when did he get it to her? It wasn't sent through the post. And it had to reach her late in the day, or there was no chance she'd bring it with her to the dance. There's only one way he could have done that—"

The telephone interrupted him.

Knott picked up the receiver and listened, with no

more than an occasional grunt. At the end he said, "Thank you, Dennis. That sounds very promising. I'll send someone from here to take a statement."

He replaced the receiver carefully and said, "How do you explain this one away? At ten past twelve, when Limbery, according to his statement, was having a snack in that motel on the Oxford road, preparatory to crossing the river at Pangbourne—in an invisible car—he was also occupying a public telephone box on Streatley Common, *south* of the river. To the growing fury of a Mrs. Mason, who wanted to use the phone. She recognized Limbery at once from the photograph. No hesitation. She said, 'When you've watched someone for twenty minutes preventing you from using a telephone, his face gets sort of fixed in your mind.'"

"She sounds a useful sort of witness," agreed Shilling.

Knott had closed the folder and was holding it in one hand. He seemed to be weighing it. He said, "I'd like you to take this lot up to the D.P.P.'s office. You can strip it down a bit. Leave out the photographs and maps, but see that you've got all the statements. Including Mrs. Mason's, as soon as we've got hers. And Dr. Farmiloe's report. And my daily summaries. And a copy of the note we found in Katie's bag. Ask for the Principal Assistant Director in Charge of Southern Region. He's a man called Adlington. He's got three chins and stutters like a machine gun, but he's very sound. I'll tell him you're coming. Give him the file to read and ask if he or the Deputy Director can see me at nine o'clock tomorrow. Understood?"

"Understood," said Shilling. He thought, The old man's playing this one very carefully. Natural enough if he's looking for promotion, I suppose. Bit uncharacteristic, all the same.

A word on the internal telephone brought in Esdaile and McCourt. Both looked as though they had been expecting the summons. The electricity in the air was unmistakable.

Knott said, "I've got jobs for both of you. Ian, I want you to talk to Mrs. Mason. Here's her address. She's got a statement for us. As soon as you've got it, let Bob have it. Eddie, I want you to get hold of Limbery. He'll either be at his office or his house. Don't make a big occasion of it. Just tell him I'd like him to step round here. If he asks why, be vague. Say that something's cropped up and I want to ask him some questions. Right?"

McCourt said, "Aye," and took himself off. Esdaile hesitated for a moment and said, "What do I do if he won't come?"

"Let's worry about that when it happens," said Knott.

Sergeant Esdaile drew a blank at the *Gazette* office and devoted some thought to his next move. To ask a hair-trigger character like Jonathan Limbery to "step round" the short distance from his office to the police station, that was one thing. To ask him to make the journey on foot, under escort, from his house in Belsize Road was quite different. It would have to be done by car. Fortunately the Chief Inspector's car was parked in the yard. Dandridge said, "Certainly you can borrow it. What do you want it for?"

"To bring in Limbery."

"Bring him in?"

"For questioning."

"Well, do it tactfully," said Dandridge.

Be vague, said Knott. Do it tactfully, said Dandridge. Bloody useful advice. If they wanted Limbery, why didn't they go and fetch him themselves? He knew the answer to that one. If there was a cock-up and someone had to carry the can, it was going to be poor old Eddie.

A crowd outside the door of number 17. Something up? No, it was just a gang of boys who had been to pay Jonathan a visit. Tim Nurse, Terry Gonville and the Havelock tearaways. Funny how the kids hung around him all the time. Better give them a minute to get clear.

Jonathan was standing inside his open front window as Esdaile drew up. Some instinct for trouble had made the boys stop and turn to stare. Esdaile cursed quietly. The last thing he wanted was an audience. He started up the front path.

Jonathan said, "What do you want, Eddie?"

"Can I come in?"

"Not until you tell me what you want."

"The Superintendent wants to ask you a few questions."

"Then let him come and ask them."

"He'd be obliged if you'd come round to the station."

"To help the police with their inquiries. Isn't that the correct expression?"

"Well—"

"Well," said Jonathan, suddenly savage, "you can give the Superintendent a message from me. He can go jump in the river. And if he never surfaces again, so much the better. Bad luck on the fishes, of course."

The boys liked this.

Esdaile said, "Look. Be reasonable. I'm not enjoying this either. I'm just obeying orders."

"Who said I wasn't enjoying it?" Jonathan swung one leg over the low sill and climbed out onto the front path. It could now be seen that he was holding a polished black walking stick in his hand, a stick with an ivory handle, which he twisted. The long bright blade came out.

"Now don't be stupid," said Esdaile, backing down the path.

Mrs. Havelock had been out shopping and had stopped to pick up Sim and Roney. She took in the scene in one comprehensive glance. Limbery, Esdaile, the rapt boys, two delivery men, a mother with a child in a stroller and, thank goodness for possible support, Gerry Gonville taking his old cocker spaniel for a walk.

She crossed the pavement in three quick strides and stepped into the telephone box.

"You're trespassing," said Jonathan, "on my property." The blade flickered. Esdaile retreated another step. "I have the right to defend my property, by force if necessary."

"You've got no right to threaten me."

"You've got it all wrong. It's not me who's threatening you. It's you and other pigs like you"—the blade flashed again—"who threaten the peace and privacy of people too timid to stand up for themselves. This time you've picked the wrong victim. Now take yourself off, you great looby."

The point of the blade was flickering in Esdaile's face. He stepped back. One of the watching boys laughed. The Sergeant, angry himself now, plunged forward.

The point of the blade slid through the top of his arm.

The only person who did not seem to be paralyzed into inactivity was Group Captain Gonville. He hitched the loop in the dog's lead over a railing, dropped his walking stick, pulled out a handkerchief, folded it into a pad and clapped it over the wound with one hand while he felt for the pressure point with his other hand.

"If he's hit an artery," he said, "we'll have to put some sort of tourniquet on it until help arrives." He had his back to Limbery and ignored him. "Let's have your tie, Terry."

"Tie?" said his son blankly.

"And quick."

Terry pulled off the school tie he was wearing. Limbery was watching them with a smile on his face. Mrs. Havelock emerged from the telephone box. Before she could say anything they heard the car coming. It cornered with a squeal of tires and stopped.

Knott got out. He moved across without haste to where Sergeant Esdaile was sitting on the pavement, looking pale but angry, his back propped against the garden wall. The Group Captain had got his son's tie into position above the wound and was tightening it. He said, "It's all right, I think. No artery. Better be on the safe side, though."

Knott nodded, picked up the heavy ash-plant walking stick and walked toward Limbery holding it loosely in his right hand.

"Put down that sword," he said.

"Not on your life."

Knott continued to advance. Limbery said, "I've stuck one pig this morning. Let's make it a double."

As the blade came at him, Knott dropped onto one knee and swung the heavy stick in a circle. It hit Limbery with a crack on the outside of his knee. He gave a scream and keeled over, dropping the sword.

Knott straightened up, put one foot on the sword and said to the larger of the two delivery men, "I'll need a hand here."

Together they lifted Limbery into the back of the car.

Knott said, "Sit in with him and see that he doesn't

try to do anything silly." He turned to the Group Captain and said, "It might be best if you used the car Esdaile came in to take him to the hospital."

"Will do," said Gonville.

Mrs. Havelock said, "I'll take all the boys home. Climb in, kids."

The crowd dispersed slowly.

15

For nearly two days the second body had been lying half in, half out of the water among the tall rushes. It was on the opposite side to the towpath, the unexplored side of the river, a mile or more below Whitchurch. To get at it you would have had to wade across a backwater and force your way through the thorn bushes and scrub elder; and since no one had happened to do this, the body had lain in peace.

The bow wave from a river steamer had lifted it and carried it into its hiding place. Subsiding, it had deposited it on an underwater snag which had caught the belt of the raincoat and held it. A pair of swans had investigated it with supercilious yellow eyes and had turned away in disgust. So far the carnivores of the undergrowth had left it alone, but they would soon be busy. Unless, of course, another wave floated the body off into deep water, when it would be the turn of fish and the submarine parasites.

The Assistant Director of Public Prosecutions said, "He's saved you a bit of trouble, anyway. No need to think up a holding charge. He's thought one up for you. How's Esdaile?"

"He's all right. A clean flesh wound. He'll be back on the job in a day or two."

"Assaulting an officer in the course of his duty and causing him actual bodily harm. You could hold him on that, while you looked around for more evidence on the main charge."

"I could," said Knott. "But I wouldn't want to. I'd prefer to go the whole way now."

The Assistant Director said, "I agree. I think you've got more than enough to justify charging Limbery with murder. Short of finding someone who actually saw him do it, I really don't see how you could get any more."

"No one saw him," said Knott. "I'm sure of that. Before the moon got up the night was pitch black. And if anyone *had* been passing, I think he'd have killed them, too. It's lucky the Havelock kids weren't by ten minutes sooner. We might have had two other bodies on our hands."

"If that's the sort of man he is," said the Assistant Director, "the sooner we have him under hatches the better. It's your decision, of course. But you can take it that I'll back you all the way on this one."

"Thank you," said Knott.

"And Philip Frost would like a word with you before you go."

The Deputy Director, Philip Frost, brother of Mrs. Steelstock and uncle of Katie, was a portly person with a manner which combined the acerbity of the barrister he had once been with the smoothness of the politicians he had occasionally to deal with.

He said, "I'd like to congratulate you, Superintendent. I read the papers last night. I think you've done an excellent job. I don't know if you realize that it was I who asked the Assistant Commissioner to give you the assignment." He smiled. "I imagine you cursed him at the time."

Knott smiled, too. He said, "I confess I'd have liked one good night's sleep after the Oxford business. However, things seem to have come out all right. I had a lot of help from Sergeant Shilling."

"Bob's a good lad. We shan't forget him. Since we've gone so far so fast, do you think we could get the committal proceedings expedited? Could you be ready in a fortnight?"

"Quicker than that, if you want."

"We'll have to brief counsel. Davenport should be all right for the preliminaries. We'll get Mavor or Masterston for the Crown Court. It'll be at Reading. It won't come on before October at the earliest. That should give you all the time you want to tie up the loose ends. If there are any."

"There are three loose ends," said Knott slowly. "If I can tie up any one of them, I'd say the case really would be defense-proof. First and most important, of course, if that print on the cupboard door above Katie's desk can be brought out sharp enough for legal identification."

"The laboratory are working on it now."

"If we can't get that, I'd like to identify the typewriter that was used. I don't imagine that it was Limbery's own machine. He wouldn't be that stupid, but—"

"Enough if you can show he had access to it. Agreed. What else?"

"The third thing's more difficult. Sergeant Shilling pointed it out to me. Part of the killer's plan must have turned on the probability—maybe simply on the possibility—that Katie would bring the note with her to the rendezvous."

"He certainly expected her to do so. That's why he searched her bag."

"Quite so, sir. But there wasn't anything in the note itself which meant that she *had* to take it with her. Things, I mean, like complicated directions that she'd have to study. It was just 'Come to the usual place.'"

The Deputy Director said, "H'm. Yes. I see your point."

"I believe the only way he could have any hope she'd bring it along was by leaving it actually *in her car*, sometime during the day. And the later the better. To follow that up, we'll have to know exactly what her movements were on Friday. There's a lot of ground still to cover there. But if we could find someone who saw Limbery near her car during the afternoon, say, or the early evening, that should go a long way towards clinching it."

"Can't expect miracles," said the Deputy Director genially. "Any of those extra bits would be useful. Agreed. But they're only extras. You've got what matters. Motive, access and a string of lies afterwards. And remember this. The defense have got to put Limbery in the box. Or risk the most damaging construction being put on his refusal to give evidence. And once he gets into the box, from all I've heard of him, he'll hang himself five times over."

"A search warrant," said Mariner. "Certainly you can have one. My clerk will make it out for you. I should have thought, after what's happened, that you'd have every right to search his house without one."

"Better be on the safe side," said Knott.

"Are you looking for anything in particular? Or shouldn't I ask?"

"No secret about it. The buzz is that he had a collection of lethal weapons. There was talk of a revolver. He used to boast to the boys about it."

"Stupid," said Mariner. "Stupid as well as vicious."

*   *   *

Number 17 Lower Belsize Road was already a focus of local interest. Photographs of it had appeared in the press. Tradesmen and passers-by slowed their pace as they came to it, or stopped altogether to stare at the closed front door and the empty windows.

When Knott arrived, with McCourt and Esdaile in attendance, a crowd gathered as though by magic. Knott viewed his audience impassively. He knew that from now on most of his moves would have to be made under the stare of publicity. He said, "Does anyone happen to know who locked the house up?"

A woman said, "Parson did it. He's got the keys."

McCourt was already on his useful moped. He said, "I'll get them for you. Shouldn't take long."

The Reverend Bird was out, but his wife was at home and located the keys for him.

"Dicky thought it wasn't right to leave the house unlocked and the windows open," she said. "You know what people are like. They'd have been trampling all over it. Helping themselves to souvenirs, probably. I hope he did right."

"We're much obliged to him," said McCourt.

"He's taken this very hard, you know. He seems to think that something which happened in church might have upset Jonathan. You heard about that?"

"Aye. We all haird about it. It wasn't in any way your husband's fault."

"So I told him. But he's very worried. He went to Reading this morning, to the prison. To see if he could help."

"That was kind of him," said McCourt and managed to extract himself and the keys.

When he got back he found that the crowd had increased. Knott was sitting on the low front wall of the garden. A number of amateur photographers had already snapped him. He said, "You've been long enough. Come on, we'll go in round the back."

Although its owner had only been gone for twenty-four hours there was already a feeling of emptiness about the house, an impression of airlessness. No air coming through the windows, no air being breathed in the rooms.

Knott spent a few minutes instructing his assistants in the technique of searching and they then split up, taking a room each. It was Esdaile who unearthed the armory. No particular attempt had been made to hide the weapons. They were in an unlocked cupboard in the bedroom. A Japanese ceremonial sword, a Gurkha kukri, a German three-edged needle bayonet, a British pattern cavalry saber, a pair of foils.

"Just a big boy scout," said Knott. "I wonder where he kept the gun. If he had one."

The two sergeants resumed their search, but they found no gun. When they got back to the sitting room Knott was staring at a photograph in a leather frame which he had found on the mantelpiece. It was a family group, evidently taken some years ago.

"Do you know who they are?"

McCourt examined the picture and said, "Aye, that's Limbery on the right. The girls would be his two sisters. I've haird him talk of them. And the woman would be his mother. She's still alive, in a nursing home somewhere."

Knott pointed to the jagged edge of the photograph. "He's cut off a piece," he said. "Why would he do that?"

"That would be where his father was standing, no doubt."

"Why cut him out of the photograph?"

McCourt thought about it and said, "It might be because he disliked him. If you want something with his dabs on it, best place will be the kitchen."

The collection of weapons was taken back to the police station and locked in a cupboard. Knott said, "If we're to be ready for committal by Monday week we've got a lot of work to do. When I was talking to the Director I said there were three gaps I'd like to fill in and I'm allotting one to each of you. Bob, I want you to concentrate on Katie's movements on the Friday. I understand she went up to town by train. When did she go? How did she get to the station? If she took her own car, where did she leave it? Was anyone seen hanging round it?"

"You're thinking about that note?"

"Right. The likeliest thing is that someone slipped it into her car. Even if it had been left locked it could have been pushed through one of the side flaps, or something like that. Then I want to know who she saw in London. It could have been that photographer chap Ruoff. I can't see, at the moment, how he fits in."

"He's got a guilty conscience about something," agreed Shilling.

"Eddie, I want you to chase that typewriter. We know the make and year of the machine. Look at all the machines in his office, of course, but it's too much to hope you'll find it there. Then ask round the various people he might have borrowed one from. And get an advertisement drafted for the local papers. Any person who possesses or has any knowledge of a Crossfield Electric to communicate with the police. I don't care how widely it gets known that we're looking for this particular machine. The wider the better."

He swung around on Ian. "I want you to concentrate on Limbery's movements that night. He was out in his car and he must have used it to put him within striking distance of the boathouse. Cars get noticed. So he'd have been careful to keep it some distance away. And he wouldn't have driven it through the village, that's certain. He'd have come in from the west."

McCourt said, "But if it was his car at the end of River Park Avenue—" and stopped. Knott was staring at him.

"*What* did you say?"

"I said, sir, if it was his car at the end of the avenue, then we *know* where he put it."

Knott said, "You're a trained police officer. You're working on this case. Am I to understand that you haven't even taken the trouble to read the file?"

"No, sir. I mean, yes, I have read it."

"Then since you took Mrs. Mason's statement yourself, you know that Limbery was on Streatley Common at ten past twelve. And since you took the statements of Miss Tress and Mrs. Havelock, you may remember that they both spoke of that car moving away from where it was parked at some time *after* twelve. Good going, don't you think? Thirteen miles in five minutes."

"I'm sorry, sir."

Having put Sergeant McCourt in his place, Knott relaxed a little. He said, "I'm not talking to Bob, because he knows all this. I'm talking to you two. Forget anything you've read about murder investigations and concentrate on this. You make your mind up who did it. You charge them. You put together the case you're going to set up in court. Then you put yourself into the shoes of the defense. You pick all the holes you can in your own case. Then you set to work and plug those holes. Right?"

"Right," said Sergeants McCourt and Esdaile in unison.

"Which reminds me. There's one little job we've got to do at once. Get into Reading, Ian, have a word with Farr and get the names of the officers who were on the traffic block on Pangbourne bridge that night. We'll want statements from them and certified copies of the records they kept."

As McCourt rode into Reading on his moped he was thinking about Knott. He didn't like him and was, in fact, afraid of him. But he couldn't help admiring him. It was the narrowness of his vision combined with the weight of his personality. It had the penetrating power of a thin but rigid blade driven by a massive force. The fact that it was driving at the wrong objective would not deter him for a moment. If he was wrong, it was for the opposition to prove him wrong. That was how justice in England worked.

When McCourt had finished his job in Reading he looked in at the general infirmary. The sister, who knew him well, said, "Not good news, I'm afraid, Sergeant. Inspector Ray had a bad hemorrhage last night We've had to move him into the intensive care unit. No one can talk to him for a bit. Is there some message?"

"Not really," said McCourt. "Just to wish him luck."

16

That evening, a string of coal barges drawn by a tug plowed its slow way up the river. The first bow wave lifted the body clear of the snag, the next one carried it out of the rushes and started it on its stately progress downstream. Had anyone been there to see it they would have noticed that it floated in an odd manner, almost as though it was wearing an old-fashioned life jacket, which kept the chest clear of the water.

"I must confess," said Mrs. Havelock, "speaking as a magistrate, that I do get tired of having young tearaways brought up in front of me and someone saying, as though it explained every form of crime and violence, 'It must be remembered that he came from a broken home.' Really, I fail to see the connection. If the father pushes off, the mother, with the help of the state, can usually cope perfectly well."

"Better than if she's spending all her time fighting with an unsatisfactory husband," said Georgie Vigors.

"Exactly. Now take Jonathan. Superficially he had a normal family background. His mother was a sweet and loving little woman. The only time I met her she reminded me of an apple dumpling. His father was a schoolmaster. Hearty, genial type. Being wise after the event, one can see that it was totally disastrous for Jonathan. His father bullied him until he was old enough to stand up for himself and hit back. Then he left him alone. I fancy Father was a bit of coward. After all, he was only twenty-six when war broke out and perfectly fit. First he claimed he was in a reserved occupation. When that wore a bit thin, he scuttled off into the Ministry of Information. I got all this from my second husband, who loathed his guts."

"I do see," said Georgie, "that it could be about the most fatal relationship a boy could have with his father. He'd be apt to grow up disliking any form of authority."

"Not just disliking it. Hating it."

"It explains a lot."

"Funking the war didn't do his old man a lot of good in the end, because he was run over by a drunken lorry driver when Jonathan was starting at Bristol University. Johnno had to come away and get a job. His mother's still alive. I imagine some of what he makes goes to help her."

The two ladies paused to consider the unsatisfactory life of young Jonathan Limbery.

"Maybe it *explains* a lot," said Mrs. Havelock at last. "But it doesn't add up to an excuse for smashing Katie's head in."

Colonel Lyon, the Governor of Reading Jail, was a conscientious man. He made a point of visiting the remand wing every day and speaking to the inmates. "They're in my prison," he used to say, "but they're not prisoners. They haven't been convicted yet. Until they are convicted, I prefer to regard them as temporary visitors."

He had kept Limbery to the last. He hoped that his visit was going to be more productive than the two previous ones, during which Limbery had ignored the warder's order to stand up, sat on his bed glowering and had refused to do anything but grunt.

On this morning he seemed to have recovered his powers of speech. He said, "It's no good keeping on at me. I've made my mind up. The state wants a sacrifice and I'm to be the scapegoat. All right. But if I'm going to be slaughtered, I'm going without bleating. The only thing I regret is the satisfaction my conviction is going to give to that bastard Knott."

The warder said, "Mind your language." Jonathan took no notice of him.

The Governor said, "That's all very well, Limbery. But if you're innocent—"

"Of course I'm innocent. I've said it often enough."

"You've said if often enough," agreed the Governor. "But if you're innocent, why not give people a chance to prove it? With the attitude you're adopting you might just as well plead guilty and have done with it."

"No you don't," said Jonathan. "You're putting words into my mouth. I didn't say I was going to plead guilty. Why should I plead guilty? I never touched the girl."

"In that case—"

"What I'm not going to have is a lot of lawyers fighting over my bones like sick jackals."

"Then do I take it you're going to conduct your own defense?"

"You're dead right I am. And I'm going to say exactly what I think of the lousy stinking police and their filthy bullying tactics."

"It's your privilege," said the Governor.

As they walked back toward his office the warder said, "Do you think he's putting it on?"

"Working up for a plea of insanity, you mean?"

"I thought he might be. You remember that man we

had who stood on his head the whole time. Said he couldn't think unless the blood was running into his brain. He tried to stand on his head in court."

"It could be a try-on," said the Governor, "but somehow I don't think it is. He's angry and he's frightened. Like a small boy banging his head against the wall to show he doesn't care."

"Maybe the parson will talk some sense into him."

"I didn't know Father Michaels was planning to have a word with him."

"Not our chaplain, sir. The one from his village. The Reverend Bird. He telephoned last night."

"Well," said the Governor, "I hope he has more luck with him than I have."

The main offices of Vigors and Dibden, Solicitors, were in Market Street, Hannington. As the practice expanded, they had opened a branch office in West Hannington village. This was two rooms and an annex, just large enough for Noel, one managing clerk and one girl who doubled as receptionist and typist. Noel spent most of his time there. He knew that when his father retired he would have to take over the main office. Meanwhile he was enjoying his independent command.

It was six o'clock in the evening and he was finishing the day's work by signing a batch of letters, when Bird was announced.

"I wonder what he wants," said Noel.

"He didn't say," said the girl. "He just said it was urgent."

"Ask him in."

Noel's first impression was that the rector was ill. His face was drained of color and there were smudges under his eyes.

He said, "You look as if you could do with a drink."

"I'm all right. Just tired. Well, thank you. But put plenty of water in it."

"I often have one myself about this time of day," said Noel. "Take the comfortable chair. Or I should say the less uncomfortable one. This office really needs total redecoration and refurnishing." He went on talking about nothing much until his visitor had downed half his drink and was beginning to look a little more comfortable. Then he said, "What can we do for you, Dicky?"

"It's not me. It's Limbery."

"I thought it might be it. You went to see him?"

"I spent the afternoon with him. It was a most unhappy experience."

"It must have been hellish. Drink that up and have another."

"Thank you, Noel. But no. I very rarely touch spirits. This will be quite enough." He took another cautious sip and said, "It wasn't very pleasant. He didn't seem able to stop talking. For the first two hours—it seemed like two hours, it might have been longer—he was preaching me a sort of sermon. His text seemed to be that hatred was more vital than love."

"Poor Dicky."

"I couldn't stop him. I don't know that I even wanted to. I thought it was probably doing him good to get it off his chest. But it was terribly depressing. Like watching a man trying to plow up the sand. Futile, sterile, pointless. In the end some good did come out of it. I managed to make him change his mind about being legally represented at the trial."

"I wondered what he was planning to do about that."

"He'd told the Governor that he was determined to conduct his own defense."

"Good God! Why?"

"I gather it was partly because he doesn't like lawyers as a class and partly because he wanted to have an opportunity of telling the judge what he thought about the police. However, in the end I persuaded him to hand it all over to you."

"To me?"

"To you personally. No one else. He said he liked you and had found you a sympathetic character in the past and he was prepared to let you do it. If you wouldn't, he'd do it all himself."

Speaking slowly, to get his breath back, Noel said, "It's quite true that we used to see a good deal of each other at one time. We used to play a lot of squash. He usually won. He's very quick on his feet and he's got exceptionally strong wrists. When he hit the ball, he really did smash it—hold up." He thought Bird was going to pass out.

"It's all right. No, really. I'm quite all right."

"Stupid of me to say a thing like that," said Noel. "I didn't mean—"

"Of course you didn't. It's just that I visualized for the first time the sort of thing that happened. Someone positioning himself behind Katie in the dark and smashing—"

"We could both do with another drink," said Noel firmly.

"Well . . . a very small one. Thank you. You will take this on, won't you?"

"I'm not by any means an expert in criminal law, but if it's me or no one, I shall have to do it."

"If it's going to be terribly expensive, I could talk to his friends. I'm sure there are a lot of people who would help."

"I'm sure there are. And equally I can think of one or

two people who certainly wouldn't. However, it may not be necessary. As far as I know, Jonathan hasn't got any money. We should be able to get him legal aid. When we've got that, we'll be able to brief top counsel. Cheer up, Dicky. You've done a good day's work."

17

The Prince Albert Lock is on the river halfway between Pangbourne and Reading, serviced by a side road from Tilehurst village. The son of Mr. Baxter, the lock keeper, came bursting into the cottage at eight o'clock that morning and was sharply told by his mother to remove his Wellingtons and comb his hair or he wouldn't get any breakfast.

Ignoring these suggestions as being frivolous or unimportant, he dropped his fishing rod on the floor, said, "Where's Dad? Oh, there he is," and pelted out into the garden. Mrs. Baxter shook her head sadly.

"A corpus, is it?" said Mr. Baxter. "Then we'd better have'un out, hadn't we?"

"Can I help?"

"I don't think your ma would like that."

"It's not fair. I saw him. In the reeds, this side of the weir."

"Well," said Mr. Baxter, who was as weak-minded as his wife with their only son. "Mind you scrub up well afterwards."

The body was lying on his back. Mr. Baxter, who had seen many corpses in his time, looked at it critically.

"Not been in more'n a few days," he said. "But what's that holding him up in front?"

His son, at the last moment, felt a distaste for the thing. He said, "I think I'll go and get my breakfast."

"That's right," said his father with a grin. "You do that."

It took him five minutes to disentangle the body from the weeds and drag it up onto the towpath. He unbuttoned the coat and then, after a brief hesitation, the shirt as well. He knew that the police disliked people meddling with a body until their own doctor had seen it, but he was puzzled by the inflated appearance of the chest.

The explanation was a stout square rubber wallet, almost the size of a small cushion.

"Funny sort of apparatus to carry about under your shirt," said Mr. Baxter.

He picked it out, dipped it in the river to wash off the dirt and slime that had accumulated on it and examined it again.

At first he thought there was no opening to it. Then he found the tiny head of the zip fastener countersunk in the thick rubber at the corner. It was too small for his clumsy fingers to get hold of. Curiosity had now got the better of discretion.

First he dragged the body by its heels through the back gate and into his garden, where it would be out of sight of passers-by. Then he went back for the wallet and carried it into his tool shed. He threaded a piece of fine wire through the eye of the zip fastener and pulled gently. The top of the wallet came open. The inside was still almost dry and the contents, which seemed to be pictures or photographs of some sort, were wrinkled at the edges but otherwise unharmed by their days of immersion.

Mr. Baxter carried them across to the door to examine them. Then he whistled softly. In the twenty years he had watched over the Prince Albert Lock a variety of flotsam and jetsam had been carried down on the broad bosom of Father Thames and deposited on his doorstep: contents of boats overturned in the upper reaches, furniture lifted from bungalows by the winter floods, on one occasion an upright piano. But, said Mr. Baxter to himself, as he separated the photographs gently and examined them one by one, blow him down if he had ever seen anything quite like this before.

He thought he had better let the police know straightaway.

Constable Leary from Reading, who respected Mr. Baxter's expertise in such matters, said, "Where do you think he went in?"

"Well," said Mr. Baxter, "it's not all that easy to say. Normally—that's to say usually—you can tell how long someone's been in by looking at his face. Being the softest exposed part, that's what the eels get at first. In this case that contraption he had under his shirt kept him floating on his back with his face clear of the water, so it's hardly been touched. You see what I mean?"

"Yes," said Constable Leary with a slight shudder. He was not as used to bodies as Mr. Baxter was.

"Another thing, see this?" Mr. Baxter disentangled a long branch of thorn from the belt at the back of the dead man's coat. "I'd say he'd been hitched up one time or another in the bushes at the edge of the bank. That makes it more difficult to judge. However, taking one thing with another, I'd say he hadn't been in above three or four days and that means he went in somewheres between Streatley and Hannington."

"Three or four days ago," said Superintendent Farr

when this was reported to him. "And there was a cheap day-return ticket to Hannington in his wallet."

"That's right," said Constable Leary. "The date was washed away. But it was Hannington all right."

"The railway could probably give us the date if you gave them the serial number. Put an inquiry through to Paddington. And let Knott have a copy of your report. I don't suppose there's any connection with his business, but you never can tell."

He was looking at the photographs as he spoke. They were enlargements, fourteen inches by twelve. The wallet had evidently been custom made to keep them safe, and it had done its job well.

"Hot stuff," said Constable Leary. "That one of the two boys. I don't know as I've ever seen anything like it."

"It's what they call hard-core pornography."

Constable Leary was about to make a joke based on the word hard, but discretion prevailed.

"There's a special squad in the Met," said Farr. "They deal with this sort of thing. We'd better let them know. He came from London, didn't he?"

"Seems so. There was that return ticket from Paddington in his pocket."

"Nothing with his name on it?"

Leary shook his head.

"He'll be a runner for one of the outfits who peddle this sort of muck. You say the face is O.K. Get a photograph taken and send it up to Central with a report. Copy to Knott at Hannington."

Constable Leary departed reluctantly. There was one or two of the photographs he would like to have looked at again. Now they would be locked away in the Superintendent's safe and he wouldn't have another chance.

* * *

Mr. Beaumorris had reached an age when he did nothing impulsively. Each action had to be judged in the light of its reactions on himself, his comfort and his convenience. Naturally there were other considerations. He liked to help his friends. He liked, even more, to discomfort his enemies. Among them he ranked George Mariner, a self-made parvenu who behaved like a snob without any real grounds for being snobbish. He disliked Superintendent Knott, too, the brute who had driven his old friend Bill Connington to take his own life.

Recently a piece of information had come into his possession. If he passed it on to the authorities it might embarrass Mariner. On the other hand it might help Superintendent Knott. A difficult problem.

He spent most of the morning thinking about it and then decided, as a compromise, to telephone the friendly Sergeant McCourt.

Ian listened without comment to what Mr. Beaumorris had to say. He had a feeling that he was being presented with an important piece of information, but it was difficult for the moment to see how it was going to fit into the plan which had started to form in his slow Scots mind as he was standing in the upper room in the boathouse staring at a spyhole in the wall.

He said, "I suppose you got all this from your girl Myra?"

"That's right," said Mr. Beaumorris placidly. "I get most of my news from her."

"Then let me see if I've got it right. While the Mariners were out at the dance on Friday night, someone telephoned their house. Polly took the call. She says it was a man. She didn't recognize the voice, but she thought it was a Londoner."

"Correct. She also thought he'd been drinking. Not

that he was drunk, you understand. But the voice was slightly slurred."

"And she's quite certain she didn't recognize it."

"Absolutely certain. It was no one she'd ever heard before in her life."

"This was about half past ten?"

"Just after."

"Did he say what his name was?"

"Yes. He said he was Mr. Lewisham."

"And he asked for Mariner by name?"

"He asked if Mr. Mariner was at home. Polly said no. He asked when he was coming back. By this time Polly was getting a bit bored with him. She simply said she hadn't any idea when he was coming back. The man said, 'Then I'll ring later.' She said, 'O.K., you do that.' And the man rang off."

"Did he say where he was telephoning from?"

"No, but Polly says it was a telephone box."

"And he didn't try again later?"

"Not while she was there. When the Mariners came back she told them about it. Before she could say much, George said, 'Wait a moment. I must get my wife to bed. She's very tired.' And he hustled her upstairs into her bedroom. Then he came down and said, 'All right. What was it?' Polly told him and he said, 'I don't know any Mr. Lewisham. It must have been a wrong number.' 'Can't have been,' said Polly. 'He asked for you by name.' To which George said, rather huffily, 'That doesn't prove anything. He probably got my name out of the phone book.'"

"But—"

"Yes," agreed Mr. Beaumorris. "It was a stupid thing to say. But Polly says he was quite clearly pretty shaken by the whole thing. However, it wasn't her business. So she pushed off."

Ian thanked Mr. Beaumorris. He said that it probably had nothing to do with the matter they were investigating but he'd certainly ask Mr. Mariner about it. He declined a glass of sherry and went straight back to the police station. The operations room was empty, but the records of the case, now occupying two bulging folders, were on the Superintendent's desk.

He got out the transcript of Mariner's statement. The passage he wanted came toward the end. *Knott: But she took off as soon as you got back? Mariner: As soon as she heard our car in the drive.*

He was staring at it for a long time. He was still sitting there when the door opened and Knott came in quietly. It was something Ian had noticed about him before. He never made much noise.

"That's right," he said. "Keep studying the record. Read it right through every day. Every word. Nothing like it for concentrating the mind." He seemed to be pleased about something.

Ian said, "I've got another report to add to it. It's on tape but I haven't had time to transcribe it yet."

"Important?"

"It could be." He told him about it.

Knott said, "The trouble is, son, you never know which bits belong and which bits don't. I remember once when I was investigating a case of arson, we kept getting reports about a man who thought he'd been brought up by a wolf pack. Used to call his father 'Baloo' and his mother 'Baghera' and went howling round the fields at night. Fascinating stuff. Nothing to do with the case, though." He opened an envelope on his desk, read the flimsy that was in it and said, "Here's another," and threw it across.

> The body of a man, as yet unidentified, was recovered from the Thames at the Prince Albert Lock this morning. He appeared to have been in the river not less than three and not more than six days. Height five foot eight. Heavy build. Weight stripped fifteen stone. He was carrying a number of obscene photographs, clearly high-class professional work featuring girls, young men and boys. These were in a wallet specially constructed to hold and conceal them. It seems probable that he was a runner or traveler for one of the studios in London who produce or retail this type of work. A photograph, face only, accompanies this report. Details of fingerprints and dental work will follow. Information about this man required by Berkshire Police, Reading. Detective Superintendent Farr.

"It's an advance copy from Farr at Reading," said Knott. "He thought I might be interested."

Ian looked puzzled.

"The lock keeper who pulled the body out—he's by way of being a bit of an expert on Father Thames and his ways. He said the man probably went in somewhere around here at the weekend."

Ian said, "Yes, but—"

"I know. Just another wolf man. All the same, we'll add it in. You never can tell. Get a third folder from Eddie. We don't want to burst the seams of that one."

"You agreed to do *what?*" said Vernon Vigors, shaken out of his usual calm.

"To represent Jonathan," said Noel. "Why not?"

"Do you feel you are equipped to do so?"

"If you mean do I know anything about defending a

man charged with murder, the answer's no, I don't. And I've had precisely two cases in the Crown Court."

"Then don't you think it would be more sensible to entrust the case to a London firm? One who have got some experience in that particular line. It's very specialized, I believe."

"There are two answers to that," said Noel. "The first is that the case will be masterminded by the counsel we choose, not by me. The second is that Jonathan adamantly refused to consider any solicitor except myself."

"He chose *you*, not the firm?"

"Apparently."

"But it's the firm that will be on the record."

"Naturally."

"Didn't it occur to you to ask me before you accepted?"

"Frankly," said Noel, "it didn't. Because it never occurred to me for a single moment that you might object."

Mr. Vigors considered this, chewing his upper lip with the teeth in his lower jaw. It was an unconscious trick, but Noel had seen it before and braced himself for trouble.

"Our firm," said Mr. Vigors, laying stress on the first word, "has built up a very sound practice in and around Hannington. We act for most of the respectable—and respected—families in the neighborhood. Did you stop for a moment to consider what they would feel when it became known that we were acting for an anarchist, who has already attacked and wounded a policeman?"

"No," said Noel.

"No?"

"I mean that I didn't stop for a moment to consider it. It seemed to me to be irrelevant."

Up to that point father and son had kept their

tempers. Regrettably, Mr. Vigors Senior was the first to lose his.

He said, the color of his face contradicting the smoothness of his voice, "We happen to be a partnership. Not a one-man band. You may have overlooked the fact that in our partnership articles, to which you signed your name when you joined Richard Dibden and myself, there was a clause which stated that any important decisions had to be taken unanimously."

"No," said Noel. "I hadn't overlooked that."

"Possibly you don't regard this as an important decision?"

"Extremely important."

"Very well, then—"

"But possibly you may have overlooked the fact that when we set up our sub-office in West Hannington, it was agreed that in everything dealt with from *this* office I was to have an absolute discretion about clients and matters taken on. I may not have got the wording quite accurate, but that was the gist of what we agreed." Noel paused and added, "In writing."

His father stared at him. His face, normally pallid, was now scarlet. Since he seemed unwilling, or unable, to say anything, Noel continued: "Since Limbery has specifically applied for *my* help, it can hardly be disputed, I imagine, that it is a matter which comes under this office and in which I exercise my discretion."

His father said, "You're determined to go on with this."

"Yes."

"And to disregard my very strong personal wishes in the matter."

"I don't like doing that. But yes."

"In that case we can hardly go on as before."

"I'm not sure what you mean."

"I mean," said his father with calculated brutality, "that since you seem to have no regard for me and for what I stand for, we can hardly meet on the same terms as we did. I shall, for instance, find it embarrassing to share a house with you."

"I'm glad you raised the point," said Noel. "I meant to tell you before. Georgie and I are expecting an addition to our family. We may have to have resident help, for a time anyway. It would be much more convenient if you could find somewhere else to live. I'm sure you understand."

His father looked at him for some seconds and then swung around and left the room without a word.

"Did you *have* to do it?" said Georgie that evening.

"I couldn't see any way round it."

"It was a bit rough."

They were close together, sharing, as they sometimes did, a dilapidated armchair. Noel put his arm around her and said, "You've got to understand this. The alternative was letting Jonathan try to defend himself. If he was allowed to do that, examine the witnesses, address the court, can you imagine any sort of justice being done at the end of the day?"

"I suppose not."

"I'm going up to London tomorrow to see our London agents. We're going to brief the best barrister money can buy. And we're going to get at the truth of this matter, if it costs me every bloody friend I've got."

18

“Have you ever sold anyone a Crossfield Electric?” said Sergeant Esdaile to Mr. Plumptree, who kept the business machinery and equipment store in Reading.

“Dozens of them,” said Mr. Plumptree. “Two or three years ago—before the fashion for golf balls got going, that is—it was one of the most popular machines on the market.”

“And you’ve got records of who you sold them to?”

“Not exactly.”

“What do you mean?”

“If I looked at my purchase and sale cards and compared them with my stock cards, I could tell you how many I sold in any one year. It would take a bit of research, but I could do it all right. But that doesn’t mean I could say *who* I sold them to. I never had any call to keep that sort of information.”

“I suppose you don’t remember selling one to anyone in these parts. In Hannington, for instance.”

“Not offhand I don’t. I’ll think about it and I’ll have a word with my lads. If I find out anything I’ll let you know.”

“Well, ta,” said Sergeant Esdaile gloomily.

* * *

Friday morning found Noel Vigors in London. He went from Paddington Station by Underground to Covent Garden and walked to Norway Court, where Messrs. Crakenshaw, Solicitors and Commissioners for Oaths, had their office. It was within a stone's throw of Bow Street Magistrates Court, where they did much of their business.

The Crakenshaws were the London agents of Vigors and Dibden. Noel had written to them and spoken to them on the telephone, but this was the first time he had been to see them. He was received by Simon Crakenshaw, who was about Noel's age but looked much older, being prematurely bald.

He said, "I read all about it in the papers. I was hoping you'd get involved and rope us in. Tell me all about it."

Noel did his best. He said, "I am a bit worried about the financial side of it. Limbery really hasn't got any money. No capital at all, as far as I know, and a very small income from that paper of his, and a lot of that goes to his mother."

"Dependent relative?" said Crakenshaw.

"I suppose she is, yes."

"Then don't worry about the money side. The poorer he is the better. We'll apply for legal aid. We ought to get a full certificate. Minimum contribution."

"Will it cover leading counsel?"

"Certificate for two counsel? Certainly. The committee will be falling over themselves to help. Charge of murder. Man with no money. The sky's the limit."

"Well, that's a relief," said Noel, "because I've a feeling we're going to need the sky."

Crakenshaw said, "If Knott's running the case you're going to need to pull out all the stops." He thought about the matter for a few moments. He said, "I think Mrs. Bellamy would be our best bet."

"Serena Bellamy? I've seen a lot about her in newspaper reports. Do you think we could get her?"

"She's the top of the tree. But I think we might. And I'll tell you why. She loathes Knott. They've had one or two fights in court already. If she sees half a chance of putting him down she'll jump at it. Murder cases aren't quite the glamorous occasions they used to be when there was a gallows at the end of the road, but they still grab the headlines and no counsel objects to a bit more of that, however well known they are."

"I see," said Noel. He found Crakenshaw's professional outlook both alarming and reassuring. "She'll find Limbery a very awkward character to deal with."

"She won't be dealing with him," said Crakenshaw. "It's you and I who have to do all that. She won't talk to him. She'll steer totally clear of him until they face each other in court."

"Why on earth—?"

"What she says is that it enables her to view the case dispassionately. It's also a complete answer to any suggestion of professional misconduct. No one can accuse her of suggesting a phony line of defense to the prisoner if she hasn't even seen him, can they?"

"But they might accuse us—"

"They might. But since we're not going to deviate one inch from the straight and narrow it doesn't arise. We've found that it's much better to stick to the rules. I know there are firms that don't. I don't believe it pays them in the long run. And once you get a name for it, the police can be real sods."

"I see," said Noel. He was beginning to realize that ten years of conveyancing and probate mixed with occasional motoring offenses might have presented him with a one-sided view of legal practice. "What do we do next?"

"I'll give you the legal aid forms to fill in. Limbery will

have to sign a declaration of means. Then we'll have a word with Mrs. Bellamy's head clerk. It's Friday now. She won't be able to see us before Monday. And you say the committal proceedings are fixed for Monday week."

"So I'm told."

"That's Knott all over. Rush the opposition off its feet. Well, we can always apply for an adjournment."

Ten minutes later, Noel found himself out in Norway Court again. He was conscious of a feeling of breathlessness.

"I've established," said Sergeant Shilling, "that Katie went up to town that Friday morning. She called on her agent, Mark Holbeck. Incidentally, I think he ought to have mentioned the fact to me when I was talking to him. Perhaps it slipped his memory."

Knott grunted.

"However, he remembered it when I put it to him. Apparently she only looked in for five minutes around midday. She told him she had a lunch date with Venetia—you know, the A.C.'s daughter."

Knott grunted again.

"I had a word with Venetia. After lunch they seem to have gone out on a shopping spree together. They had tea at Venetia's house and Katie pushed off saying she'd be just in time to catch the six twenty and she'd better not miss it, because she'd promised to go to a ghastly local hop and if she came in late everyone would think she was trying to put on an act."

"Shrewd thinking," said Knott. "When does the six twenty get to Hannington?"

"It doesn't. You have to change at Reading and get the slow train. That's scheduled to reach Hannington at ten past seven. Which it did. I've checked."

"Then she'd be home by half past?"

"She'd have to extract her car from the station car park, which takes some doing, as it's small and the cars are pretty well jammed together. But if she went straight home, she'd certainly be there by half past. Then, I imagine, bath and change."

"Eat?"

"Probably not. If she had a good lunch. There were refreshments at the dance."

Knott thought about it. It seemed straightforward. The connection with the Loftus girl might be tricky. On the other hand, if he pulled off this one it must do him a bit of good in quarters that mattered. He realized that Shilling had something else to tell him.

He said, "While I was at it I found out that Limbery was in Reading that morning. Mariner told me. He was there, too. He's still a consultant with his firm and goes up occasionally. Actually they were on the same train, both ways."

"Times?"

"Eight forty up. Two fifty back. Mariner first class, Limbery second. But even if they'd been in the same carriage I don't imagine they'd have chatted to each other."

"No love lost there," agreed Knott.

He was visualizing Hannington Station, which he had already inspected. The opening in front of the nineteenth-century station building and the cramped car park to the left of it packed with commuters' cars. He said, "I imagine Limbery drove to the station?"

"We know he did."

"How?"

"Because Mariner, who came out of the station building at the same moment, saw him walking off into the car park to fetch his car. Correction. Assumed that he was going to fetch his car."

"Why didn't he follow him to get his own car?"

"Because his wife had taken him to the station and was meeting him."

"A pity. He might have told us how close to Katie's car Limbery's was parked."

Shilling followed this reasoning without difficulty. He said, "You think that's when he slipped in the note?"

"If her car was parked next to his it would have been a perfect opportunity."

"We might be able to find out. The eight forty up is the regular commuters' train. Those two chaps who work in London—Tony Windle and Billy Gonville—chances are they'd have been on it."

"Find out."

Jack Nurse said, "It's an absolute scandal. I only heard the news this morning. I can't imagine what young Noel can be thinking of."

"What's he done now?" said his wife.

"What he's done is to take on, totally off his own bat, and without consulting anyone, the defense of that madman Limbery."

"Why not?" said Sally. "Someone had to do it."

"Why not? Because Vigors and Dibden is a respectable firm, miss. That's why not."

"You mean that someone who's accused of a crime has to go to an unrespectable firm."

Mr. Nurse sometimes found it difficult to cope with his daughter's logic. He fell back on generalities. He said, "Like all young people, Noel thinks he knows better than his elders."

"Perhaps he does, sometimes."

"I imagine I may be permitted to know more about legal topics than you do, young lady."

"I know one thing about the law. A man's presumed

to be innocent until he's proved guilty. I think Noel was quite right to stick up for him."

"You do?"

"Certainly. That's what proper lawyers are for. To stick up for people who can't stick up for themselves."

"Then you think I'm talking nonsense?"

"In this case, yes."

"Now, Sally," said her mother hastily. "You don't really mean that."

It was too late. Storm signals had been hoisted.

"I certainly do mean it," said Sally. "I think it's absolutely foul the way vile old men like George Mariner and Vernon Vigors have assumed, without a particle of proof, that Jonathan killed Katie."

"Vile old men, eh?" said her father. His foot was tapping the floor. "Perhaps you'd like to add your father to the list."

"If you insist on joining the club, yes."

"I see."

"Sally," said her mother, "you mustn't talk like that to your father."

"I'll talk to him in any way I want."

"In that case," said her father, "you'd better pack up your things and take yourself off to somewhere you'll be appreciated."

"Jack!"

"Since you treat me like dirt," said Sally, "the sooner I stop polluting your house the better."

"You can't go away like this," said her mother. "Where will you go?"

"To London," said Sally, who was as close to tears as her mother was. "Patricia Cole will let me share her flat. She told me so."

"She won't want you at this time of night," said her

father, who saw that he had gone too far. "Cool down. We'll talk about it in the morning."

"I've done all the talking I'm going to do," said Sally and slammed out of the room.

"Bit of luck finding you two here together," said Sergeant Shilling.

Tony Windle and Billy Gonville looked at him cautiously. Sergeant McCourt they knew and, to a certain extent, trusted. They were not so certain about this smooth-faced young man from London.

"Anything we can do for you?"

"Just to think back to Friday morning. I imagine you both went up to London as usual."

"As usual."

"That would be the eight forty."

"As usual."

"And both went down to the station in your cars."

"We both went down in Gonville's car. Mine was out of action."

"Yes. I remember. Your local practical joker had put yours out of action. By the way, have there been any other incidents of that sort?"

"If there have, we haven't heard of them."

"Odd. Mariner, Vigors and you."

"Not really," said Tony. "Most people round here lock their cars up at night. Vigors and Mariner hadn't got round to putting their cars away. The damage was done during the evening. That's why everyone thought it was kids. We haven't got a garage, so mine was easy meat. While he was at it, the joker might have fixed Billy's, too. They're parked together in our back yard."

Billy said, "Is Scotland Yard worried about it?"

"Not really. But it was cars I came to ask you about.

When you parked yours at the station, did you happen to notice Limbery's car?"

They looked at each other. The conversation so far had been casual enough. Were they now getting to some point that mattered?

"As a matter of fact, I did," said Tony. "It's a ropy old Morris Traveller. A respray job. It was parked at the far end."

"By the pedestrian access?"

"Just beyond it."

"I understand that Katie went up to town that morning on the eight forty. I wondered if you happened to notice where *her* car was parked."

So that's it, said the two young men simultaneously to themselves. It was Windle who answered. He said, "We could hardly have noticed Katie's car. It wasn't there."

"Oh?"

"Walter ran her down to the station. I expect her mother fetched her. That was the usual arrangement when she went to town."

"But—" said Shilling.

"I know," said Tony. "She had a car of her own. But she doesn't seem to have been keen on using it. Lately, that is. She drove round in it a lot when she first got it. New toy. Then she seemed to get tired of it."

"The fact is," said Billy, "she liked other people to do things for her. If Tony's car hadn't been out of action she'd have expected him to drive her to the dance that night. Although it was only four hundred yards straight down the road."

"Is that right?" said Shilling. An idea was beginning to shape itself in his mind. He thought he would try it out on Knott.

When he was gone, Tony heaved himself out of his chair, took two large glass-bottomed pewter tankards out of the sideboard and filled them from a cask in the corner. He handed one to Billy, who sank half of the contents in two gulps and then said, "It *is* odd, when you come to think of it."

"Very odd," said Tony. "For the first few months of this year she was hardly out of that car. Drove it all over the place, took it up to London. Then—it didn't happen gradually—she just seemed to stop using it."

"Do you think it could have been her? Young Roney—?"

"It might have been. He said it was a small red car. Of course, they're common enough."

He was referring to something that had happened in the first week of March.

Roney Havelock, walking home from school in the dusk, had been hit by a car driving on sidelights only. That part of the street, between River Park Avenue and West Hannington Manor, was unlighted. When he saw that the car was going to hit him, Roney had jumped for safety. Some outlying portion, possibly the driving mirror, had caught in his coat and hurled him onto the side of the road. He had cracked his head on a fencepost and knocked himself out. The next motorist to come past had been his mother, who had picked him up, taken him straight to the Hannington Infirmary and telephoned the police. By that time Roney, who was suffering from concussion, had been able to make a statement. He hadn't noticed the car until a moment before it hit him. It was small and red. That was all.

"There could be nothing in it," said Tony. "Katie's car is small and red—"

"Lots of them about."

"But it *was* then that she practically gave up using her car, particularly after dark."

"The police never pinned it onto anyone."

"That's right," said Tony. "They started making a lot of inquiries. I remember Ian coming to talk to me about it. My car's red and smallish. Luckily I'd got an alibi. Then, somehow, they seemed to lose interest."

"I notice," said Billy, "that you didn't mention any of this to the Sergeant just now. All you said was Katie had given up driving lately. March isn't exactly lately."

Tony finished his beer, took both mugs and refilled them. He said, "If Katie did knock young Roney down, she may not even have known that she'd touched him. And it can't have anything to do with her getting killed five months later."

"I suppose not."

"And anyway, I don't trust Shilling. And I don't like his boss."

"The White Rat."

"He's simply in it for what he can get out of it. I was talking to Pritchard at lunch yesterday. You know the chap I mean?"

"Conk Pritchard?"

"No. That's his brother. This was Dozey Pritchard. Their father's something in the Solicitors' Department at Scotland Yard. He was saying that if Knott pulls this off he's a snip for promotion to Commander. All he wants is a conviction. It doesn't matter to him whether he's got the right man. It's a race between him and another chap on the Murder Squad called Haliburton. He was the one who pulled off that kidnapping job at Exeter, remember?"

Billy considered this, staring into his tankard as though he could see the truth rising with the bubbles from its amber depths. He said, "Do you think Johnno did do it?"

Tony said, "No, I don't. Do you?"

"It's out of character. Sticking poor old Eddie through the arm in front of an admiring audience. That was

Johnno all over. But lurking on a dark path and beating Katie's head in. I just can't see it. And who the hell's that?"

The telephone was in the hall. Billy went out. A one-sided conversation followed, which consisted mostly of Billy saying, "What?" and "Oh" and finally "Hold on a second." He came back and said, "Well, what do you know? That's Sally Nurse on the telephone. She wants to know if she can come round and spend a couple of nights here."

"Has her house burned down?"

"She's had a fight with her father and walked out. A friend in London had offered her a share of her pad, but the friend's gone abroad and locked the place up. Won't be back till Monday."

"I don't mind, if you don't," said Tony. "She can use the sofa."

"Safety in numbers," said Billy with a grin. "All right. I'll tell her."

"I didn't get a lot out of them," said Shilling. "Except that it's clear Katie's car wasn't in the car park that day. I checked that with Walter. But I did get the beginnings of an idea."

Knott grunted. He preferred facts to ideas. But he had enough respect for his assistant to listen.

"It's that business about the practical joker. He drained old Vigors' radiator and he let down Mariner's tires and then, sometime on Thursday night, he immobilized Windle's car by pinching the distributor."

"Wolf man," said Knott.

"Well, it might be, of course. But it just occurred to me. Suppose the first two were dummy runs and it was only the third one that mattered. If Windle's car hadn't been out of action, he'd have driven Katie to the dance.

That's for sure. Since he couldn't, she had to use her own car."

"Couldn't Walter drive her?"

"Walter would be taking her mother. If she went with them, she'd be tied to them for the evening. No, failing Windle, I think she'd be bound to take her own car. Not a certainty, I agree, but highly likely."

"Yes," said Knott. And again. "Yes. I take your point."

"That was a perfect setup for the killer. Katie's up in London. Her car's standing all that day in her stable-yard, which is easy to get at and nicely hidden from view. All he's got to do is to slip the note through the window. Katie finds it there *when she comes out to drive to the dance.* She wouldn't want to leave it lying about. Not with all the LYPAH business in it. Natural thing would be to tuck it away in her bag. It's almost the only way he could be certain it *would* finish up there."

Knott was thinking about it, twisting it this way and that, slotting it into the pattern he had created.

He said, "It's all right in one way. He'd have to know quite a bit about Katie and her habits. The fact that she'd probably get her brother to drive her to the station instead of taking her own car. And the supposition that if Windle's car wasn't available she'd take her own car to the dance. And that's the sort of knowledge Limbery would have. In another way it doesn't fit quite so well. It argues a very careful forward-thinking killer."

"Not a hotheaded fool," agreed Shilling. "A cold-blooded bastard."

19

"I don't see why we shouldn't take it," said Mariner.

"Be your age, George," said Mrs. Havelock. "You know what you're told. If you have any personal connection with the accused, you can't sit."

"Is that right, Gerry?"

"On the nail," said Group Captain Gonville. "It would be quite impossible for any of us to sit. We all know Jonathan."

"Far too well," said Mrs. Havelock.

"Then what do we do?"

"Ask Henry."

Henry was their clerk. He was also their mainstay. He knew all there was to know about law and procedure. Mrs. Havelock sometimes thought that he would have made a very good judge.

"I'll give him a buzz," said Gonville. The magistrates were meeting in his drawing room.

When he came back, he said, "Henry's already fixed it. He's getting Appleton from Reading."

"Pity," said Mariner. "This was one case I was really looking forward to taking."

And that, said Mrs. Havelock to herself, is just why you're not going to be allowed to take it.

* * *

That same morning the weather broke. It was the first rain since mid-July and was generally welcomed. As Superintendent Farr came into the temporary operations room behind the Hannington police station a spout from a blocked drain above the door shot a cupful of water down his back. He took off his coat and said, "Well, that's a bloody friendly way to welcome a colleague."

Knott and Shilling were working at their desks. Knott said, "Come in, Dennis. I can see by that happy smile on your kisser that you've got something for us."

"I have and all," said Farr. "And seeing I was coming in this direction, I thought I'd give it to you myself." He extracted some papers from his briefcase. "First, the Met have put a name to that bod that was pulled out of the river. Lewson. Known to the criminal fraternity as Gabby. He and his brother Louie both worked for this photographer, Rod the Sod Ruoff."

"When I saw the photograph," said Shilling, "I thought it reminded me of someone. It must have been his brother I met when I went up to the studio to ask him about Katie. Chucker-out and general dogsbody."

"Right. And they both have a bit of form. Nothing sensational. Insulting behavior. Drunk and disorderly. Just a pair of barroom cowboys."

"An odd pair to be working for a studio," said Knott.

"It's an odd studio. Society beauties and television personalities and a sideline in porn. I'll send the photographs over and you can see for yourself."

Shilling said, "I suppose 'Gabby' was short for Gabriel."

Knott looked at him sharply. He suspected that his assistant sometimes pulled his leg. He said, "I don't get it."

"Gabriel was the messenger of the gods. Gabby seems to have been a messenger boy for Ruoff. Taking the merchandise round to the customers. I should think there was an element of blackmail about it, too, wouldn't you?"

"I thought the same thing," said Farr. "Some respectable citizen buys a few naughty photographs. Then he gets cold feet and doesn't fancy having any more. So Gabby turns up at his house one evening with a wallet full of prime stuff. The last thing our respectable citizen wants is a fuss on his own doorstep. So he buys the lot to keep him quiet."

"You could be right," said Knott. "But has it got anything to do with my case?"

"Next point," said Farr smoothly. "There was a ticket in Gabby's wallet. A cheap day-return ticket to Hannington. The date was washed off, but the number on the ticket was still legible. Paddington says that it must have been issued latish that Friday. They can't be certain of the exact time, but around five or six. Since it was day-return, presumably Gabby planned to go back to London the same night. The last train back is the fast from Swindon, which stops at Hannington at ten minutes before midnight. That would give him about six hours. For whatever he was planning to do."

"All right," said Knott. "All right. That means that he was hanging around this part of the world at the time Katie was killed. That still doesn't mean—"

"Wait for it," said Farr. "I've kept the punch line for the last." He took out another sheet of paper. "We've got the pathologist's report on Lewson. Dr. Carlyle, from Southampton. He did the autopsy on Katie, too. He says, 'An examination of both wounds leaves me in little doubt that they were made by the same weapon. The shape and size of the fracture, which it was possible to measure with precision, suggests a thinnish steel pipe, with some protuberance, or knob, at the end of it. In both cases it was swung downwards and sideways into the head, and the fact that the depth of penetration was the same in both cases suggests that the same hand struck both blows, although that last point is, of course, only surmise.'"

The three men looked at each other. Knott's face was ugly. The case, which had looked straightforward, seemed to be branching out in unexpected directions. It was an unwelcome development.

"Of course," said Farr, "it *could* still be unconnected. Or it could be connected in some way which doesn't make any real difference to your case. All the same, Charlie, I think it might be a good idea to sort it out before the defense starts sniffing round it. It'd be normal tactics for them to raise as many side issues as possible. Muddy the water. Put up a smokescreen. You know what I mean."

Knott grunted. He could see the force of Farr's suggestion. It was his belief that defense lawyers would try every dirty trick in the book. And the less plausible their case, the dirtier and trickier would their conduct of it be.

He said, "We'll have to tackle this from both ends. We want to know what Lewson was doing down here that evening. The first place he'd make for would be the nearest pub. That's routine stuff. One of Dan's boys can tackle that. We'll give him a photograph and tell him to start at the railway station. The London end must be your pigeon, Bob. I asked Division to keep an eye on Ruoff's place. See if they've got anything for us. If they could think up an excuse to look at his records, we might be able to find out who his customer in Hannington was."

Shilling said, "I've got any amount of things to finish here. I could go up on Monday."

"Soon as you can," said Knott. They all had a lot to do. He was beginning to regret that he had offered to open the committal proceedings so quickly. It would entail a loss of face if *he* had to ask for an adjournment. Probably the defense would save him the trouble by asking for one themselves. They must be further behind than he was.

Walter Steelstock was standing in the front doorway of West Hannington Manor staring down the drive. The rain was sweeping across the lawns in a gauzy curtain. The farmers might want it, but it was a bore that it should have happened on a Saturday afternoon. He had organized a game of tennis with the two Havelock girls and Billy Gonville. If the game had gone well, he had thought of suggesting a trip into Oxford that evening. Certain plans, which involved Lavinia, were beginning to form in his mind. These followed the sequence which he had been taught in the Cadet Corps at school. Intention. Method. Movement of own troops. Movements of enemy. The enemy, in this case, was his mother. He heard a sound behind him and spun around.

Peter was coming downstairs and taking evident care to do so without making too much noise.

Enemy troops? His mother in the drawing room?

Peter jerked his head toward the dining room and Walter followed him in, closing the door quietly. He noticed that Peter's face was white. That was either excitement or fear. They affected him in the same way. When he was younger, in moments of stress he had sometimes passed right out. The doctor had talked about puberty and growing pains and had told them not to worry about it. In the last two years there had been no recurrence of the trouble. Now he looked ghastly.

Walter said, "For God's sake, sit down, Pete, or you'll fall flat on your back. What's up?"

Peter sat down, put his elbows on the table and said, "Will they . . . will the court . . . make out that Johnno killed Katie?"

"I should think it's quite likely."

"Why?"

"Why would they find him guilty, you mean?"

Peter nodded. Walter, observing the staring eyes and the sweat standing out on his forehead, thought that he looked like a frightened horse. He lowered his voice and spoke slowly. He said, "It's the note that was found in Katie's bag."

"You mean a note from Johnno asking Katie to meet him that night."

"That's the obvious assumption."

"But—" said Peter. And then evidently changed his mind. "Is that all?"

"The rest seems to be circumstantial. The fact that he was known to be a wild character and that he had been very keen on Katie and had quarreled with her that time at the Tennis Club."

"That was my fault."

"Why?"

"He was coaching me at tennis at our court. I kept saying to him that there was plenty of time. And then —there wasn't."

"I don't see that it's anything to get worked up about," said Walter. "He's such a casual chap that he's always late for everything. If it hadn't been you, it'd have been some other reason."

Peter hardly seemed to be listening. He said, "Is that all they've got against him?"

"There's a sort of theory—I'm not sure where it came from—that he's put up a cock-and-bull story about where he actually was that evening and the police can prove that he's lying. It's something to do with the job he says he was on for the paper. That's all I know about it. We shall have it served up piping hot when it comes to court."

"And then it'll be too late to do anything about it."

"Anything about what?"

"I mean, once he's sworn to his account of what he says he was doing it'll be too late to go back on it."

"A lot too late," said Walter grimly.

"It's quite extraordinary," said Dicky Bird, "but it looks as though we shan't have a single treble in the choir tomorrow. They've fallen by the wayside, one after the other. Two of them have got bad colds, another one's going out with her parents. Tina Gonville says she's sprained her ankle, although I'll swear I saw her skipping down the street this morning—"

"There's nothing coincidental about it," said his wife.

"What do you mean?"

"Roney and Sim Havelock have been going round saying they'll scrag anyone who sings in your choir."

"Why on earth—?"

"It's something to do with what you said in church last Sunday. They've got the wrong end of the stick, of course. But they've convinced themselves that because you were sympathetic about Katie, you must be antagonistic to Jonathan. He's their hero."

He stared at her. "I didn't mean—"

"Of course you didn't. It's mad."

"It's very unsettling," said her husband.

When Knott wanted his assistants he summoned them on the internal telephone. As they got up to comply, their own outside telephone rang and McCourt stopped behind to answer it. When he reached the operations room he found Dandridge and Esdaile examining a dozen photographs which had been spread out on the table. He said, addressing himself to Dandridge, "That was Superintendent Farr on the telephone. Bad news, I'm afraid. Inspector Ray died this morning."

"I was afraid of that," said Dandridge. "I had a call

from his wife last night." Shilling and Esdaile gave a sympathetic murmur. Knott grunted.

By this time, McCourt had reached the table and Esdaile moved aside to let him see the photographs. McCourt stared at them bleakly for a moment, then swung around, walked to the door and went out.

"What's up now?" said Knott.

Esdaile said, "Ian's upset."

"You mean that stuff turned him up?"

"That's right," said Esdaile.

Shilling said, "When he was with the Met, his first posting was West End Central. He got his face shoved into a lot of shit there. I guess it upset him."

Knott seemed more interested in the feelings of Sergeant McCourt than he had been in the death of Inspector Ray. He said, "Do you mean that sex upsets him? Is that it, Bob?"

"Not straight sex. I mean, he's quite O.K. as far as that sort of thing's concerned. He had one or two rather smooth girlfriends when he was up in London, I seem to remember. They rather go for that ascetic Scots look. What he couldn't take was perversion. Maybe it was being brought up in a manse."

"It takes them both ways," said Knott. "I remember one youngster—I was in recruit class with him—his father was a canon and I wouldn't have trusted him with my sister *or* my kid brother. I suppose that's why Ian pulled out of the Met?"

"I guess so," said Shilling. "I think it was the Pussycat Case that finished him. It was about that time, if you remember."

"I remember it," said Knott with a faint grimace of distaste.

"He asked for a transfer soon after and got himself a job down here. I believe his folk live down here."

Knott said, "I thought they were Scotch."

"His father was. His mother's English. She came down here when the old man died."

"I think he's O.K. now," said Eddie.

"Better put those photographs away," said Knott.

McCourt came back. He looked pale, but otherwise collected. He said, "Sorry about that, sir," addressing the apology to Dandridge, and sat down quietly by the table.

"Right," said Knott. "Now I want to recap. We've got a certain amount of information about this porn peddler. I'm not at all sure how he fits into our case, or whether he fits into it at all. But if the pathologist is right and he was killed at the same time as Katie and by the same weapon, we've obviously got to fit him in somewhere. Over to you, Dan."

"Well," said Dandridge, "we've discovered that he got here by the seven forty. That's one of the through trains from Paddington. It wasn't crowded and anyway the man on the gate knows most of the regulars, so he spotted this chap at once. He seems to have drifted off into the town and gone on a pub crawl. He put in an hour at the Station Tavern, moved on to the Masons Arms, where he had something to eat, and finished up at the Crown."

"Where's the Crown?" said Knott. He had got up and was examining the large-scale map.

"It's on the corner of Eveleigh Road," said McCourt. "It's near my lodgings. I often drop in there in the evening for a bit to eat and a pint."

"Is the landlord reliable? I mean, would he make a good witness?"

"Old Scotty. Yes, I would say he'd be all right."

"What time did this chap leave?"

"Apparently he went out twice. Once to use the phone. At least he asked where the nearest box was. So that's the supposition. The second time was when the pub was closing. He was about the last man out."

"Which would be when?"

"Officially eleven o'clock."

Ian said, "Scotty's fairly strict about that sort of thing. It wouldn't be later than a quarter past."

Knott was still examining the map. He said, "It's beginning to add up. In parts, anyway. Eveleigh Road runs down to the river. Lewson rolls out at a quarter past eleven, not exactly drunk, but tolerably full of whisky. Wherever he was making for, and I guess that's fairly obvious now, he'd be likely to use the towpath in preference to the main road. If he'd looked at the map he'd know he could get back to the main road easily enough by using Church Lane or River Park Avenue. But for that pathologist's report—and pathologists are sometimes too bloody clever by half—I'd guess that he slipped on the bank, which is pretty steep there, cracked his head on something sharp, rolled into the river and was drowned."

"He wouldn't be the first," said Dandridge. "Is something bothering you, Ian?"

McCourt had been trying to speak for some time. He said, "Did you say the man's name was Lewson?"

Knott grinned at him. "It's all right, son," he said, "we've all noticed it. Lewson. Lewisham. I don't doubt he was planning to call on the chairman of your Bench and sell him a few more dirty photographs."

20

"Well, Mr. Vigors," said Mrs. Bellamy, "we've got a lot of work to do and not much time to do it in."

The sun was shining directly into her south-facing chambers in Crown Office Row, lighting up the spines of the law books which crammed the shelves, focusing on one patch of blinding scarlet which Noel could see was a set of *Famous Criminal Trials*.

"I'm afraid that's right," said Noel. "I was only consulted late last week. I imagine we could ask for an adjournment."

"We could," said Mrs. Bellamy, "but I'm not sure that I shall advise it. We'll keep our options open for a little longer, I think."

Ever since he came into the room, Noel had been teased by a resemblance. It was some minutes before he placed it. Mrs. Bellamy was a perfect female counterpart of Oliver Cromwell. There was the same calm sagacious face, the heavy jowls, the impression of rustic, kindly competence, a kindliness qualified by the steel of the eyes and flatly contradicted by the rat-trap mouth, a mouth which had said, *I would cut off his head, were he three times king*.

On this occasion this formidable woman was doing

no more than studying a long list of names and was seeming to find it puzzling.

"We shall need your local knowledge, Mr. Vigors," she said. "What we have here is a list, seemingly arranged in alphabetical order, of the witnesses the Crown intends to call. Rita Black, Fire Officer Burt, Dr. Carlyle, Joseph Cavey, Arnold Cowie . . . A more considerate opponent than Detective Chief Superintendent Knott would at least have set them down in the order in which he intended to call them. We might then have had some notion of the parts they were intended to play in his carefully staged melodrama. Detective Sergeant Esdaile, Dr. Farmiloe—that's a name I remember. What's Jack Farmiloe doing in your part of the world?"

"He retired there last year."

"Anything he says will be gospel. Sim Havelock, Detective Chief Superintendent Knott, Police Constable Luck, George Mariner, Mary Mason, Sally Nurse, Olivia Steelstock, Walter Steelstock. Olivia is the mother, Walter the brother, I take it? Quite so. Noel Vigors. Hullo! Slightly unusual to call the solicitor acting for the defense as a Crown witness."

"I noticed that," said Noel. "Maybe because I can give evidence of when Katie left the dance—or maybe to talk about a quarrel that took place in the Tennis Club."

"We shall have to think about that. Anthony Windle, Chief Superintendent Wiseman and that's the lot."

"I can place the locals for you," said Noel. He ran his finger down the list. "Cavey's the caretaker of the village hall and part-time barman at the Tennis Club."

"The man who found the body?"

"Right. Arnold Cowie is editor of the Reading *Sun*. Limbery covered local features for him. Including that fire. Which no doubt accounts for Fire Officer Burt.

Sergeant Esdaile is local C.I.D. Sim Havelock is a small boy, son of Mrs. Havelock, one of the Hannington magistrates."

"How small?"

"Eight or nine."

"I detest child witnesses," said Mrs. Bellamy. She looked as though she could have eaten two for breakfast. "You can't cross-examine them, and the court believes everything they say. P.C. Luck? Is he one of yours?"

"Not that I know of."

"You and Sophie had better check the local forces. Reading, Swindon and Oxford for a start."

Sophie was one of the two girls who had been introduced to Noel when he came into the room. She nodded and made a note. Both girls were dressed in the formal black and white of the profession and he assumed that they were pupils in the Chambers. The masculine formality of their dress did not conceal the fact that they were both easy on the eye.

"George Mariner's the local bigwig. I know nothing about Mary Mason. Sally Nurse is the daughter of our managing clerk, Jack Nurse. She was at the dance that night and was thought to have a crush on Katie. Copied her clothes and getup. The Steelstocks you know about. Tony Windle was a rather casual boyfriend of Katie's. Superintendent Wiseman—I don't know him."

"He is the number-one fingerprint expert at Scotland Yard," said Mrs. Bellamy. "A very competent man. Dr. Carlyle is the pathologist. He's attached to the Southampton General Hospital. Haven't you got a friend in those parts, Laura?"

The second girl said, "I know one of the sisters at the hospital. She helped us in that abortion case last year."

"See if she can get alongside Dr. Carlyle. I'd very much like to see a copy of the autopsy report *before* it's produced in court." She returned to the list. "It looks as though the jokers in the pack are Rita Black and Mary Mason. Unfortunately two rather common names. Local directories might help."

"Couldn't we ask Knott?" said Noel.

"We could. And he could tell us. He could even give us copies of their statements. But we can't force him to do so. And since I'm sure he'd refuse, I don't intend to ask him. He is not a man who believes in making life easy for the opposition."

Simon Crakenshaw, who had been sitting quietly in one corner of the room, caught Noel's eye at this point and winked at him.

"All we've got to work from," said Mrs. Bellamy, "is the statement of the accused. Unless Rita Black and Mary Mason are surprise witnesses who actually saw the crime committed, which I doubt, they must be connected in some way with Limbery's account of what he did that night. The editor fits in with that. He'll probably be called to say that Limbery's story of the fire was so superficial that he needn't have been there at all. Or not for very long. One of the others could be connected with the roadhouse where he says he had a snack. Better check on that, Laura."

Laura made a note.

Mrs. Bellamy put both documents down and sat back in her chair, which creaked in protest. She said, "We've got one other line which has got to be followed up hard. Katie was a client of a well-known—I should say notorious—London photographer called Ruoff. I was involved in a case with him about four years ago."

There were numbered box files on the shelves inside the door. Sophie had one out and open on the desk almost before Mrs. Bellamy had finished speaking. Her fingers riffled through the papers and found the one she wanted.

"He ran a series of parties which were described, with more accuracy than usual, as orgies. Young people of both sexes were given drinks which had been hocussed with some drug which left them barely conscious. They were then stripped and photographed in interesting positions. Oddly enough the objective didn't seem to be blackmail. At least that was never suggested. The photographs were sold to private clients who were prepared to pay highly for them and to fringe magazines which specialized in that sort of thing. The victims didn't complain. One imagines they were ashamed of having gone to that sort of party at all. They may not even have been sure of what had happened to them. It was the prosecution of one of the magazines which brought the matter to light." She closed the folder.

"What happened to Ruoff?" said Noel.

"He was bound over and had to pay a heavy fine. Most people thought he should have gone to prison. He was very ably defended. By me."

Noel was on the point of making a comment, but noticed that Sophie and Laura were looking particularly impassive and decided not to.

"However, he was punished. In another way. As the hearing went on, the names of some of his victims became known. And their friends laid for Ruoff. He was beaten up at least once and he had to hire two barroom bullies to look after him. Men with criminal records. Names here, somewhere."

"In the newspaper clippings," suggested Sophie.

"Right. Here they are. The Lewson brothers. Now you see where we're going?"

Noel saw nothing, but managed to look intelligent.

"Superintendent Knott is a man who likes to keep his

cases simple. From the witnesses he's calling, it's clear he sees this as a local killing. He'll want to cut the London end right out. That makes our tactics clear. We plug the London connection for all it's worth. And it's worth a good deal. This is a case of violent crime. Down at West Hannington you've got a lot of nice people?"

Noel said, "I certainly wouldn't have described any of them as violent criminals."

"Right. While up in London, in what we might call the other half of Katie's life—Quite a good expression that—the other half of Katie's life . . ."

Noel saw her mentally trying it out on the jury.

"As I was saying, up here we've got a pornographic photographer who's already been in trouble with the police, two professional criminals and others, for all we know, in the background. That's a hotbed that's more likely to spawn a murder."

"How do we investigate it?"

"We use private detectives. Captain Smedley will be our best bet. He'll put a couple of good men onto it. They'll find out anything that's there."

"I know Katie's agent, Mark Holbeck," said Sophie. "I could have a word with him."

"Good girl. The more we can dig up the better. I'll be frank with you, Mr. Vigors. Nothing we find may have any connection with the killing. But we have to fight with what weapons we've got. And where we have no weapons to our hand, we have to manufacture them. In the Mancini case—you remember it?—the Brighton trunk murder—Norman Birkett had to defend a pimp who was found with a body of the girl he'd been managing stowed away in a trunk with her head bashed in. What did he do? He started to talk about morphine. Got Roche Lynch, the Home Office analyst, to admit that owing to the putrefaction of the corpse it was impossible to tell *exactly* how much morphine there was in the body. By the time he'd finished, the jury didn't know whether she'd died of an overdose of drugs or had fallen down the steps or been hit on the head with a hammer. A masterly performance. Well, we mustn't sit round chatting. We've all of us got a lot to do."

Simon Crakenshaw walked back up Middle Temple Lane with Noel. He said, "Did you see her eyes light up when she observed that Knott was going to give evidence? She's been waiting for this opportunity for months."

"I did wonder," said Noel, "whether her main object was to get Limbery off or to put Knott down."

"Oh, both," said Simon. "Both, I think."

The car which drew up outside the Hannington police station was a black three-and-a-half-liter Rover. The man who got out of it matched the car. He had the air of distinction which derives from height, leanness and a military cast of countenance. In fact, although Mavor was known by his friends at the bar as "Brigadier Mavor," he had been too young for the war and had never been in any branch of the Army. His father had been a master printer from the Midlands and a notable trade union organizer.

Dandridge brought him through into the back room and both Knott and Shilling jumped up when he came in. He shook hands with them.

"This is a surprise," said Knott. "We were told that Davenport was going to take the committal."

"So he was," said Mavor. "There's been a change of plan. I'm going to take it. The Director felt that Davenport wasn't quite up to Mrs. Bellamy's weight."

"Do you mean to tell me," said Knott, "that that lesbian bitch has got in on the act? For God's sake! How's Limbery going to pay for her?"

"Legal aid."

"The criminal's charter. Is there any other country in the world as daft as we are? Law-abiding citizens pay money out of their taxes for lawyers to fiddle acquittals for the criminals who rob their houses and rape their daughters."

"You ought to stand for Parliament, Charlie," said Mavor. "Let's sit down, get the papers out and do some work. Better have the troops in as well."

Dandridge and the two sergeants were brought in and introduced. Papers were spread and Knott expounded the case of the Queen against Jonathan Limbery, interrupted from time to time by questions from Mavor. These were not always directed at Knott. All five of them came under fire from time to time. When some fact was not clear, Mavor seemed to take it in his teeth and shake it until he had worried his way to the center of it or, as happened occasionally, decided that there was no hard center to it, when he would spit it out.

At the finish he said, "The main outline's clear enough, Charlie. The only piece I can't make out is how Lewson comes into it. If it wasn't for the pathologist's report, I'd write it off as coincidence. But Carlyle's not a fool. If he's convinced that both wounds were caused by the same weapon, he'll stand up in the box and say so."

"Always supposing he's asked."

Mavor thought about this. He said, "You mean, leave the second body out of it altogether?"

"It's no part of our case. We haven't been asked to investigate it. Why should we bring it in?"

"Logically you're right. But I don't like it. It's a loose

end. You leave a loose end lying, someone's bound to trip over it."

"Is there any reason," said Shilling, "why it shouldn't fit into our case quite neatly? We know that Lewson left the Crown at about a quarter past eleven and probably went along the towpath. He probably meant to turn up Lower Church Lane. That would be the logical way to get to Mariner's house. But suppose he missed the turning. It was a dark night and he was fairly full of whisky. That would bring him to the boathouse at the exact moment when the murder was taking place. Limbery has killed Katie and has the weapon still in his hand when Lewson lurches onto the scene. Curtains for Lewson."

"I think that's almost certainly what did happen," said Knott. "In fact, if we have to bring Lewson into the story at all, that would be my explanation. But I still think it would be better to keep him out of it."

Mavor swung his head slowly, looking at each of the men around the table in turn, as though they were a jury and he was estimating their response to some proposition which he had put forward. His eyes came to rest on McCourt. Here he seemed to sense an element of resistance.

"You've been very quiet, Sergeant," he said. "Let's have your ideas. Don't be bashful. Imagine that you're counsel for the defense. If there *is* another theory which fits the facts, much better have it out now and push it around."

McCourt shot a quick look at Knott, who remained unresponsive. Then he said, "It was that car, sir. The one that was parked at the end of River Park Avenue. The wheelbase corresponds exactly with Mr. Mariner's Humber Diplomat."

"How do you know that?" said Knott. "You been round measuring it?"

"No, sir. I got the specifications from the factory."

"And that's all?"

"Not quite."

"Let him have his head," said Mavor, who had been studying McCourt.

"It seems that Lewson was planning to call on Mr. Mariner with those photographs."

"A fair assumption."

"Well, I don't think our Mr. Mariner is a nice sort of man at all. For instance, he's made a sort of spyhole in his office at the Boat Club so that he can watch what goes on. It looks straight down onto that pile of punt cushions under the window. Even at night, if there was a bit of moon, he'd be able to see clear enough."

"You mean he's a voyeur," said Mavor. "It's very likely. It fits in with the dirty pictures. But it doesn't mean he killed Katie."

"No, sir. Not by itself. But I think he did."

There was a short silence. Out of the corner of his eye McCourt could see Sergeant Esdaile gaping at him and Shilling with the beginnings of a smile on his face.

Knott said, "How? And why?" He said it with no more apparent feeling than if he had been opening a debate on some theoretical subject.

"He could have got there in time. In fact he's almost the only person at the dance who could have done so. He was first away, just as soon as he saw that Katie had taken the bait. It would be a matter of minutes to drive back to his house. The business of the telephone message maybe held him up for a few minutes, but no longer."

"Wouldn't his wife hear him driving off?" said Mavor.

"She's very deaf, sir. And she takes sleeping pills.

You'll find Miss Tress mentioned it in her statement. They're quite strong. You can only get them on a doctor's certificate."

"I suppose you checked this, too?" said Knott.

"Aye. I'd a word with Dr. Farmiloe."

"Go on," said Mavor. "Mariner drives down to the river, parks his car, walks along and smashes in Katie's head. Now why would he do a thing like that?"

"It's a bit difficult to be sure about that, sir, without knowing exactly what the relationship between them was."

Knott grunted and said, "If there was a relationship."

"Oh, I think there was," said McCourt. He seemed to be gaining confidence as he went along. "If you remember what Windle said—it's in his statement there."

"Don't read it," said Mavor. "Play it to us. It's always clearer that way."

It took a minute to fit the tape into the machine and locate the place. Then Tony Windle's voice came out, startlingly lifelike: "'The most you'll ever end up as is "something in insurance." That's no good to a girl like me. What I need is people with influence. People who can help me out when I get into trouble. I've got friends like that up in London. And I've got at least one *very* useful friend down here.' I asked her who it was and she wouldn't tell me."

McCourt clicked off the machine. Mavor said, "Fill me in, please. That was Tony Windle, the local boyfriend, talking? And he was reporting something Katie had said to him?"

"That's right, sir."

"Play the last bit again."

Tony's voice said, "'And I've got at least one *very* useful friend down here.' I asked her who it was and she wouldn't tell me."

Mavor said, "And you think this *very* useful friend was George Mariner?"

"I know he was useful to her once."

"Oh? Tell us about that."

"It was the time when a boy was knocked down by a hit-and-run motorist last March. A small red car. I'd been told to look into it. I'd eliminated a number of other possibilities and I'd concluded there was enough evidence to question Katie. I told Inspector Ray."

"Ray?"

"He was in charge of C.I.D. here," said Dandridge. "He died last week. Stomach cancer."

"And Ray told you to lay off?"

"That's right."

"And you think Mariner had been leaning on him?"

"I think so, sir."

"It's only supposition."

Unexpectedly, Sergeant Esdaile said, "The Inspector and Mr. Mariner were very close. If anyone could influence him, it would be Mr. Mariner."

"Suppose you're right. It puts Katie in Mariner's debt. What was the payoff? Did she give him a turn or two on the punt cushion?"

"That might have been the way it started. But I don't think it stayed like that. Katie was a girl who didn't like anyone to have a hold over her. She preferred—Well, sir, it's all in Mark Holbeck's statement."

"Then I'd better reread it," said Mavor. During the three minutes that it took him to do so there was silence in the room, broken only by Sergeant Esdaile's heavy breathing and an occasional creaking as Dandridge shifted uncomfortably in his chair.

"What Holbeck's statement tells us," said Mavor, "is that Katie was a girl who liked to have the whip hand."

"That's right, sir."

"And how did she get the whip hand over Mariner?"

"I think that's in Holbeck's statement, too, sir. You remember he said that Ruoff was angry because Katie had stolen something on one of her visits to him. Suppose what she stole was evidence that Mariner was one of his customers. His name in an address book, an account, something like that. It didn't mean that Mariner was doing anything criminal—"

"He started as Mr. Mariner," said Knott. "I think I prefer it that way."

"I'm sorry, sir." McCourt's face was as scarlet as if it had been slapped. "It didn't mean that Mr. Mariner was doing anything criminal. But if the story had got out—"

"Chairman of the Bench," said Mavor, "churchwarden, big white chief. You've made your point, Sergeant. Do you think she was blackmailing him?"

"Not for money. She had plenty of her own. I think what she had was a sort of power complex. She liked to have people on the end of a string and give it a tweak from time to time."

"And you think she tweaked Mariner once too often? So he typed out this come-hither note, laid for her and killed her?"

"I thought he might have done."

"It's a theory. Like the case we've been working on so far. They're both theories. That's right, isn't it?"

Not knowing what was coming, and not caring to risk another rebuff, McCourt contented himself with nodding.

"So what we have to do is to compare them. Like the washing powders on television. Give them a practical test on Junior's soccer shorts and see which of them washes whitest."

In the next few minutes McCourt realized one fact clearly. It was not his impressive appearance alone which had elevated Mavor to the position of Senior Treasury Counsel.

"So far as motive goes, you'd agree that the motive you put forward for Mariner will work equally well with Limbery? If Katie had proof of some homosexual activity—there are hints of this in a number of statements—then it would give her the same sort of hold over him. And since he was the more violent character of the two, he was more likely to have reacted by killing her. All right? So far as motive goes, we'll call it fifteen-all. Now let's think about opportunity. Your timetable is feasible, but it's damned tight. Dr. Farmiloe, who doesn't make mistakes about things like that, gave the *likely* limits as eleven ten to eleven forty. When he says that, he's really putting his money on sometime halfway between. Say eleven twenty-five or eleven thirty at the latest. It was *after* eleven when Mariner left the dancehall. He had to get his car out, get his wife on board, drive home, get her out again and install her in her bedroom. Then cope with the maid and the telephone call. Then, I imagine, take a peep at his wife to see she really was asleep. Then get the car out, drive it by the back way, I imagine, to River Park Avenue and park it. Then walk two or three hundred yards to the boathouse. If I'd been asked, I wouldn't have put him there before twenty to twelve."

"If he didn't go there to kill Katie," said McCourt, "why did he go?"

"That's obvious," said Knott. "He saw her slipping off, guessed she was going to meet Limbery and decided to treat himself to an eyeful. Bang in character."

Mavor nodded. "So he arrives sometime after half past eleven. By which time Limbery could have killed Katie *and* Lewson and got clear. Mariner waits at his spyhole for twenty minutes or so. No luck. Nothing for peeping Tom this time. He pussyfoots back to his car, arriving there a few minutes past twelve, and drives off, being heard by Miss Tress, whose extrasensory perception tells her that a dirty old man is passing her bedroom window, and is noticed driving back *without lights* by the vicar and his wife. All right so far, Sergeant?"

McCourt said, "Aye, it'll work that way, too."

"Thirty-all so far? Right. Now I'll give you three reasons why your theory of Mariner as murderer doesn't work at all. First, because the murderer, as we suppose, visited Katie's house later that night and broke open her desk to find the note which he hadn't found when he ransacked her bag. Or what he thought was her bag. Why should Mariner have bothered? The note didn't incriminate him. It pointed away from him. It pointed to Limbery."

"The breaking in could be unconnected with the killing. There'd been an attempted burglary once before."

"Ingenious, but unconvincing. Take the next point. The latest reasonable time for the killings was half past eleven. Here's Mariner with two corpses on his hands. So tell me this. Why did he hang around for half an hour?"

"Searching Katie's bag."

"Twenty seconds."

"Hiding the weapon."

"If he didn't throw it into the river higher up, he'd take it home with him."

"Perhaps Dr. Farmiloe was wrong about the time."

"It's not a supposition I'd bank on myself. But let me show you the third hole in your case. To my mind it disposes of it. Haven't you forgotten that telephone call?"

McCourt started to say something and then stopped.

"Work it out, Sergeant."

"You mean the call Lewson made to Mariner's house? The one that Polly took?"

"And told him about. He may or may not have known who Lewson or Lewisham was, but he knew this much. *Someone had telephoned him asking for him by name and proposed to call on him later that evening.* If he was proposing to go out and treat himself to an eyeful of what was going on in the boathouse he wouldn't necessarily have put it off. Suppose the man does turn up. His wife's in bed, deaf and drugged. There's no one else in the house, which is an isolated one. He can ring the bell and thump the knocker as much as he likes. In fact, if he does know who Lewson is, all the more reason for being out when he calls. He knows Lewson can't hang around too long. He'll be planning to take the last train back to town. Another reason, incidentally, for not coming back until after twelve. *But now try it the other way round.* Imagine he's going out to commit a carefully planned murder. Knowing that a man is going to come to his house and will stand up afterwards in court and say, 'Wherever else Mariner was at half past eleven he wasn't at home. I thumped on the knocker for five minutes. I could hear the dog barking. If he'd been there he must have heard me.'"

"You started at fifteen-all," said Knott with a grin. "I think we've reached game, set and match. Retire gracefully, Sergeant."

McCourt was saved from answering by the telephone. It was the outside line on Shilling's table. He listened with a look of mild surprise on his friendly face.

"It's for you, Ian," he said. "Walter Steelstock on the line. He wants a word with you. He says it's urgent."

"Me, personally?"

"You, by name."

Knott said, "If it's urgent, you'd better jump on your fiery steed and gallop round there."

After he had gone, there was a moment of silence, broken by Mavor, who said, "He's a bright lad. There were one or two very good points in that theory of his. Got a logical mind. Only wants a bit more experience."

"He told me," said Esdaile, "that he was planning to be a lawyer. It didn't work out. His father died."

"Wouldn't there be more scope for him up in the Met?"

"He tried it," said Shilling. "It went sour on him. He got dipped head first into the cesspit of Soho and it didn't mix well with a simple Scottish upbringing."

Knott said, "As if this case wasn't complicated enough, without detective sergeants thinking for themselves." He said this with ferocious good humor. "Don't you start getting ideas of your own, Eddie."

"Me?" said Esdaile. "I just do what I'm told. I spend most of my time looking for typewriters."

"The machine that note was written on," said Mavor thoughtfully. "If you could find that, it really would be a clincher."

When McCourt reached West Hannington Manor, Walter had the front door open for him. He said, "Come in quietly, if you don't mind. Mother's in the drawing room. We didn't want to disturb her."

He led the way up the broad thick-carpeted staircase and along a passage to a door on the left, at the end. It was a bedroom which had been converted into a mixture of study and workshop, a boy's room full of books, papers, trophies, toolkits, records, posters and photographs.

"I've got the Sergeant for you," said Walter and

backed out, closing the door quietly but firmly behind him.

Peter, who had got up as they came in, indicated the only chair and said, "Won't you sit down." He sounded as breathless as if he had just finished a hundred-yard sprint.

McCourt said, "Thank you," and seated himself with deliberate slowness. His hand on the side farthest from Peter slid in his coat pocket and switched on the recorder. "I gather you've something you wanted to tell me."

"I heard," said Peter, "that is, Walter told me—Is it true that no one knows where Johnno—where Limbery—was that night?" He was speaking in a high, unnatural voice.

"If it's the Friday night of the killing you mean, we have had an account from Limbery of his movements."

"But he can't *prove* where he was?"

"His story is unsupported at the moment."

"Well, I can tell you where he was. And I can prove it. He was with me."

McCourt said in his most unemphatic voice. "Aye. Well, perhaps you'd like to tell me about that. Before we start, why don't you sit down. I'll have to ask you a few questions. It'll maybe take a little time."

Peter squatted on the end of the bed. The action of sitting down seemed in some sense to relax him. He said, "It was about ten o'clock—a bit later. Mother and Walter had gone out to this dance and Mrs. Basset always has Friday evenings off, so I was alone downstairs when the telephone rang. It was Johnno—Mr. Limbery."

"Let's call him Johnno," said McCourt.

"He told me he'd been sent out to do a story on a fire. He was going straightaway. Would I like to come with him for the ride? I said yes, I would. There's a door in the wall at the bottom of our garden. It leads out into Brickfield Road. We keep it locked, of course, but I knew where the key was. And I left the scullery window unlatched. I'd often got in and out that way before." He smiled, in a way that made his sullen face suddenly attractive. "I guessed we might be late getting back, you see, and I wanted to be able to slip in without disturbing the others."

McCourt nearly said, Would your mother have minded you going out like that? but he had the sense not to interrupt. Peter was talking more easily now, but there was explosive material not far below the surface.

"When we got to Streatley we could see the fire. It was the other side of the river, just outside Goring, blazing away like anything. We drove up as close as we could and parked the car and Johnno got out and talked to one of the firemen. They were doing what they could, but until the other brigades arrived they couldn't do all that much."

"That would be the local brigade?"

"I should think so. I don't know exactly what was happening, because I stayed in the car. Johnno made a few inquiries and we pushed off."

"You realize, don't you," said McCourt, "that if your story's going to be a help to Johnno, we have to be a wee bit careful about times. For instance, you said Johnno rang you about ten o'clock, or a bit later. How much later?"

"Not more than a minute or so. The ten o'clock news had just started. I turned it off when the telephone rang."

"Then he drove straight round? So you'd have been on your way by ten past ten and that would get you to

Goring—when? By half past, assuming you went straight there."

"That would be about right, I think. I couldn't swear to the exact time."

"As a policeman, I'm always suspicious of people who swear to exact times. About how long were you at the fire?"

"Well . . ." said Peter.

He's tightening up, thought McCourt. To help him, he said, "I imagine you must have been away before the roof fell in, or Johnno would have put it in his report?"

"Yes, we were away before that happened. I shouldn't think we were there much more than half an hour."

"That brings us to eleven o'clock. What next?"

"Then we drove back to Streatley Common and parked there for a bit. Johnno was writing up his notes. He'd brought his battery-powered record player with him. He usually carried it round in the back of the car. The kids liked playing it."

"So you had a pop concert and he wrote his article for the paper?"

"That's right," said Peter. Easier now.

"And this lasted how long?"

Tension again. "I think it must have been an hour. Perhaps a bit more."

"Well, that takes us to around a quarter past twelve. What happened then?"

"Then we drove back to a telephone box. It was quite funny actually, because soon after he'd started a woman came out of one of the houses and she wanted to use the phone and she got absolutely furious and started hammering on the glass and Johnno took no notice at all."

"You'd be able to identify the house this woman came out of?"

"Yes. I think I could. I think it was the one opposite the telephone box, on the other side of the road."

"Did she see you?"

Peter thought about this one. He said, "I'm not sure. I was sitting quietly in the car. I think perhaps she didn't see me. She was concentrating on getting angry with Johnno."

"What then?"

"Then we put on a few more records and talked for a bit and drove home."

"How long was the second session?"

"I can't remember exactly. I was pretty sleepy by then."

"It's important, so let's see if we can work it out. We know Johnno got home at a quarter to two. He'd have dropped you a few minutes before. Right? That would get you home sometime after half past one. I suppose everyone was in bed."

"There was a light on in Mother's room. I wondered why. Of course, I didn't know—"

"Of course not. Let's say twenty minutes for the drive back. That means you'd have left Streatley at one fifteen, near enough. How long was Johnno on the telephone?"

The question seemed to jerk Peter back from some secret place into which his thoughts had wandered. He said, "How long? Well . . . I don't know. I don't think it can have been much more than ten minutes. I expect it seemed much longer to the lady."

"I expect it did. That would mean that your second session was a bit shorter than the first one. Half past twelve to a quarter past one. Say, three quarters of an hour."

"Yes, I should think that would be about it."

McCourt was planning his strategy carefully. He said, "You're fond of Johnno, aren't you, Peter?"

"Yes, I am." A touch of defiance.

"And I guess he's fond of you."

"You'd know soon enough if Johnno *wasn't* fond of you."

"Not a man to hide his feelings, I agree," said McCourt with a smile. "I suppose you first got to know him when he taught at Coverdales."

"He didn't teach the form I was in. But he ran a sort of unofficial music club. A pop group, really. I was a member of that. The boys all liked him. He didn't get along too well with some of the masters, though."

"And then you saw more of him, of course, when you were at home."

"He came round here a good deal."

"To see Katie."

"To see both of us, I guess. Mother froze him out after a bit. She didn't approve of him at all."

"Different generations, different points of view," said McCourt easily. He was coming to the point now and he had to tread with care. There was a question that must be asked. He knew it and he fancied Peter knew it too. Chief Superintendent Knott would have had no doubts and no hesitation. He would have banged the boy over the head with it and gone on banging until he had got the answer he wanted. Looking at Peter's flushed but obstinate face, he thought that a slow approach might be more productive than brutality.

He said, "I'll tell you frankly what's worrying me, Peter. You're a great friend of Johnno's. In fact you're one of his fan club. Like all the boys round here, as far as I can make out. Everyone will know that. If you come forward now with this story, people are going to ask two obvious questions. First, if your account is correct, why is it totally different from Johnno's own account?"

Peter said, "Is it?" It was either good acting or his astonishment was genuine.

"It certainly is. You won't expect me to go into details, but really your account doesn't tie up anywhere at all with his. But the second question is even more important. *Why haven't you said something before?* You know—everyone's known—for the last ten days what Johnno's accused of doing and when he was supposed to have done it. Why didn't you come forward at once? Why didn't you say, 'He couldn't have done it. He was with me the whole time'?"

Peter said nothing.

"Don't you see, it makes what you're doing now look like a last-minute effort to save Johnno's skin."

Peter still said nothing. He seemed to be enmeshed in his own thoughts.

With genuine compassion in his voice, McCourt said, "I expect I oughtn't to be saying this, but I will. If you want to go back on what you've told me, now's the time to do it. Before you get involved to a point where you *can't* go back."

Peter seemed to be nerving himself. McCourt waited patiently as the seconds ticked by in silence. Then Peter said, "Unless I can answer both those questions, you're not going to believe what I've told you. No one's going to believe it. Is that right?"

McCourt said, "Aye. That's about the strength of it."

"The answer to both questions is the same. Johnno wouldn't tell you and I couldn't. Because of what went on in the car."

For a long moment McCourt didn't seem to understand him. Then he said, in a voice suddenly hard, "Be careful what you say now."

"You wanted the truth. I'm going to give it to you. I've always been in love with Johnno and I think he's always been in love with me."

"Love?" said McCourt. The single syllable spat out like a small explosion.

"Yes, love. Why shouldn't he love me? What's wrong with it?"

McCourt said nothing.

"People thought he came round to our house to see Katie. It wasn't true. He came to see me. I don't think I realized how far it had gone. I mean, he hadn't actually done anything to me before. Being together there in the car that night, it just happened. He put one arm round me and started to kiss me. I kissed him back."

"Was that all?"

"No, it wasn't all."

"Did he undress you?"

"Yes."

"And you let him do that?"

"I didn't let him do it. I helped him." The defiance was back in Peter's voice.

"I don't think we need the details right now," said McCourt. He put a hand into his jacket pocket and switched off the tape recorder. Then he got up and said, "You called it love. I call it filth."

He walked across to the door and went out, leaving Peter sitting on the end of the bed with fat tears rolling down his cheeks.

"*Well*," said Mavor, "and what do you make of that?"

Shilling had departed for London and the Superintendent was alone with Mavor. McCourt's tape recorder stood on the table between them.

"I'd been expecting something of the sort," said Knott. "When a case stirs up a lot of local feeling, you're always liable to get it. Someone comes forward with a last-minute alibi."

"Then you don't believe the boy's story?"

"Not a word of it."

"You realize it can't have been a last-minute effort. They must have concocted it together, before you pulled Limbery in. Otherwise Peter couldn't have known about the episode at the telephone box."

"At first sight that was a convincing touch," agreed Knott. "But it doesn't necessarily mean they concocted the story together. I think what happened was that Limbery told Peter about the woman wanting to use the telephone box and dancing with rage and banging on the glass. Told it to him as a good story, maybe they had a private laugh over it. When Peter had to invent his version he fitted in that bit. Limbery couldn't use it himself. He needed a story which kept him at the fire much longer. Well past the time of the murder. And he stretched it a bit further with that snack at the motel—where no one seems to have remembered him, incidentally."

"Friday night crowd. Quite possible."

"Perfectly possible. And if he hadn't come back, by bad luck, across the wrong bridge we might never have been able to shoot his story down at all."

Mavor thought about it. He said, "There was one point in Peter's version that I found almost totally incredible. Did you notice? *He said that he didn't get out of the car when they arrived at the fire.* Can you believe it? Sparks flying, timbers falling, men rushing about. Damn it all, he'd come out to see the fire. Can you imagine any boy staying shut up in the car?"

"Exactly," said Knott. "You find me a single independent witness who saw the boy at the fire, or anywhere else that night, and I might pay some attention to it."

"We shall have to give it to the defense," said Mavor.

"Even if we're not going to use it?"

"Unless you want to go into the Court of Criminal Appeal and come out on your ear. It's an alibi defense. Normally it comes the other way round. This time we've got it first. Certainly it goes to them. And if you feel inclined for a bet, I'll give you two to one in pounds that they don't use it."

Knott considered this generous offer, but said, "No, I've a feeling you're right. It's a messy enough case as it is. They won't risk messing it up further."

Inspector Dandridge at that moment was saying the same thing, in different words, to McCourt. "It's a nasty case," he said. "You don't want to make it any nastier by being too clever. Our job's to put one side of it. The prosecution side. We play that straight down the middle. Sure there are alternative solutions and little bits that don't fit. That's a job for the defense. They'll produce them quick enough, don't you worry."

McCourt, who had been unusually silent since his return from the Manor, said he would bear this advice in mind.

It was past nine when Sergeant Shilling reached London, and the dusk of a late August day was clouding over with a threat of more rain. As he parked his car a flurry of drops blew along the street. He turned up the collar of his raincoat and trudged back along the pavement to Ruoff's front door. A hammering with the bull's-head knocker produced no answer.

In the silence which followed, he thought he heard a very faint sound inside the house. It was an indeterminate noise which might have been made by feet going up or down stairs.

He hammered once again on the knocker. This time the silence was complete. He tried the door handle. The door swung open.

Shilling was conscious of a prickle of apprehension, a capillary reaction to a situation which was abnormal and might be dangerous. Normal householders do not leave their front doors on the latch after dark. Nor do they retreat upstairs when a visitor announces himself. The street was a quiet one, one of London's backwaters, with a privacy and a seclusion that must have suited Ruoff's dubious trade.

No point in hanging about, said Shilling to himself. He went in, but left the front door ajar, giving himself enough light to see the foot of the stairs and the photograph of the giant hand pointing upward.

"Excelsior," said Shilling. He climbed the stairs and paused on the first landing to listen again. In the silence he heard a single very faint creak, as though someone had shifted his weight from one foot to the other, trying to make no noise as he did so. The fact that it was so cautious encouraged Shilling. The man who was ahead of him had as little right in the house as he had. Less, possibly. Shilling climbed the next flight. He was now on the bedroom floor. The door on his left was wide open. Shilling looked in.

This was the master bedroom. The blinds were drawn, but enough light from the streetlamp outside filtered in around the edges for him to see the outlines of the room: the row of white painted cupboards along one wall, the big double bed and an ornate brass lamp on it.

He saw something else, too. A bundle lying on the bed, a shapeless inanimate bundle. Sergeant Shilling knew what it was and cursed under his breath. Then he stepped up to the bed, felt for the switch and turned on the light.

The man was dressed in vivid orange and green pajamas. His hands had been tied, his wrists lashed together with a dressing-gown cord and pulled up into the middle of his back. His ankles had been hobbled with a second cord which was attached to the rail at the foot of the bed. He was lying half on his side, with his face turned away.

Shilling walked around to the other side of the bed. He had known the truth before he saw the engorged face and staring dead eyes. Whatever secrets Rodney Ruoff had possessed, they were not going to learn them from him now.

A noise made him look up.

Three men had come into the room.

21

Shilling knew one of them, a man with close-cropped gray hair and a red face, who said, "Good God, Bob, what the hell are you doing here?"

"I came to ask him some questions," said Shilling, looking down at what lay on the bed.

"Too late now," said the gray-haired man, who was Detective Chief Superintendent Forster. "I suppose it was something to do with what's happening down in Berkshire. It was Charlie Knott who put us onto watching this place."

"What happened to *him?*"

"No mystery about that. One of his boyfriends did it. Kid called Billy. Real age eighteen, mental age eight. Like I said, we had the place under observation. Sergeant Lillee here saw the kid leaving late last night."

"Early this morning," said Sergeant Lillee.

"We knew all about Rod's little games, so there was nothing unusual about it. However, when there was no sign of life, no one going in or out all day, blinds still drawn, we began to wonder what was going on and we went in to look. The Sergeant found him about half an hour before you arrived. He left young Parrish in charge and came for me."

"So it was you pussyfooting about on the stairs, was it?" said Shilling.

"That's right," said Parrish. "Tell you the truth, I thought at first it was Billy, come back to have a look. Mind you," he added hastily, "it was pretty dark."

"What are you going to do now?"

"We're pulling in Billy. No difficulty there. He'll tell us all about it. We shan't even have to ask him."

"You can't help feeling sorry for the stupid bastard," said Shilling. He looked at the bundle on the bed. "I suppose this is an occupational risk with an old poof."

"That's right," said Forster. "He lets the boyfriend tie him up. Master and slave scene. Then the boyfriend gets a bit too excited and finishes him off. It's happening all the time."

"It couldn't have happened at a worse time. I badly needed to ask some questions and he was the only one who could give me the answers."

"There *is* a tie-up with Charlie's business, then?"

"There could be," said Shilling. "But God knows whether we shall ever find out now what it was."

"I'll tell you something," said Sergeant Lillee. "You weren't the only people who were interested in this outfit."

Shilling and Forster stared at him.

He said, "When I was watching the place on Friday night—I was using a room opposite—I saw a man hanging about. I thought I recognized him, so I said to myself, I'll go down and take a closer look. Might have a word with him."

"For God's sake," said Forster. "This isn't a six-part serial. *Who was he?*"

"Chap called Blaine. Works for Captain Smedley's outfit. Used to be in X Division."

"Captain Smedley?" said Shilling.

"Private inquiry agency," said Forster. "Only uses ex-policemen. Very hot stuff."

"Bloody hell," said Shilling.

"It's not going to please Charlie, is it?"

"That's the understatement of the year," said Shilling. "This is going to be apple pie for the defense. Their tactics are obviously going to be to muddy the water, and here's a dirty great stick to do the muddying with. What we must do now, no way out, is find out what the tie-up really was. We can't ask Rod, but there is another possibility. We go through his papers."

Forster thought about it.

He said, "I don't see why not. As long as we do it together. The technical whiz kids will be here any moment now. They'll want to take over this room, and the pathologist will want the body. You and I could start working on his papers."

"There's a sort of office upstairs in the studio," said Parrish. "Lots of books and papers there. Photographs, too."

"Then let's get started," said Forster. "Take us all night, I wouldn't wonder."

"I *had* got other plans for tonight," said Shilling. "I'll have to do some telephoning. She'll be bloody furious."

"Tell her you're saving it up for next time," said Forster.

The second telephone call which Shilling made was at seven o'clock the next morning. It caught Knott as he was shaving. He washed the soap off his face and sat on the edge of the bed swinging his stubby legs and listening to what Shilling had to say.

"Tell me again about those names," he said.

Shilling told him, reading them off a list he had in one hand.

"He seems to have been in touch with half the celebrities in London. Not all stage and screen people, either."

"He was a well-known photographer," said Shilling. "They meet all sorts."

"And the only names which connect up in any way with this business are Katie herself and George Mariner. We already knew he was a customer."

"And Venetia Loftus, as was."

"Yes," said Knott thoughtfully. "And Venetia Loftus. Who is she now?"

"Venetia Arkinshaw. Married to an artist. Lives in Putney."

"Yes," said Knott. He was in no hurry about that one. He was turning over the possible ramifications of involving, even indirectly, the daughter of the Assistant Commissioner in a case which was, God knows, messy and complex enough already.

He said, "She was a particular friend of Katie's, wasn't she?"

"They were at school together. And kept up afterwards."

"And Katie was lunching with her on the day she was killed."

"That's correct," said Shilling, and added, to himself, Not my decision, thank God.

"All right," said Knott at last. "Go and have a word with her. I needn't tell you to go carefully. Don't lean on the fact that Venetia was one of Ruoff's clients. There could be dozens of innocent reasons for that. Keep it general. Anything she can tell us that might help."

"Right."

"And one other thing. *Tell her father what you're planning to do*. If he objects, don't do it."

* * *

The door of the house in Putney was opened by a young man wearing a beard and a smock.

He said, "I gather you've come to grill Venny. Her old man's been on the telephone to her for hours. Has she done something frightful?"

"She hasn't done anything at all," said Shilling with elaborate cheerfulness. "It's just that we think she may, indirectly, be able to help us with some information that she may have picked up at second hand."

"When you wrap it up like that," said the young man, who was Philip Arkinshaw, "it sounds absolutely terrible. However, I gather her father's told her she's got to spill whatever beans there are. Come on up."

He led the way to the first-floor drawing room and left Shilling with Venetia, a pleasant-looking person, of Katie's age and type, but with more than a hint of the maturity that marriage and housekeeping seem to bring.

She said, "Dad's been on the phone. I gather you want to know about Rodney Ruoff."

"Anything you can tell me."

"Is it right he's been killed?"

"Yes."

"Who did it? One of his boyfriends?"

"The local police seem to think so."

"He had it coming to him. He really was a sod."

"In the original sense of the word," said Shilling with a smile.

"That's right. In the original sense of the word. He's no loss to anyone. How does he fit into your business? What was his connection with Katie's death?"

"That's where we hoped you could help us, Mrs. Arkinshaw."

"Well, I'll do what I can. It was—let me think—three or four years ago. I can't remember the exact date.

It was when Rodney was starting to promote Katie. Show her photographs around and talk to people who could be useful. And in case you're thinking anything else, Sergeant, so far as Katie was concerned, that was all it was. He hadn't got any other ideas about her. To start with, he hadn't much use for girls as girls. Only as models."

"Strictly for show and not for use."

"Right. And it *was* a sort of safety factor when you went to one of his parties."

"Wild parties, I imagine."

"Orgies, Sergeant. No other word for it. Fun though, in a creepy sort of way. You met all sorts. Upper crust and lower crust. You were always encouraged to bring guests. As long as they were young and beautiful. Going to them was the thing to have done among the young of our set at that time. It was a sort of dare, if you understand me."

She spoke of it, thought Shilling, as though it was thirty years ago, not three.

"Katie and I reckoned that if we brought our own drink with us and kept together we'd get away more or less intact."

"Your own drink?"

"That was the important thing. If Rod had his eye on anyone he used to fix their drink. God knows what he put into it. Some sort of drug, I imagine. So what we used to do was take a medicine bottle full of something fairly harmless in our evening bags—outsize evening bags being rather the fashion at that time. Then, if the drink looked suspicious, we'd tip it quietly into a vase and refill from our own supply."

"You could do that?"

"When Rod's parties got under way you could do anything. Even if someone had noticed you, they wouldn't have batted an eyelid."

"And what was Ruoff's idea?"

When Venetia hesitated, Shilling said with his most candid smile, "It's all right, Mrs. Arkinshaw. I'm older than I look. And I did spend a year at West End Central."

Venetia said. "You sound like an S.S. boy saying, 'I did my year at Buchenwald.'"

"It wasn't quite as bad as that. But we did have to deal with some fairly incredible perversions."

"This wasn't incredible. You might call it commercial. He'd get some boy or girl hooched up to the eyebrows and take them off into one of the bedrooms. Maybe a boy on his own, or two boys, or two girls. He'd get them to take off their clothes and pose for him."

"The commercial angle being?"

"Certainly not blackmail. I don't think that was ever the idea. What he wanted was photographs he could sell to the porn merchants here and abroad. A lot of the really way-out pictures went to Denmark and Sweden. Another thing, if the person concerned *was* at all well known—I don't mean a celebrity, but someone who might have friends who'd kick up a fuss—he usually managed the picture so that the face was unrecognizable. He was a good enough photographer to do that. He couldn't always manage it. It was when he slipped up on that, once, that he got into trouble, I believe."

"That's right," said Shilling. "And got off with a fine. Which no doubt the sale of the photographs paid for ten times over."

While he was saying this, he was thinking that a lot of what he was hearing he knew before. Some of it was new. But none of it really took them much further. Venetia was offering information readily enough. But his instinct told him that she was keeping something back. There was one locked room in the house. One secret cupboard that hadn't been opened. And the tantalizing thought was that if he could see into it he would see the whole truth.

He said cautiously, "When I was talking to Katie's agent, Mark Holbeck—I expect you know him?"

"Yes. I know Mark. I thought Katie rather went for him at one time, actually."

"Not reciprocated?"

"I gather not."

"Well, Holbeck mentioned some occasion when he'd met Ruoff at a party. This was fairly recently, I gather. When he mentioned Katie's name, Ruoff blew up. He said she'd stolen some of his property and refused to give it back. The implication was that he couldn't take any steps to get it back either. I don't suppose you'd have any idea what it was?"

"No," said Venetia slowly. "But I could guess."

"Yes?"

"It's what I was telling you. About the photographs Rod took. If the face was recognizable—particularly if it was someone . . . well . . . someone who was normally rather respectable—Rod couldn't flog it to a porno magazine. But the chances are he'd keep it. Suppose Katie was at the studio one day on business and was left alone for a moment. It would have been just like her to open drawers and cupboards and poke about to see what she could find. She was noted at school for being light-fingered where other people's property was concerned."

"Yes," said Shilling. "Yes."

The door of the secret cupboard was half open.

"If it happened to be someone she knew. Someone at Hannington, say. Someone respectable. Naturally she'd have kept it. And as like as not she'd have let the person concerned know she'd got it. Not to make money out of him. Just to feel that he was in her power and had to dance when she pulled the strings."

"Yes," said Shilling again.

"But I'm afraid that's only guesswork. I don't really think there's anything more I can tell. It was a long time ago and in retrospect rather silly, I'm afraid. I'm a sober married woman now."

A gesture indicated the nicely furnished drawing room, a photograph of the infant on the mantelpiece, the carapace of respectability.

Shilling accepted that he was being dismissed. He said, "Thank you very much, Mrs. Arkinshaw. What you've told me could be very valuable. If you do think of anything else, telephone Hannington 343. Direct dialing. You'll be put straight through to Superintendent Knott or myself, or if we both happen to be out, Inspector Dandridge, or one of the sergeants, Esdaile or McCourt. Don't bother to show me out, please. I can find my own way."

Venetia held the door of the drawing room open and watched him make his way down the narrow but elegant stairs toward the front door.

It was as well for Sergeant Shilling's peace of mind that he was unable to see the expression on her face.

"It's plausible," said Knott. "But it needn't necessarily have been Mariner. Lot of respectable people in Hannington."

"Although we already know there *was* a connection between Mariner and the Ruoff crowd," said Mavor.

"I know, I know," said Knott. He sounded both angry and obstinate. Shilling recognized the tone of voice. He had heard it before in other cases.

"But it doesn't *prove* anything. Suppose everything we

think is true. Suppose he's a dirty old man and Katie found a picture of him with his clothes off. Suppose she used it to tweak him. Suppose she even used it to get him to lean on Inspector Ray about the hit-and-run case. Suppose all of that. It still doesn't make him a murderer. He's not the murdering type. Limbery is."

"There's only one objection to that," said Knott. "I can't imagine why Mariner would agree to take his clothes off, or even more why anyone would want to take a photograph of him when he had."

"You can't tell with men of that age," said Mavor. "One of our high court judges—Well, no, I'd better not tell you about that."

There was a knock on the door and McCourt came in. His face was whiter than usual. He had a slip of paper in his hand. He said, "A message has come through from Central. They've had a report from the Forensic Science people who've been working on those prints we sent them. The ones from the door of the cupboard above Katie's desk."

"Well?" said Knott impassively.

"They're sending you a written report. I jotted down the gist of it. They've managed to bring up two prints, a thumb and an index finger, sharp enough for identification. Neither of them corresponds to Limbery's prints."

"I see. Anything more?"

"They tried them on the main computer. No record."

"Well, that's that. Thank you, Ian."

McCourt placed the paper quietly on the table and went out. Mavor had been watching him. He said, "I've got two pieces of advice for you about that young man. The first is that Dandridge ought to find him something to do. Something quite unconnected with this case, I mean. There must be plenty of routine work piling up. The second is, don't call him as a witness."

"I wasn't thinking of doing so," said Knott. "But why? Do you think he's turning sour?"

"Not sour exactly," said Mavor. "But he's got a very Scottish conscience. Abstract notions of right and wrong. It makes him an uncomfortable bedfellow in a case like this where there's a lot of wrong and not much right."

22

By the time McCourt had crossed the yard and reached the room he shared with Esdaile his face had changed from white to red. He shut the door with explosive firmness and said, "I see."

"See what?" said Esdaile.

"I see," said McCourt. "That's all he said: 'I see.' I tell him that the bottom's knocked out of his case and that's all he can say: 'I see.'"

"I wouldn't go as far as that," said Esdaile placidly. "I never thought that burglary at Katie's place had necessarily got anything to do with her killing."

"Not necessarily," said McCourt. "But it seemed pretty clear. The killer searched her bag for the note he'd sent. He couldn't find it, so he went to her house to look for it."

"Maybe," said Esdaile. "Maybe not. Don't forget, she was burgled once before."

"All right," said McCourt. "Let's suppose it was just a coincidence. I don't believe it. But suppose it was. Are we going to give the facts to the defense? Are we going to say to them that when we started we thought this fingerprint was so important we took the door right off its hinges and sent it up to the Science Laboratory and wasted their time on it for a fortnight and now it doesn't turn out to be the one we wanted, we're going to forget about it?"

"No need to get worked up," said Esdaile. "It's nothing to do with you or me."

"Of course it is. It's to do with us and everyone else in the police. If we don't play the rules, who is going to?"

Esdaile looked at him curiously. He said, "If you feel like that, you ought to resign."

"That would just be running away."

"For God's sake," said Esdaile. "What *are* you going to do?"

McCourt relaxed and grinned. "What I'd like to do is to catch the killer and hand him to Superintendent Knott on a plate, clearly labeled and garnished with watercress. And there's only one way to do that. We've *got* to find that typewriter."

"Don't talk to me about typewriters. I've started dreaming about typewriters." Esdaile opened his desk and took out a thick file. "I worked out the other day, I've asked two hundred and ten people if they've ever owned or sold or seen a Crossfield Electric. I've actually traced two dozen of them and none of them produced a sample which looked anything like that bloody note. It wasn't worth sending them up to the Documents Division. Even I could see they were no good."

McCourt seemed to be thinking of something else. He said, "When you were making these inquiries, Eddie, how did you do it?"

"How?"

"I don't mean with the shops. They'd know what you meant when you talked about a Crossfield Electric. I meant with private people. Look. Say the husband was out and you asked the wife whether her husband used to have one. She'd say, 'Oh, I know he *had* a typewriter, but I can't remember exactly what sort it was.'"

"I showed her a picture, of course."

"Have you got a picture?"

"Dozens of them." He fished out a handful of catalogues and pushed one across. McCourt examined it. It seemed to fascinate him. He stared at it for so long that Esdaile said, "What's up? The bloody thing isn't even beautiful. Now if I'd been going round with the photograph of some smashing girl—"

"Eddie," said McCourt, "I've seen a machine just like this one."

"I've seen two dozen. I told you."

McCourt ignored him. He said, "Do you remember? I told you two or three weeks ago I had to go and see the Master Mariner. It was when that joker tried to wreck his car. He kept me waiting for twenty minutes in what he calls his business room. I had plenty of time to admire the fixtures and fittings. *I'll swear he had a typewriter just like this one.*"

Esdaile said slowly, "He must have bought it up in London, then. Because if he'd bought it anywhere local I'd have been given his name by the shop that supplied it. Are you sure?"

"Absolutely sure."

"Another thing," said McCourt. "There's been a lot of publicity about this. A notice in the press and so on. If he really has got a Crossfield Electric, why hasn't he come forward to say so? If he was innocent he'd have told you about it and you'd have gone up and taken a sample of the type face and cleared it and that would have been the end of it."

The two sergeants looked at each other.

"What are you going to do about it?" said Esdaile at last.

"Think up some excuse and go up and have a look for myself. If he keeps me waiting, which he usually does, I'll slip in a piece of paper and run off a sample."

"Suppose he hears you?"

"If it's an electric typewriter it'll be pretty quiet."

"I hope so," said Esdaile. "Because if he catches you taking samples behind his back and if they turn out to be innocent samples, he really will have a stick to beat you with. He plays golf with the Chief Constable, too."

McCourt said, "If the samples match, it'll be a long time before he plays golf with anyone."

"We have quite a few points to consider," said Mrs. Bellamy, "and one or two very useful leads." Her voice had a purring quality. She's a cat, thought Noel, a big well-muscled tabby cat, sleepy-looking, but murder to any mouse that strays within reach of her claws.

"First of all, we've got Captain Smedley's reports. There's no doubt at all that the killing of Ruoff has got some connection with Katie's death. Otherwise why would Sergeant Shilling, who must have more than enough work to do down at Hannington, be snooping around Chelverton Mews?"

"The papers this morning," said Simon Crakenshaw, "all carried the same story—some sort of official handout, I suppose. That a man was assisting the police with their inquiries and a charge was expected shortly."

"No doubt," said Mrs. Bellamy. "But it still leaves my question unanswered. Here's another one. What was Lewson, one of Ruoff's bodyguards, doing down at Hannington? And how did he come to fall into the river with a hole in his head which had been made by the same weapon which killed Katie? Your pathologist was absolutely clear about that, Laura?"

Laura showed her pretty teeth in a grin and said, "Absolutely, Mrs. Bellamy. As a matter of fact he was rather annoyed about that. Apparently Knott didn't entirely trust his opinion. He sent his report up to Summerson for checking. That's the sort of thing that just isn't done among top-class pathologists."

"Knott never had an ounce of tact. What did Summerson do?"

"He sent the report back with a scribble at the bottom of it. 'I agree with every word of this report and wonder why it was necessary for me to see it.'"

"Excellent," said Mrs. Bellamy. "That gives us several different lines of attack. Next we have to think about this last-minute alibi that the prosecution has kindly presented us with."

"I'm not too clear about the rules," said Noel. "I suppose they passed it on to us because they had to."

"In theory," said Mrs. Bellamy, "the Crown has to present the defense with any relevant information. However, there's no need for them to do so before the committal proceedings. Then they must expose the whole of their case. But they'd have been severely criticized if they hadn't passed on this particular piece of information as soon as they got it. And I think they had another reason. They were fairly certain we wouldn't dare to use it."

Noel said in tones of incredulity, "But I thought—"

"You thought that the boy's story was a complete defense to Limbery, Mr. Vigors."

"Well," said Noel. "*If* it's true, surely—"

"Whether it's true or not is unimportant. In the last analysis what matters is whether the court believes it. He'd be savagely cross-examined, asked for prurient details, which he'd be ashamed or unwilling to give, contradict himself at half a dozen points and finish by bursting into tears. And at the end of it all, when he'd been publicly crucified, do you know what conclusion the court would come to? They would conclude that conduct of this sort *had* taken place, possibly more than once, but *not* necessarily on the night in question. And this presents the Crown with one enormous advantage, one ace in their hand which they didn't possess before. You might almost call it the ace of trumps. Motive, Mr. Vigors. Motive."

"I suppose so," said Noel unhappily. Although no hint of expression had appeared on their well-drilled countenances, he felt certain that Sophie and Laura were laughing at him.

Mrs. Bellamy said, in more accommodating tones, "You mustn't believe all the nonsense that's talked about motive. Every judge in a murder case tells the jury that there's no onus on the prosecution to prove motive. I sometimes wonder how he can say it without laughing. There may be no onus, at law, *but motive is the one thing the jury understands*. They don't believe that people commit murder for no reason at all. Show them a reason and you show them a guilty man. So far the one motive they've got is a piffling one. A lovers' quarrel! Six weeks before! No one in their senses is going to believe in that as a motive for murder. But give them a real motive. Let Peter tell his story and suggest that Katie had got to know about it. Hell hath no fury like a woman who's been thrown over for another woman. But a girl who's been thrown over for her own brother! A girl like Katie, who had a tongue like a whipsaw and enjoyed using it and watching people squirm. There's a background to murder that any jury could understand."

Simon said, "I see the force of that. But can we do without Peter's evidence? The court *might* believe him. And it *is* an alibi."

Mrs. Bellamy considered the point, her thick white hands resting on the table in front of her. She carried an armory of rings on both hands thick as knuckle dusters.

"It's really a balance of chances," she said. "If the Crown case was a strong one, I'd agree with you, we'd have to use the boy. But I don't think it is a strong one. The more I look at it the weaker it seems. Are you by any chance a bridge player, Mr. Crakenshaw?"

Simon, who knew that Mrs. Bellamy was a bridge player of international repute, thought it safer to say, "I play a little."

"Then you know that the secret of good defense lies in working out what cards your opponent holds. So let's see what cards the Crown has got."

She ticked them off, one point at a time, the rings on her fingers sending out flashes of blue light as she did so.

"They've got the note. That's their strong card. I imagine they hoped to spring it on us, but luckily we know all about it."

Noel nodded. It was Walter who had given him that useful piece of information.

"Forewarned is forearmed. The evidence that it came from Limbery is internal and we know that they're not too confident about it. If they had been, they wouldn't have wasted all that time looking for the typewriter. What else have they got? Opportunity. Limbery wasn't at the dance. Five hundred other inhabitants of Hannington weren't at the dance. Is that a reason for suggesting they killed Katie? His account of his movements that night is inaccurate. Suppose that it is. People aren't always meticulously accurate when talking to the police. Particularly when they haven't been charged and have no reason to suppose they are going to be. Motive? As things stand, so weak as to be unbelievable. I'm really surprised at Knott risking a charge if that's all the ammunition he's got."

Surprised, thought Noel. But pleased, too. She's looking forward to her old enemy making a fool of himself.

He said, "Do I gather from what you've said that you propose to go the whole way in the Magistrates Court?"

"And lift restrictions on reporting?" said Simon.

"We've asked for an old-fashioned committal," said Mrs. Bellamy. "No need to make our minds up on the other points until the last moment. We'll keep our options open."

McCourt had decided that a simple and adequate excuse for calling on Mariner was to take along a copy of the photograph of Gabby Lewson and ask him if he recognized it. This could reasonably be tied into an inquiry about the telephone call from the mysterious Mr. Lewisham.

Two things prevented him from carrying out this plan immediately. The first was that he suddenly seemed to have a great deal of work to do—routine matters which had been pushed to one side while the murder investigation was proceeding. It was not until late on the Wednesday evening of that week that he managed to get away and visit the Croft. Here he met the second difficulty. Polly, who answered the door, told him that Mariner was not at home.

"Gone up to London for two days," she said. "Left this morning. Coming back Friday night."

"Do you know what he's up to?"

"Search me," said Polly. "I heard him telling Mrs. Mariner something about business."

This was awkward. If he asked to be allowed to inspect Mariner's study, Polly would be bound to ask him why he wanted to and he could think of no plausible excuse for doing so. Not that Polly would have objected. He suspected that she disliked Mariner almost as much as he did.

She said, "If it's urgent, he's staying at his club. You could get hold of him there."

McCourt said, "It'll keep. I'll try again on Friday evening."

* * *

The thought of what he had to do worried Noel Vigors so much that he found it difficult to get to sleep. He was desperately sorry for Peter. He had known and liked him ever since he was a shy six-year-old wincing under his father's hearty verbal onslaughts. He suspected that what had brought Peter and Limbery together was the fact that they had both been afflicted with bullying and inadequate fathers.

Peter's statement of what had happened on that Friday night when Katie was killed had had the ring of truth. Noel was more than half inclined to believe it. That, as he informed his pillow at two o'clock in the morning, was personal feeling; and it was his duty as a professional man to be impersonal and dispassionate. Intellectually he accepted the arguments put forward by Mrs. Bellamy for not calling the boy. He accepted that she was more experienced in these matters than he was. He tried not to be influenced by the fact that he disliked her.

Georgie grunted sleepily and said, "Wassup?"

"Too hot."

She said, "Take off one of the blankets," turned over and went to sleep again. He wished he could have discussed the problem with her, but that was professionally impossible. He turned onto his other side and started to count sheep going through a gate until these became clients going through the door of his office. He got a couple of hours of unrestful sleep.

Next morning when he reached the Manor, Peter, who had been warned of his visit, was waiting for him. They walked down together to the wooden shack beside the tennis court which was a repository for tennis and croquet gear and they sat on a bench in front of it.

Peter said, "I heard you'd taken on this case. I was glad about that. Johnno would have made an awful mess of it if he'd tried to do it himself. Is it true you've got a Q.C. from London?"

"Quite true. I saw her yesterday."

"Her? You mean it's a woman? Funny. I always thought of Q.C.'s as men. Do you think a woman will be able to stand up to the police?"

"I can't think of anyone Mrs. Bellamy isn't capable of standing up to."

"I expect you wanted to talk about my—about me—giving evidence."

Noel thought that there was no point in trying to break it to him gently. He said, "As I told you, we had a conference on the case yesterday. Mrs. Bellamy has decided that it would be better not to call you."

He had wondered how Peter would take it. Many people, having offered to give evidence, evidence which would involve them in public ridicule, if nothing worse, might have been relieved when their brave offer was refused. The reaction he had not looked for was anger.

The blood mounted in the boy's face, coloring his pale and freckled skin. He said, "Why, Noel? Why? Why?"

Noel said, "The police don't usually try to help the defense in a case like this. So when they told us what you'd said, we came to the conclusion that they *wanted* you to give evidence. That it would actually help their case. You'd be cross-examined viciously about exactly what had taken place between you and Limbery. They'd ask you for a lot of details. You understand? Then they'd suggest that this part of your evidence was very likely true. *But that it hadn't happened on this particular occasion*. That you'd made all that up, to help him. Do you see?"

Peter muttered something under his breath. His mouth was set in a hard line that reminded Noel of Mrs. Steelstock.

Noel said, "If they could convince the court that their version was right, it supplied a sort of motive . . ."

Noel was aware that he was getting into deep water. Fortunately for him, Peter didn't seem to be listening. He was busy with his own bitter thoughts. He said, "When I told Sergeant McCourt what had happened, I thought the police would have to drop the case. All he's done is tell everyone about it."

"Not everyone," said Noel. He was listening more to the tone of voice than to the words. He wondered if there was any age at which you could be more deeply hurt than at sixteen. "I know about it. And our counsel knows. They wouldn't—they couldn't—say a word to anyone else."

"All right. I trust you. But I don't trust the police. They'll talk about it and make jokes about it and soon it'll get out. Johnno warned me, never trust the police. Never, never, never. They'll always do you down if they can. I hate them. All of them. Particularly that smug Sergeant. I thought he'd understand. He's always been friendly. And he—he looked at me as if I was a piece of dirt he wanted to scrape off his boot."

When Noel got home to lunch, as he did on most days, Georgie said, "What's up? You look as if you'd been run over by a traction engine."

"Not a bad guess," said Noel. "I can't tell you about it now, but I will when it's all over."

"It's this bloody case, isn't it?"

"Yes."

"I wish to God, if Katie was going to get murdered, she'd had the decency to do it up in London, where she really belonged."

This made Noel laugh, which may have been what Georgie had intended.

23

"I wish Peter wouldn't spend all his time cooped up in that room of his," said Mrs. Steelstock. "He's hardly come out of it for the last two days. It can't be healthy. Couldn't you get him to take some exercise?"

"I've tried," said Walter. "He just tells me to leave him alone."

"What about a game of tennis?"

"He doesn't want to play tennis."

"What can be wrong with him? He's been like this ever since that policeman came to see him. Do you think he can have said something to upset him?"

"I think he may have done," said Walter. "The only things he's said to me have been about the police. He's very bitter."

"About all of them?"

"Yes. About Sergeant McCourt in particular."

"Odd," said Mrs. Steelstock. "He always seemed to me to be one of the nicer ones. Nicer than that horrible Superintendent from London, anyway. Whatever can he have done to him?"

"Term will soon be starting. He'll have to snap out of it then."

* * *

It was late on Friday evening when McCourt arrived at the Croft and rang the bell. Polly opened the door to him. She said, "His Majesty is taking his bath. As soon as he emerges I will inform him of your presence. Perhaps you would care to await him in his throne room. I mean his study."

"O.K. I hope he won't be too long."

"Fifteen minutes minimum, I should guess," said Polly. "He's a careful washer."

That should be long enough, said McCourt, but this was to himself.

As soon as he was alone in the study he moved across quietly to the desk where he knew the typewriter was kept. The desk was locked. It did not look like the kind of lock that would respond to such simple methods as were available to him. Moreover, if he succeeded in opening it he was far from certain that he would be able to relock it. One thing he did notice. If there was an electric typewriter in the desk, it was no longer plugged into the wall socket.

It was a full twenty minutes before George Mariner appeared. Even before he began to speak, McCourt noticed the change in him. His face seemed to have lost some of its smooth rosiness and his eyes were deeper in his head. He looked like a man who has sustained a shock. A man who was unused to shocks and lacked the resilience to deal with them.

Mariner said, speaking hurriedly, "Sorry to keep you waiting, Sergeant. Something about this case, I suppose. Is it true that the committal proceedings are starting on Monday?"

"Unless the defense asks for an adjournment."

"That's unusually quick, isn't it?"

"It is quick," agreed McCourt. "No doubt there will

be a considerable delay before the case can reach the Crown Court. If it goes forward."

"But I suppose it means that the Superintendent is very sure of his ground."

McCourt did not feel prepared to comment on this.

Mariner said, "Well, now, what can I do for you?"

"There are one or two loose ends we would like to tidy up, sir, if we can. This is one of them."

McCourt slid his hand into his pocket and laid the photograph of Gabby Lewson on top of the desk. Mariner looked down at it. His eyes flickered for a moment. He said, "It's not very pleasant, is it?"

"Well, you see, he'd been two, three days in the water. He'll have had a little cosmetic treatment, I don't doubt."

Mariner was still staring at the photograph. He said, "It's difficult to be sure, with him in that state. But I don't think— No, I'm quite sure. I've never seen him before."

McCourt repocketed the photograph. Mariner seemed glad to see it go. He said, speaking more normally, "Was there any reason to suppose I should have known him?"

"We did at one time connect him with that telephone call that came to your house on the night Katie was killed. Polly thought he called himself Lewisham. This man's name is Lewson. It would have been easy for her to make a mistake."

"Polly doesn't make mistakes. If she said Lewisham, that's what it was."

"And the name meant nothing to you?"

"Nothing at all. Might I ask why the police should attach such importance to this particular telephone call?"

"It's like this," said McCourt. "*Any* stranger who was

in this neighborhood at just the time Katie was killed and is unaccounted for is bound to be a subject of inquiry. If our first idea had been right and 'Lewson' and 'Lewisham' were one and the same person, then you might say that he *was* accounted for. In the river. On the other hand, if Mr. Lewisham exists, as a separate person, we're bound to try to locate him."

McCourt wondered, as he said it, if this would sound as thin to Mariner as it did to him. Apparently not. Mariner had followed the explanation carefully and now said, "Yes. I see that. But I find it difficult to help you."

"You're quite sure that the name means nothing to you? You have so many different interests. If I might make a suggestion, why not have a look in your address book? A busy man jots names down and forgets them."

"If it'll set your mind at rest, Sergeant," said Mariner. He took a bunch of keys out of his pocket and unlocked the desk. McCourt moved unobtrusively up behind him. There was a typewriter in the desk. It was a new portable machine and bore no resemblance whatever to the typewriter that McCourt had seen there three weeks before.

"Lamprey, Levett, Ligertwood, Livingstone. No Lewisham, I'm afraid, Sergeant."

"Another dead end, I'm afraid," said McCourt politely. "But thank you for trying."

"Really," said Colonel Lyon, "I don't think I've ever read such a letter. I hardly know what to do about it."

In times of doubt he was used to consulting his head warder, a reliable and experienced officer.

"Might I have a look at it, sir?"

"Certainly."

The letter had arrived at the prison that morning,

addressed to Jonathan Limbery and marked "Personal and Confidential." These words were three times underlined.

"I had to open it, of course."

"Of course, sir."

"From West Hannington Manor and signed 'Peter.' That would be the dead girl's brother."

"That's right, sir."

The head warder was experiencing some difficulty with the handwriting, which had started reasonably enough but had deteriorated as passion took hold of Peter's pen.

> *"The police are playing their usual dirty tricks. Sergeant McCourt is the worst of the lot. I used to like him, but now I hate him more than all of them. When he came to see me I told him about what happened in the car that night. He spat in my face.*

"Really, sir! That doesn't sound like Sergeant McCourt. A very steady officer, I'd always understood."

"There's worse to come."

> *"I'm sure he was the one who persuaded them not to call me as a witness, so if they do convict you and send you away, you'll know who to blame. For that and anything else that happens. I hardly know what I'm writing. Perhaps they won't even let you see this letter. Goodbye, my dearest, dearest Johnno.*

"Might have been written by a girl, sir."

"It's a very curious letter altogether," said the Governor. "I don't think I can show it to him."

"Certainly not."

"Then what am I going to do with it?"

"If I were you, sir, I should tear it up and forget about it."

"I don't think I can do that," said the Governor unhappily.

The Reverend Bird looked sadly around the church. The congregation was an unusually large one for Sunday evensong, but the front row of the choir stalls on each side was empty. Although the local boys had refused to join the choir he had had a happy little group of girls, including his own daughter. Now even she had refused to perform. "I should be all by myself and look silly," she had said.

He had prepared a sermon on Church Unity, a subject which was being much canvassed by his bishop at that time. But before plunging into ecumenical argument he felt that he must say something more directly to his troubled flock. He had sensed that they were deeply divided, young against old, children against parents. He had heard of the discords in the Vigors family and of the sudden departure of Sally Nurse for London. He had caught a glimpse of Peter, white-faced and miserable, coming out of the gates of Hannington Manor and had felt an impulse to run up to him and put an arm around his shoulders, an impulse which he had been just sensible enough to resist.

The committal proceedings hung like a black cloud across all horizons.

He said, "Long before I was born and before most of you were born, a man called Wallace was tried and convicted of the murder of his wife. It was a well-known case. Criminologists still argue about whether he was guilty or not. There is still doubt. But one thing about which there is no doubt at all is that owing to the intense local feeling which the case aroused he didn't get a fair trial. He appealed against his conviction. On the Sunday before his appeal was heard the Anglican Bishop of Liverpool prescribed a prayer to be read in all the churches of his diocese. I should like to read it to you. It ran, 'You shall pray for the people that their confidence in the fair dealings of their fellow men may be restored and that truth and justice, religion and piety, may be established among us. Finally you shall pray for all who await the judgment of their fellow men and commit them to the perfect justice of Almighty God.'"

After a brief silence, during which the congregation seemed to be holding its breath, he said, "And now to my text . . ."

Walking back after the service with Mr. Beaumorris to pick up her car, which she had parked in the open space between his cottage and the Rectory, Mrs. Havelock said, "I thought Dicky Bird was better than usual tonight. All the same, I think he might have told us the end of the story. Did the man get off?"

"I rather think that he did," said Mr. Beaumorris. "And died less than two years later of a very painful disease."

"So much for the justice of God," said Mrs. Havelock.

Mr. Beaumorris was surprised to see a light in his front room, and even more surprised to find Sergeant McCourt waiting for him, with Myra in attendance.

McCourt said, without preamble, "I fear that this visit is totally irregular. But I am here to ask for your help."

"Then won't you sit down. Are you asking for Myra's help as well?"

"Yes."

Mr. Beaumorris, who made it a rule of life never to

be surprised at anything, said, "Very well, then let us all sit down."

"First I ought to explain why what I am doing is irregular. I am doing it without consulting my superior officer, Inspector Dandridge. And without informing Superintendent Knott. In fact, what I am doing may turn out to be contrary to his interests."

"My dear Ian," said Mr. Beaumorris. "You don't mind me calling you Ian, I hope, particularly as we are meeting on such an irregular basis." The old man snuffled happily. "If what you are proposing to do is likely in any way to discommode or embarrass Superintendent Knott, you are assured of my unstinting help. Of Myra's, too, I am sure."

"It's kind of you to say so. Then this is what I want. It would be difficult for me to go to Mariner's house and speak to Polly. Do you think you could persuade her to come down here for half an hour? I take it there'd be no objection to her coming out with you on a Sunday evening."

"We're not slaves," said Myra. "Of course she'll come, if she wants to. What am I going to tell her?"

"Tell her," said McCourt, "that there's one piece of information which may affect the result of the case tomorrow and that she's the only person who can give it to us."

"Don't be too long," said Mr. Beaumorris, "or I shall be dead of unsatisfied curiosity before you get back." He added, "You can take my bicycle if you like." But Myra was already hurrying down the street.

When Polly arrived, McCourt said to her, "On the night Katie was killed, the night of the Tennis Club dance, I had to go round to some of the bigger houses and warn people to be careful about locking up. You remember?"

Polly nodded, her face impassive.

"I waited for Mr. Mariner in his business room. There was an electric typewriter on his desk. It's no longer there. He's got a much smaller portable machine."

"That's right. He bought it in Reading, about a week ago."

"Then what happened to the other machine?"

Polly thought about it. McCourt said, "It's a heavy brute of a thing. He couldn't have walked out with it. It might still be in the house, of course—"

Polly shook her head. She said, "It's not there. I'd have seen it if it was."

"Then if it's gone, either he took it away in his car or someone came and fetched it. Can you remember whether he's had a visitor, with a car, in the last ten days?"

Polly said, "I don't think—" And then, "Oh yes. There was one. Commander Bellairs."

The name meant nothing to any of them.

"He's not in the Navy now. In fact, he's quite old. He runs that boys' club up in London. The one that Mr. Mariner is boss of. And come to think of it, that was rather funny. Usually he's fussy about visitors. He doesn't like going to the door himself."

"So I noticed," said McCourt.

"They ring the bell and I let them in and fetch him. Even if he sees them coming, he likes to do it that way."

"Stuffy old pig," said Myra under her breath. The others ignored her. McCourt said, "So what was funny about this occasion?"

"What was funny was I didn't see him come or go. I just happened to notice his car parked outside the front door. That's how I knew it was the Commander. Mr. Mariner must have let him in and out himself."

"And when was this?"

"Sometime last week."

"Can you remember which day?"

"Thursday, I think. Yes. I'm sure it was Thursday. I was cleaning the silver when the Commander arrived and that's the day I do it."

"And it was *after* the Commander's visit that Mr. Mariner bought the new typewriter."

"That's right. He went into Reading on the Saturday morning and brought it back with him. Why is it important?"

"I'm not entirely sure yet," said McCourt. "But if what I think is true, it might be the most important thing that's happened so far."

24

"You are charged," said the clerk, "that you did on the fifteenth day of August last at West Hannington in the County of Berkshire murder Kate Louise Steelstock."

"Absolute nonsense," said Jonathan.

"The accused pleads not guilty," said Mrs. Bellamy.

"You are further charged that on the twenty-third day of August at West Hannington aforesaid you did wound Detective Sergeant Edward Esdaile with intent to commit grievous bodily harm contrary to Section Eighteen of the Offenses Against the Person Act 1861."

"Nuts to that and any other charges you can dream up," said Jonathan.

Mrs. Bellamy, who had remained on her feet, said, "The accused pleads not guilty to both charges. Might I add that we have asked for committal proceedings in the old style under Section Seven because it is our intention to demonstrate, to your satisfaction I trust, sir, that there is no case to answer on the first charge and that there was such provocation on the second charge as to render a charge under Section Eighteen untenable. We have requested that reporting restrictions should be lifted so that this may be demonstrated publicly at the earliest possible opportunity."

Mr. Appleton nodded. The reporters scribbled.

The Reading Magistrates Court was a large one, which was lucky, since it was packed to suffocation point. Intending spectators who had thought, by arriving at eight o'clock, to be certain of getting in had found a queue already stretching down one street and around the corner into another. The constable on duty had advised them to go home. "Some people have been here all night," he said, "and a lot came down by the six o'clock train from Paddington."

The only people from West Hannington who got into the courtroom were Mrs. Havelock and Group Captain Gonville. As magistrates they had been given privilege tickets and were wedged into a narrow space between the Bench and a much enlarged press box. Mrs. Havelock had left Sim in the witness room with Roney to keep him company.

Mavor rose as Mrs. Bellamy subsided. ("Just like the weatherman and his wife," whispered Mrs. Havelock. "One goes in when the other comes out.")

"It is not my intention," said Mavor, "to make an opening speech. I shall call the witnesses before you, only reserving the right to intervene from time to time in order to place their evidence into its proper context so that the charges may be better understood. Broadly speaking, they will cover three different topics. First, matters directly connected with the charges. Secondly, matters arising out of a certain note, which I will put in evidence at the appropriate time. Thirdly, matters referring to the account given by the accused of his movements on the night of August fifteenth and the early morning of August sixteenth. Sergeant Esdaile, please."

Sergeant Esdaile produced the plans he had drawn and the photographs he had taken and these were explained to Mr. Appleton, who placed them carefully on the table in front of him. Mavor then said, "I should now like to turn to the second charge. Would you please tell us, Sergeant, what happened on August twenty-third."

Sergeant Esdaile did his best, but Mrs. Havelock couldn't help thinking that he succeeded in turning what had been a fast-moving and exciting episode into something which sounded curiously dull and unconvincing.

Mrs. Bellamy said, "I understand, Sergeant, that you have fully recovered the use of your arm."

"That's right."

"And have been back on duty for the week past."

"That's right."

"Could you tell the court what you have been doing?"

Sergeant Esdaile looked surprised.

"I don't mean all of it. What have you been mainly engaged in?"

"Mainly I've been pursuing inquiries about a typewriter."

"And have your inquiries been successful?"

"No, ma'am."

"One of the places you looked would have been in the office of the accused."

"Yes."

"And you would have inquired of the friends and acquaintances of the accused whether they possessed the particular machine you were looking for. Again without success."

"That is so, ma'am."

"Did you dislike the accused?"

The sudden switch threw Sergeant Esdaile completely. He gaped at Mrs. Bellamy, who repeated the question.

"I didn't like him or dislike him. I didn't really know him very well."

"If you didn't dislike him, why was it that, on the

occasion you have told us about, when you were told to bring the accused in for questioning, you called him"—Mrs. Bellamy looked down at her brief for a moment—"a long-haired communist agitator and a bastard who did nothing but stir up trouble?"

"I never did."

"Did you consider it part of your duty to use expressions of this sort?"

"I told you I never said anything like it."

"I shall be calling two witnesses who heard the words," said Mrs. Bellamy and sat down.

"Remembering that you are on oath and that you are a police officer," said Mavor, "I should like to have your assurance that you never used the expressions we have just heard."

"Certainly not," said Sergeant Esdaile. He sounded more surprised than indignant.

"Thank you. Mr. Joseph Cavey."

Mr. Cavey described his discovery of the body. He produced no surprises and was not cross-examined.

He was followed into the box by Dr. Farmiloe, who gave his evidence in the clear, unhurried manner of one who has performed the same function many times before. He referred from time to time to a sheaf of notes which he held in his hand.

"In summary, then," said Mavor, "your conclusion was that the girl had been killed by one blow, on the back of the skull, at a time which you estimate, on the grounds which you have explained to the learned Magistrate, to have been between a quarter past eleven and a quarter to twelve."

"My possible estimates were rather wider than that. But that is the most probable timing."

Mrs. Bellamy said, "Your experience, Doctor, entitles your estimates to be received with respect. But I should like to clarify one point. Your post here, and your post when you were in practice in London, is that of Police Doctor."

"I'm not sure that officially there is any such position. I am on call to the police and receive a small fee for my services. They could, of course, use any other doctor if they wished."

"Having you on the spot," said Mrs. Bellamy with a slight smile, "they would be very foolish if they did call in anyone else. But that is not my point. You are not, I think, a pathologist."

"That is correct."

"And there are a number of pathologists in the country—the leading ones, naturally, are in London—whom the Crown habitually calls on in murder cases."

"In cases involving death or severe bodily damage."

"Quite so. They are usually referred to in the press, again incorrectly, as Home Office pathologists."

Dr. Farmiloe nodded.

"If I might make their respective functions clear, sir," said Mrs. Bellamy, turning to the Magistrate, "since they are sometimes misunderstood. The main duty of the Police Doctor is to certify the fact of death. It was extremely sensible that Dr. Farmiloe also turned his attention to ascertaining the time of death, since you will understand from the explanations he has given you that the sooner this is done the more accurate the result will be. But"—Mrs. Bellamy paused for a moment and looked around the crowded room—"it is no part of his function to determine the cause of death. That is a matter for the pathologist?"

Since there seemed to be a question mark at the end of this statement, Dr. Farmiloe nodded again and said, "I think, in fact, it went to Dr. Carlyle at Southampton."

"Then I can defer questions on it until Dr. Carlyle produces his report for us."

Mavor, who had been fully aware for some time of the direction in which Mrs. Bellamy was heading, rose to his feet and said, "In view of the fact that Dr. Farmiloe, who has great experience in these matters, was able to tell us that the cause of death was a blow on the head, we saw no reason, sir, to trouble you with an additional report."

Mr. Appleton thought about this. He was a large red-faced man who, when he was not dispensing justice, looked after four hundred acres of mixed arable and sheep farm. He said, "I don't follow this. Has Dr. Carlyle made a report?"

"Yes, sir."

"And he is the Crown Pathologist for this district?"

"Yes, sir."

"Then I would like to see it."

Mavor already had it in his hand. He said, "Certainly, sir. Before putting it in, perhaps I might read you the passage which is in point. 'The cause of death was severe damage to the brain tissue from a single deep and well-marked fracture of the skull.' There are other comments, but that is the main conclusion."

He handed it to the usher, who handed it to the clerk, who passed it up to Mr. Appleton. Mrs. Bellamy, who had remained standing, said, "Might I suggest that it would be better if the learned Magistrate saw *both* Dr. Carlyle's reports."

A moment of silence.

"As far as I know," said Mavor, "he made only one report."

"If those are your instructions, then I can only say that you have not been instructed fully. I have here a copy of a report on a second death which occurred at about the same time and approximately the same place, in which Dr. Carlyle makes a most instructive addendum to his first report."

Mavor looked at Knott, who shook his head like an angry bull tormented by gadflies.

"If you have *not* been supplied with a copy," said Mrs. Bellamy sweetly, "I have several here." She extracted a number of documents, handed one to Mavor and one to the usher, who looked inquiringly at the Magistrate.

"I should like to see it," said Mr. Appleton. He felt that an attempt was being made to pull the wool over his eyes and resented it.

"The passage is at the end," said Mrs. Bellamy.

Mr. Appleton read it through and said, "I think this is most relevant. Why was it not produced?"

Mavor, who had been conferring with Knott, said, "I understand that the police view is that since there was no connection between the two deaths there was no point in troubling you with it."

"It's not a question of troubling me. My function is to arrive at my best estimate of the evidence. How can I do that when part of it is kept from me?"

"There was no intention—"

"This report says, 'On close examination of the depressed fracture in this case, I was struck by the marked similarity to the fracture in the earlier case and concluded that they had both been made by the same instrument.'"

The press box was drinking this in with the gratification of puppies presented with an unexpected meal. Mr. Appleton glanced at them and said, "Since these proceedings are being publicly reported, I should perhaps explain that this second report concerns a body, since identified as a Mr. Lewson, which was recovered from the river some miles below Whitchurch. There seems to be evidence that it entered the water at Hannington on the evening that Miss Steelstock was killed." He turned to Mavor. "Did that not seem to you to be important?"

"Having considered the matter carefully, sir, we came to the conclusion that Dr. Carlyle must have been mistaken."

"I see."

"Although," said Mrs. Bellamy, "his conclusions were supported by Dr. Summerson, who is possibly the most experienced pathologist in the country. There is a note by him to that effect, at the foot of the report."

"In spite of that," said Mavor stolidly.

"I have said this before and I will say it again," said Mr. Appleton. "It is not the job of the police to pick and choose what evidence they will give. It is their duty to present all the evidence. Have you any more questions, ma'am?"

"No more questions," said Mrs. Bellamy, subsiding gracefully.

"George Courtenay Mariner."

Mr. Mariner took the oath in a confident voice, identified himself and proceeded to describe the quarrel which had taken place in the Tennis Club bar. Mrs. Bellamy appeared to be so far uninterested in what he was saying that she spent most of the time in a whispered colloquy with Sophie. It was clear, however, that her attention had not wandered, for when Mavor said, "Was there, to your knowledge, an earlier occasion when the accused engaged in an altercation with a Mr. Windle?" she was on her feet in a flash.

"I must object to that," she said.

"If your objection," said Mavor, "is that evidence about the earlier occasion would better be given by Mr. Windle himself, I can assure you that it is my intention to call him."

"My objection, as my learned friend well knows, is that

the earlier episode can only be referred to as evidence of the general character and disposition of the accused. It cannot be adduced in committal proceedings."

Mr. Appleton looked lost. His clerk rose to his feet and said something to him. Mr. Appleton nodded several times and said, "The objection is supported."

"I have no questions for this witness," said Mrs. Bellamy. She managed to say it in a tone of voice which implied that his evidence was unimportant and irrelevant. Mariner looked surprised and left the box. It was difficult to say whether he was relieved or disappointed at not being cross-examined.

"I should explain," said Mavor, "that my next witness, Arthur Simpson Havelock, is a boy of nine. His mother is in court and if you feel it advisable that she should stand near the boy, we should have no objection."

"He'll be all right," said Mrs. Havelock, "as long as you don't frighten him."

Sim, looking minute but quite self-possessed, took the oath. The Magistrate, who knew Mrs. Havelock and all her children, said, "Look at that gentleman, Sim. The one standing up. He's going to ask you some questions."

"All right."

"How old are you, Sim?"

"I'm nine."

"And you're old enough to understand that this is a law court and that you're giving evidence and must speak truthfully."

"O.K."

"You see Mr. Limbery. Over there. You know him, don't you?"

"Yes."

"Did you ever see him with Miss Steelstock?"

"With Katie?"

"Yes."

Mavor waited patiently. His training and his instincts had been against calling the boy, and if his evidence had not been vital to his case he would not have done so.

Sim said, "Do you mean about seeing them at the boathouse?"

"If you saw them at the boathouse, then you can tell us about it."

"Well, we did." Sim paused and added, "We saw them twice. Once was in May and once was in July."

"And what were they doing?"

The court held its breath.

"They were lying on the ground. The second time we didn't see much because they went into the boathouse."

"When you did see them, Sim—on the first occasion—can you tell us what they were doing?"

"Not really. It was getting dark."

"I see. So it would have been sometime about nine o'clock."

"About then."

"Were they lying close together?"

"Quite close, yes."

Out of the corner of his eye, Mavor could see Mrs. Bellamy watching him like a hawk. He thought that the last answer was almost what he wanted. If he went any further he might spoil it. He said, "Thank you," and sat down.

Mrs. Bellamy said, "When you were answering the gentleman, Sim, I couldn't help noticing that you said, '*We* saw them.' Was someone with you?"

"Roney was."

"Is Roney your brother?"

"Yes."

"I suppose he's younger than you?"

For the first time Sim smiled, exposing a gappy set of

front teeth. He said, "Roney isn't younger than me. He's eleven. Nearly twelve."

Mrs. Bellamy looked at the Magistrate, but he already had the point. He said, "I take it that the other boy is being called?"

Mavor's sigh was almost audible. He said, "I understand, sir, that there was some sort of difficulty about the older boy."

"What sort of difficulty?"

"He wasn't willing to give evidence."

The Magistrate looked puzzled. He said, "If the two boys were together on both occasions, surely it would have been preferable to have called the older boy. There's no rule that I know of against issuing a subpoena to a minor."

"It would be unusual," agreed Mavor. "But I know nothing against it."

"Is the boy available?"

Mrs. Havelock said, "He's in the waiting room."

"I should like to hear his evidence."

Mavor hesitated. He said, "I shall have to take instructions, sir."

"Very well."

Two whispered conferences began. The first between Mavor, Knott and the solicitor acting for the police; the second between Mr. Appleton and his clerk.

"Like amateur theatricals when something goes wrong," said Group Captain Gonville. "The only difference is they haven't got a curtain to lower. Are they going to let Roney loose on us?"

"They're in for trouble either way," said Mrs. Havelock grimly.

As the conferences came to an end, the Magistrate said, "I'm told that I've got no right to call for any particular witness. That's not my job. It's up to the prosecution to produce exactly what evidence they wish. I'm going to say this, however. If the older boy, who could clearly corroborate his brother, is *not* going to be called, I shall have to regard what the younger boy says as being, to a certain degree, suspect. I don't mean that I shall disregard it altogether, but I shall accept it only with considerable caution."

Mavor said smoothly, "We have decided that there is no reason why the other boy should not be asked to give evidence. If he refuses to speak, no doubt the court will have to decide whether it has any power to make him do so."

"Obdurate witnesses used to be pressed between heavy weights," said the Group Captain. "Perhaps he'll be too nervous to say anything."

"Don't you believe it," said Mrs. Havelock.

After this preamble, Roney's entrance into the witness box had something of the effect of a star actor whose entrance onto the stage has been carefully delayed and prepared for him by the supporting cast. He smiled cheerfully at the crowded court and took the oath in a clear and confident voice. A murmur from the female members of the public, although not formulated into words, clearly expressed the mass view that he was a sweet little boy.

"We have one or two questions to ask you," said Mavor. "I'm sure you realize the importance of giving truthful answers."

"Yes, sir."

"Your brother has told us that you were with him on two occasions, once in May and once in July, when you saw Mr. Limbery with Kate Steelstock near the boathouse."

"That's right, sir. We saw them there."

"Could you tell us what they were doing?"

"Just sitting together talking."

"Sitting?"

"Sitting on the ground."

"They weren't lying down?"

"Oh no, sir. Just sitting. Talking and laughing."

"You're sure they weren't lying down."

"Quite sure."

"You realize that you are giving evidence on oath."

"Yes, sir."

"And if you don't speak the truth, the consequences can be very serious."

"That's right," said Roney. "It's called perjury and you can be sent to prison."

"Then let me repeat the question. Are you sure that they weren't lying together on the ground quite close to each other?"

"I won't have this witness intimidated," said Mr. Appleton. "He's told you once. What's the point of getting him to say it again?"

Roney flashed a grateful smile at Mr. Appleton and said, "He isn't frightening me, sir. Mother told me that if I had to give evidence, I'd only got to tell the truth and no one could do anything to me."

The crowd loved this. Mavor said, "Very well," and sat down. Mrs. Bellamy said, "I'd like to ask you a question, Roney."

"Yes?"

"You were just outside Mr. Limbery's house in Belsize Road when a policeman came to ask him some questions."

"Sergeant Esdaile. Yes, I saw him."

"Were you close enough to hear what the Sergeant said to Mr. Limbery?"

"Oh yes, quite close enough."

"Then could you tell us what he said?"

A slow flush crept up over Roney's pale cheeks. He said, "It was rather rude."

"We're quite used to hearing rude words in this court," said Mr. Appleton. "No one's going to be shocked. Just see if you can remember."

"Well, sir, he said something like Johnno—I mean Mr. Limbery—being a long-haired nuisance. Then he called him a bastard. I can't remember what came before bastard, but it was a sort of rude word."

"Thank you," said Mrs. Bellamy. "Thank you very much."

At about this time, Sergeant McCourt was looking for the Surrey and Berkshire Dockside Mission. He knew of its existence and like other charitable-minded inhabitants of Hannington had contributed small sums toward its upkeep. He had stopped doing so when he discovered that George Mariner was running it.

The mission house had not been easy to find, being tucked away in a back street in Stepney; and when found, it had not been easy to enter, since the front door was locked and bolted. Exploration down a side street had led him to the missioner's flat and persistent hammering on the door had produced the missioner's assistant, an earnest young man with a crew-cut, wearing overalls liberally splashed with fresh whitewash.

"Excuse my appearance," he said. "Just trying to smarten the place up. Police? Good heavens, what have they been up to now?"

"Nothing to do with your young charges," said McCourt. "I just wanted to find out if you had recently come into possession of an electric typewriter."

"Quite recently. Last week, in fact. Don't tell me it was stolen. Mr. Mariner—"

"It was Mr. Mariner gave it to you?"

"That's right. He knew our old one was broken. He'd just bought himself a new portable and told Commander Bellairs to come down and collect his old one. Why?"

"It's just a matter of checking a lot of local machines. We want to find out how one particular note came to be typed. That means elimination of all other possible machines."

"Elimination?"

"That's right."

"It sounds mad to me. But come in."

If McCourt had looked back as he followed the young man in he might have noticed an inconspicuous person busy lighting a cigarette ten yards down the pavement. Had he been even more alert, he might have noticed that the same person had been hanging about outside the barrier of the arrival platform at Paddington, but his mind was fixed on his quest.

As the door shut behind McCourt, the person showed signs of activity. He moved quickly back into the High Street and without actually running, but without wasting any time at all, reached a telephone box, dialed a number, said, "Blaine here," and asked for Captain Smedley.

The Captain listened to what Blaine had to say, thought about it for a moment and said, "Good show. I guessed it would be worth keeping an eye on that young man. Stay with him."

Most of the excitement in the afternoon was caused by one man and two women fainting. They were carried out of the packed and stifling hall, but this had not diminished the crowd, since three more people from the head of the queue were allowed in.

Mavor had been dealing with the discovery and identification of the note. Listening to him as he pieced together the evidence of Sally Nurse, her father and mother, Sergeant Shilling and Walter Steelstock, Mrs. Havelock had appreciated for the first time how a prosecution case had to be built up. Not by one or two dramatic witnesses but by a lot of humdrum people contributing each their own small share, a brick at a time in the edifice of the Crown.

The only light relief had been Walter's bashful explanation of what he understood LYPAH to mean. The press had enjoyed that.

As the afternoon drew toward its close, Mrs. Steelstock was in the box. She had identified her own signature on the envelope which contained the note and Mavor was now moving on, cautiously, to a different topic.

"Can you tell us," he said, "from your own observation, something of the relationship between your daughter and the accused?"

"To start with, they seemed to be good friends."

"Yes?"

"More recently I should have said that any feeling my daughter may have had for Mr. Limbery had ceased."

Jonathan, who had appeared to be dozing in the dock, sat up.

"You mean that he had ceased to be friendly?"

"Yes."

"How had this happened?"

"I'm not sure I follow you."

"I mean that where a friendship between a young man and a girl ceases, it is usually because one of them cools off."

"It was Kate who dropped Mr. Limbery."

"And that," said Jonathan, "is a damned lie."

Mavor ignored him.

"Could you suggest a reason for her doing so?"

"Certainly. She had come to the conclusion that he was an immature and self-important young man."

"And that is a bloody lie. What does an old crumb like you know about young people, anyway?"

Mr. Appleton said, "You must not interrupt the proceedings."

"Have I got to sit here and listen to a lot of crap talked about me by people whose heads are stuffed with maggots?"

"There's a remedy for that. I can have you removed from the court and the proceedings can go on without you."

Jonathan subsided with a grunt.

Mrs. Bellamy said, "Tell me, Mrs. Steelstock, would you have described Kate as a confiding girl?"

Mrs. Steelstock circled around it for a bit and then said, "Sometimes."

"I am right in thinking that she didn't live at home."

"She had her own house. Yes."

"Did she tell you about all that happened up in London? All about her television program and her friends up there."

"Well, no."

"Did she discuss Mr. Limbery with you?"

"Not in so many words."

"If she didn't discuss him in words, how *did* she discuss him?"

"I meant," said Mrs. Steelstock coldly, "that I gathered what her feelings were by her conduct."

"What conduct?"

"She no longer invited him to the house."

"But she could, of course, have been meeting him elsewhere?"

"I suppose so."

"Thank you."

*   *   *

"No doubt at all," said Mr. Mapledurham. "Not a scrap of doubt. Capital 'T' slightly worn at the foot, lower-case 'b' tilted. 'S' fractionally out of alignment. Those are the obvious ones. A careful analysis would probably give you half a dozen more."

"You're quite certain it's the same machine?"

"Swear to it in any court of law."

"You might have to do just that," said McCourt.

A quarter to four. The first day's proceedings would be coming to an end soon. The quicker he got back to Hannington the better.

A quarter past four. The Magistrate looked at the clock. He said, "I understand from your opening remarks, Mr. Mavor, that you will next be calling what you described as your third set of witnesses, dealing with the movements of the accused on the night of the killing."

"That's right, sir," said Mavor. "I shall call Superintendent Knott to put in a statement made by the accused and follow that with three or four witnesses who will deal with various aspects of that statement."

"I normally rise at four thirty, but in the circumstances—" The Magistrate looked around the room at the public—overheated, drooping and sated.

"It would perhaps be convenient to start with this new section of evidence tomorrow," agreed Mavor. He was unaffected by the heat. Like a naval officer, he did much of his work on his feet in uncomfortable surroundings.

The usher said, "The court will rise."

As they were going out, Mrs. Havelock said to Group Captain Gonville, "I should call that level pegging so far."

"A lot's going to depend on Knott. I could see that

female gorgon licking her lips when she heard he was going to be called as a witness."

"It's odd, isn't it, how the whole thing seems to have developed into a private battle between the two of them. Jonathan seems to have been relegated to the role of extra."

"An extra, if you like," said Group Captain Gonville. "But not a non-speaking part."

"It's interesting," said Knott shortly, "but it's not conclusive."

McCourt stared at him. The Superintendent's face was more gray than white and the lines of fatigue and strain were bitten into it, but his voice was as flat and as expressionless as ever.

"The Documents Division was quite definite, sir. They're reporting in writing. It'll be with you first thing tomorrow."

"I'll read it with interest, son. But what does it actually prove, except that the note was written on Mariner's typewriter? Anyone could have got at it. He made a habit of keeping people waiting. I could have typed it. You could have typed it. The Chief Constable could have typed it. So what's to prevent Limbery snatching a chance when he was alone there?"

"Why would he do that?"

For a moment Knott looked as though he wasn't going to answer. Then he said, "If you were planning to send a note and you didn't want it found, but there was a chance it might be, wouldn't you type it on someone else's machine? Particularly if you loathed his guts." He climbed to his feet and lumbered out.

McCourt turned on Shilling, his face set in unusual lines of anger. He said, "So the charade goes on."

"Curtain up at ten sharp tomorrow."

"And nothing can stop it?"

"I don't say it couldn't be stopped," said Shilling, carefully, "but it's going to take more than this last bit of evidence to do it. After all, there's some truth in what he said. Almost anyone could have used the machine. All you had to do was ring the bell. Polly lets you in and you've got anything from two to twenty minutes available, according to who you were. When I called recently I was kept waiting for twelve minutes."

"Yes, but why did he—?"

"I know what you're going to say. The answer's panic. When he heard that inquiries were being made, he had to get rid of the machine. Stupid thing to do, but understandable. And his conscience wasn't all that clear if he'd been out doing a spot of voyeuring. And a word of advice. I don't think I should try any more bright suggestions on the old man. Not just at this moment."

"I heard he had some rough handling in court."

"That wouldn't worry him. It's something else."

He stopped and McCourt noticed that his face was unusually grim.

"The Steelstock boy has killed himself. His mother found him when she got back from court. He'd cut his throat with one of his father's old razors and made a filthy mess of it. He left a note, too. Blaming the police in general and you in particular."

25

It might have seemed impossible that the crowd should be larger, but on the second morning the waiting line stretched far back, down the street beside the court building, along the back of the building and fifty yards out into the road beyond. The people at the head of the queue had been there all night. They had left the court at the end of the hearing and had immediately taken up their positions outside the door. There were half a dozen policemen on duty now.

The crowd was not only larger. It was in a different mood. Somehow the news of Peter's death had got out. It was a garbled account passed by word of mouth. Katie's kid brother had killed himself. It was something to do with the police. They hadn't wanted him to give evidence (or, in another version, they had wanted him to give evidence). They had bullied him. They had tried to break him down. The boy could take no more and had cut his own throat.

The crowd was angry.

When the police judged that the courtroom was full and tried to shut the door of the public entrance, there was a scuffle. A woman said, "Why won't you let us in?" A big red-faced man who had his foot in the door preventing it from being shut said, "We know why. You don't want us to hear the truth, do you? How many more kids are you going to kill?"

The policeman at the door summoned help and they got it shut. The crowd outside refused to disperse. When Knott arrived he was recognized and a storm of hissing and booing broke out. Knott ignored it and pushed his way through toward the side entrance. The policeman on duty there held the door open for him. He said, "I don't know what's come over them."

"Mass hysteria," said Knott.

"I understand, Superintendent," said Mavor, "that the accused made a statement."

"He made two, sir. An earlier statement in answer to some questions which I put to him in the course of my investigation. A later and more formal statement after he had been charged and cautioned."

"The second statement was taken down?"

"In his presence, sir. And signed by him as being correct."

"Then perhaps you would read it out to us."

"'As the result of a telephone call from the news editor of the Reading *Sun*, I left my house at approximately ten o'clock that evening—'"

"The evening he referred to being August fifteenth?"

"That is correct, sir. '—at approximately ten o'clock that evening and drove over to Quantocks Paper Mills outside Goring to report on a fire which I was informed had broken out there. I proceeded to the scene of the fire, arriving at about half past ten. I was engaged in making notes and conversing with the fire officers until about a quarter to twelve, when I drove to a call box on the Oxford road and dictated my report over the telephone to the newspaper. I then had a quick snack at the

King of Clubs roadhouse, which is also on the Oxford road. I left the roadhouse at approximately a quarter to one and proceeded back via Whitchurch and Pangbourne, getting home at about half past one.' Signed and witnessed."

"Thank you, Superintendent. I'll put in a copy of this statement." A document was handed up to the Magistrate, who added it to the pile on his desk. "Now tell us, Superintendent. Did this statement coincide with the earlier informal statement which you mentioned?"

"It was a good deal shorter, sir. But it coincided in every material particular."

"Then I would like to draw your attention, sir, to three points in it. First, that the accused says he spent an hour and a quarter at the scene of the fire. Secondly, that he telephoned his account to the paper from a call box on the Oxford road. Thirdly, that he returned home through Whitchurch and Pangbourne, which would involve crossing the Thames at this point. It is the contention of the Crown, sir, that the accused has lied, and lied deliberately, on all these three points. The remaining witnesses will be directing their testimony to those matters."

Knott made a move to leave the box, but Mrs. Bellamy was already on her feet.

"I have one or two questions which I should like to put to this witness. I was not clear whether this was to be his only appearance, or whether he is to give evidence on other points later."

"If you have any questions to put to the Superintendent, do so now by all means," said Mavor.

"Thank you."

Mrs. Bellamy had brought out a pair of old-fashioned pince-nez glasses, which she perched on her nose, alternately looking through them at her notes and over them at the witness. There was something mesmeric about the bobbing up and down of her head.

("Like a wasp eating marmalade," whispered Mrs. Havelock.)

"Could I direct your attention to the pathologist's reports which we have had read to us. *Both* reports, Superintendent. Particularly the second one. You remember it?"

"Yes."

"A report by one eminent pathologist, endorsed by a second, a very eminent one, which stated that *two* people had been killed by the same weapon, at about the same time and probably by the same person."

"It was not a statement. It simply suggested the possibility."

"When two eminent experts suggest a possibility, you don't think it becomes a probability?"

"I think it remains a theory."

"But it was a theory based on facts. The shape and depth of the wound."

"Yes."

"Relevant facts."

"If you like."

"And is it not your duty to inform the defense of all relevant facts which come to your notice?"

"It would only have been relevant if the accused was charged with the second killing."

A man at the back of the court said loudly, "Nonsense."

The Magistrate looked up. Then he said, "I'm afraid I don't understand that myself, Superintendent. If there was evidence that the same man had killed two people, surely this was relevant."

"All that we had to go on was a theory put forward by Dr. Carlyle that the blows could have been produced by the same instrument. We did not consider this to be strong enough evidence definitely to connect the two."

"In other words," said Mrs. Bellamy, "you thought you knew better than Dr. Carlyle."

"If you want to put it that way."

"And than Dr. Summerson."

"Yes."

"Who are acknowledged experts in their own field."

"I agree."

"And what training in forensic pathology have you had, Superintendent?"

"I have listened to a lot of pathologists giving evidence and have believed exactly half of them," said Knott.

("Not bad," said Group Captain Gonville.)

"This second man, whose death you regarded as unimportant, has been identified, I believe, as being a certain Gabriel Lewson, employed as a runner by a society photographer named Rodney Ruoff. Is that right, Superintendent?"

"That is so."

"And did you also regard it as totally irrelevant that Ruoff was himself murdered a few days ago?"

"We hardly thought it likely that the accused had had any part in that killing, since he was in custody at the time it occurred."

"Quite so. But did it not occur to you as a relevant fact that *three* people, all of whom were closely connected, should have been killed within a few days of each other?"

Knott said, "There was no connection known to us—" and stopped.

"You were going to say that there was no connection between Miss Steelstock and Ruoff?"

"No close connection."

"Although he was her photographer and the man who had set her on her way to stardom."

"No close connection," said Knott obstinately.

A murmur came from the crowded listeners. It was difficult to distinguish words, but "rubbish" was certainly among them. Mrs. Bellamy listened to it with her head cocked. The reporters wrote, "Raking cross-examination," and "Police witness under fire."

"Let me repeat a question I put to you earlier," said Mrs. Bellamy. "You do agree, I hope, that if facts *are* relevant, it is the duty of the police to share them with the defense?"

"Yes."

"The object of a criminal trial is to elucidate the truth, not to secure a personal victory for a particular policeman."

"The object of a trial," said Knott, "is to determine whether the accused is guilty of the crime he is charged with. Not to examine any other crimes which may have taken place in the neighborhood at the time."

It was a good answer, in a debating sense, but, thought Mrs. Havelock, it was too long. It was the first small sign that the Superintendent was getting rattled.

Mrs. Bellamy said, "Of course. That's right. And that is what I meant by the word 'relevant.' Relevant to this crime. Now am I not right in thinking that a considerable part of the police investigation was devoted to trying to trace the typewriter on which this famous note was typed?"

"It was one of the things we tried to do."

"Was not one of your sergeants sent round all office suppliers in the neighborhood with a description of the make of typewriter?"

"Yes."

"And an advertisement put in the press?"

"Yes."

"Would you not describe that as a persistent investigation?"

"All our investigations in a murder case are persistent."

"And were they all as successful as this one?"

Knott looked at her for a long moment. The color was creeping into his face. He said, "I'm not sure that I understand."

"Then I must make myself clear. Did not one of your officers go up to London yesterday and visit a certain mission house in South London? Did he not find a typewriter there and take a sample from it, which he subsequently handed to the Documents Division in your own Science Laboratory for testing?"

"I believe that is correct."

"And what was the result?"

"I'm afraid I can't tell you."

"Why not?"

"I have not yet received an official report."

The noise from the courtroom was like the hiss of expelled breath which has been held too long. Someone shouted, "The man's a liar." A woman sitting close behind Mrs. Havelock said, "Make him answer," in tones of such venom that Mrs. Havelock looked around startled. It was a woman she knew quite well, a mother of three children and normally as placid as an apple dumpling. Now her face was transformed by fury.

Mr. Appleton looked around the room, from side to side, waiting until the noise had died away. Then he said, quite pleasantly, "I have no doubt you are as anxious as I am to hear the rest of the evidence in this case. But, I have to warn you that if there is any further interruption, I shall adjourn the hearing and continue it with the press in attendance but with no members of the general public there at all. Have you any further questions for this witness, Mrs. Bellamy?"

"There is one further matter which I should like to explore. It concerns the statement which we have heard read out to us. A statement alleged to have been made by the accused."

"A statement which was made by the accused," said Knott. He was back on balance again.

"Could you explain to us exactly how it was obtained?"

"The accused was asked if he wished to volunteer a statement. He did so. And it was written down."

"Sentence by sentence, as he spoke it?"

"Yes."

"I am only raising the point because certain parts of it sound more like a police version of what the accused *might* have said than a verbatim record of what he *did* say. For instance"—Mrs. Bellamy adjusted her pince-nez—"'I proceeded to the scene of the fire, arriving at about half past ten . . . and conversing with the fire officers.' That hardly sounds to me like something the accused would actually have said."

"He did say it."

"'I left the roadhouse at approximately a quarter to one and proceeded back via Whitchurch and Pangbourne.' Did he say that, too?"

"Yes."

"I thought it was only policemen who 'conversed' and 'proceeded.' Ordinary people 'talked' and 'went.'"

"That's what he said."

"You're sure this wasn't the sort of statement which is obtained by the police asking a series of questions which suggest the answers they want."

"Quite sure."

"More lies," said Jonathan.

"I am pressing the matter because I am going to suggest that at this point you inserted two or three words which the accused never said—'via Whitchurch and Pangbourne.'"

"He said them in his formal statement and in his earlier informal statement."

"Which was not taken down verbatim?"

"No, but it was tape-recorded."

For the first time Mrs. Bellamy looked taken aback. She recovered quickly. She said, "If this was done without the knowledge and consent of the accused, I do not see that it can be referred to in evidence."

"I understand," said Mavor, "that the tape itself will demonstrate that the accused was informed that his words were being recorded."

"Before or after he made his statement?"

"The passage occurs towards the end."

"And until then he knew nothing about it and had not consented to a recording being made?"

"He had not consented, but he made no objection."

Mr. Appleton conferred with his clerk. He said, "When the accused made this earlier statement, had he been charged?"

"No, sir."

"Then I don't think it can be given in evidence in this court."

Mavor said, "We accept your ruling, sir." He had not thought they would get away with it, but it had been worth trying. And the intervention had robbed Mrs. Bellamy's cross-examination of some of its sting.

"I shall resume at two o'clock," said Mr. Appleton. "And might I ask spectators, if they intend to remain in court over the interval, not to leave a quantity of debris on the floor. Yesterday it took the attendants half an hour to sweep up."

"It looks as though we should finish this afternoon," said the Group Captain. "I thought Mrs. Bellamy made the best of the running this morning. How do you think the chances stand now?"

"Still fifty-fifty," said Mrs. Havelock. "Thank God it's Appleton who has to make his mind up and not us."

At three o'clock that afternoon, Sergeant Shilling, who had been left in charge of the operations room, sustained two shocks, both of them severe.

The first shock arrived in the form of a telephone call. Shilling recognized the voice. It was a detective sergeant called Whittaker who worked in the Fingerprint Section at Central. Wrong. Not Whittaker. Whitmore. He seemed to be amused about something.

He said, "You remember that print you sent up to us?"

"The one off the cupboard door."

"That's the one. Well, guess what!"

"Tell me," said Shilling. Already he could feel a faint tickle of uneasiness.

"You know we tried it on the main computer. No luck there at all. Not a chirrup. This morning, just for laughs, we put it on the Sock List."

Shilling's hand tightened on the telephone. He understood well enough what Whitmore was talking about. The Fingerprint Section maintained a separate record, known as the "Scene of Crime," or "S.O.C. List." On it were recorded the prints of all those people who might have legitimate business at the place where a crime had been discovered. Not only police officers in all the forces in the country, but pathologists, police surgeons, photographers and the like. It was useful as an eliminator and could be keyed, if necessary, into the main print computer.

"Looks like he's been a bit careless," said Whitmore. "He'll collect a rocket from Knotty." Shilling was hardly listening to him. His mind was racing ahead, trying to absorb and work out the shocking implications of what he had heard.

"Don't be too hard on him," said Whitmore. "We all make mistakes. We'll be sending you a written report by hand this evening."

Shilling said, "Thank you," and rang off. He was still staring blindly at the telephone when a second and greater shock followed.

He had been aware that something was happening across the other side of the courtyard. Someone had arrived. He heard Sergeant Bakewell's voice saying, "It's just across here, sir. I'll show you the way."

Then the door was opened and Terence Loftus, Assistant Commissioner of the Metropolitan Police, stalked into the room.

Mrs. Mason said, "Of course I'm sure. You don't stand for twenty minutes outside a lighted telephone box without being able to recognize the man who's deliberately keeping you waiting. I can assure you it fixes his face very firmly in your mind."

She glared at the man in the dock. Jonathan rewarded her with a charming smile.

"And you're quite certain about the time?" said Mavor.

"Perfectly certain. You see, my sister doesn't like being dragged away from her television set before midnight. Then she has to put the dog out. We have a standing arrangement, that if I want to ring her I do so at five or ten minutes after midnight. That suits us both. I don't go to bed early myself."

Mavor was on the point of saying, "Thank you very

much," when he noted that a disturbance was taking place near the side door. A uniformed policeman was forcing a passage through the crowd for a tall gray-haired man whom Mavor had no difficulty in recognizing. By this time everyone in the room realized that something was happening.

Mavor said, "It seems there may have been a development of which I ought to be apprised. I wonder if you would allow me to hold up the proceedings for a moment."

"Certainly," said Mr. Appleton courteously. He, too, had recognized the newcomer, who was talking to the solicitor for the police. Mavor joined the conference. Most of the talking was done by the gray-haired man. He made a gesture of chopping the desk in front of him with the edge of his hand, a karate blow.

Mavor returned to his place, placed the last paper he had been using neatly on top of his brief and said, "I understand that the Crown will offer no further evidence on the first charge."

A curious sound broke from the packed ranks of the spectators. It was like a communal gasp, followed by an outbreak which started as a murmur, escalated into something more menacing and died away suddenly when it was observed that Mrs. Bellamy was on her feet.

She said, "I should like to understand that. Does it mean that the charge is withdrawn?"

"The first charge, yes."

"In that case, since, as I have indicated, there is evidence of considerable provocation on the lesser charge, I should like to make an application that the prisoner be released forthwith on bail."

The response from the courtroom made it clear that there was strong popular backing for this suggestion.

Mr. Appleton turned to Mavor, who had Knott now at his elbow, whispering fiercely.

Mavor said, "The second charge may be a lesser one. It is nevertheless a very serious one. Wounding a member of the police force. It would, I submit, be most unusual to afford bail on such a charge. However, the decision must be left to you, sir."

"Has he surrendered his passport?"

"I haven't got a passport," said Jonathan. His voice was so high-pitched as to be almost out of control.

"Something missing up top," said the Group Captain. "*I* wouldn't let him loose. Not for a minute."

"On condition, then," said Mr. Appleton, "that you report every evening before six o'clock to the Hannington police station and if you break that condition your bail will be automatically canceled, I am prepared to grant the application."

Jonathan had listened to this with a smile twitching his lips. Now he threw back his head and laughed. It was a horrible sound, part spite, part hysteria, with very little humor in it. Fortunately it was drowned by the roar of cheering which broke from the court.

There was a scene of confusion as the reporters fought to make their way out through the side entrance and the people at the back shouldered and elbowed their way through the slower spectators. The police had bolted the door to prevent a further invasion from the street and it took some seconds to get it open. Then the crowd belched out and the noise of the cheering spread down the waiting queue and flowed out into the streets of Reading, flowed down a dozen telephone wires into the offices of great papers and out to millions upon millions of readers.

The police had blundered. The man they had accused of the killing of Katie Steelstock was free.

26

"Thirty years of police work," said the Assistant Commissioner, "have convinced me that it is always the most trivial causes which lead to the most disastrous results. If my daughter, Venetia, had known that Sergeant McCourt was stationed at Hannington, she'd have told me a fortnight ago what she told me yesterday morning and most of our troubles would never have happened."

Knott grunted. They were alone in the Assistant Commissioner's office. Knott's face was still gray, but some of the life had come back into his eyes.

"It appears that she got friendly with McCourt when he was in London. They met over some trouble with a dog. A nice-looking boy, with an easy manner. She took him along to one of Ruoff's parties. Ruoff gave him the full treatment. Hocussed drink and private photographic session in the bedroom. My daughter went looking for him and came in right at the end. McCourt was pretty well flat out by that time, though he realized afterwards what had happened and this must have been what finally decided him to change the filth of London for the clean countryside. When Ruoff gathered that his latest model was a police officer he was scared stiff. He'd just had one brush with the law and was lucky to get away without a prison sentence. He assured my daughter he'd destroy the photograph."

"But he didn't," said Knott.

"He didn't," agreed the Assistant Commissioner. "He kept it and Katie found it when she was rummaging through his cabinet and took it away. It was apple pie for her. She had that puritanical young man on the end of a string, with a hook in his mouth she could twitch whenever she felt like it."

Knott was thinking it out slowly. He said, "Then it was really the photograph and the note that he was looking for when he broke into her house late that night."

"It was the photograph he was looking for, though I don't doubt he'd have been glad to destroy the note, too. He'd had to word it to make it seem as though it came from Limbery. He knew Katie was still hot for him and would come running. On the other hand, he'd no wish to get Limbery into trouble."

Knott said, "He must have known it might be found. That's why he typed it on Mariner's machine."

"That's what all his later maneuvers were about. Shifting the blame onto Mariner. If anyone had to be a scapegoat for his crime, he'd rather it was someone he loathed than someone he liked."

Knott was still thinking back. He said, "There was an earlier attempted burglary at Katie's house. I suppose that was him too."

"I imagine so. He simply *had* to destroy that photograph. Once it was gone he'd be safe, or so he thought. He reckoned that Ruoff wouldn't dare open his mouth. He didn't realize my daughter knew about it. Another thing he didn't know was that Ruoff had kept the negative. Forster found it when he was going through his effects. It's not a pleasant picture."

There was a long silence.

"I'd guess," said Knott at last, "that if she'd just used that photograph to tease him he wouldn't have killed her. It was when she forced him to lie and cheat about that running-down case that she signed her own death warrant. He suggested, you remember, that Ray had taken him off it at Mariner's instigation. But he didn't make the suggestion until he knew that Ray was dead."

"A ruthless, single-minded young man," said the Assistant Commissioner.

"Well placed to do what he had to do. Out and about at all hours on that moped and no questions asked. Put Windle's car out of action on the Thursday night and the other two as well, no doubt. Called on Mariner, who was sure to keep him waiting, and used his typewriter. Dropped the note in Katie's car. He'll have done that when he called at the Manor that evening."

"Right. And walked down the towpath, in the dark, from his conveniently placed lodgings in Eveleigh Road and waited for Kate. If she didn't turn up, no harm done. But she did."

"So did Lewson," said .Knott. "That's clear now. Maybe he recognized McCourt, maybe he didn't. McCourt was taking no chances. So he killed him, too. And went home to bed."

"A cool customer."

"But not so cool right now."

"How is he?"

"The doctors say he'll live."

When Jonathan was released he had gone back to the remand wing for bail formalities. There he had been given back his belongings, and the letter from Peter. He had read it, gone straight back to his house, dug up the revolver he had buried in his back garden, met Sergeant

McCourt in the road and shot him three times through the body. He had then given himself up.

"A pity he didn't shoot a bit straighter," said the Assistant Commissioner. "Now we shall have it all to do over again. If he'd worn a thicker pair of gloves when he broke down the door of Kate's desk I don't believe there'd be even a prima facie case against him."

Knott said, "I remember telling him that he ought to keep up to date on the techniques of his profession."

"It'll be the devil of a case to run," said the Assistant Commissioner. "A lot of assumptions but no proof." He thought about it for a bit. "I think I'll give it to Jim Haliburton."

The grunt which Knott gave might have meant anything, or nothing at all.

Cheat! cheat!